D1555065

BLACK DOG

ESCAPE

Don,
Thanks for your
support and Friendship!

W.L. BACH

Lance Bach

ENDURE ALL PUBLISHING LLC

Dedicated to those men and women in uniform who put their lives on the line to keep America free. Their service is not free. It comes with a cost that we all must bear.

BOOK ONE

ONE

—— ⚜ ——

The blacked-out MH-47 Chinook helicopter creaks and groans as it ascends the dark, forbidden valley in Afghanistan. The crew had stripped the aircraft of excess equipment to be able to climb to this altitude. The monstrous motors decelerate and I feel the pilot slowly turn the big machine. My heart rate increases. I unstrap the seatbelt and chamber a round into my MK-17 sniper rifle. The helo lurches as the rear ramp opens onto a ten-foot ledge protruding from a sheer rock wall. I stride quickly down the ramp and leap to the ledge below. Looking back, I see that the pilot is holding the nose of the helicopter in mid-air above the valley floor with only the ramp touching the ground. The crew chief gives me a thumbs up, reaches for a button and the ramp begins to close. The Chinook drops off the mountain like a black whale diving below the surface of the ocean.

The oxygen is deathly thin at this altitude, causing me to inhale with deliberate force. The cold air hits the back of my throat like needles. The *whoop whoop* of the rotors slowly fades as the helicopter descends into the valley. I need to move quickly away from this insertion point in case anyone heard the Chinook. I patrol towards the other side of the rocky mountain top, heading for the firing position I'd picked out on the map back at the Tactical Operations Center.

It's early October; the mountains around Deh Rawod are already encased in the bleak landscape of winter. The waning crescent moon highlights dirty white patches of snow. The jagged shale rock slips under my weight. I walk on the balls of my feet to avoid sending a rock down the hillside and alerting the villagers.

I make my way around the eastern side of the mountain above the target, shift to my knees, then down on my stomach, the sniper rifle cradled in my arms. Belly-crawling towards my destination, I clear my jumpy mind and focus only on moving like an animal—feeling the soft spots with my hands, moving my knees up, inching forward—*rest, breathe, creep forward*. Two hours later, I reach the location and carefully raise the rifle into the firing position. It fits there in the same way my old German Shepherd lays his head on my shoulder.

I let out a slow breath of icy steam, adjust the scope on the MK-17 sniper rifle, and aim 600 meters down the rocky hillside into a medieval, mud-walled compound. The chill wind blows across my face. I estimate a ten-knot crosswind and 50 degrees of declination to the target. I turn the knobs on my scope to compensate, slide my eye back to the black rubber eyepiece and peer down the valley into the compound below. The sharp wind carries the pungent smells of juniper, cedar and a cooking fire from somewhere down the valley.

I check the scope; the target's vehicle is still there. Mullah Jalami has been trying to coerce local village elders to support attacks on Americans. He came to our attention after a raid three weeks ago, fingered as the local Taliban emir by one of the detainees. Now it was time to put him out of business for good.

Jalami would exit the meeting in the mud hut sometime this evening and move to his Toyota Hilux pick-up truck, escorted by bodyguards. I calculate that I have five seconds to make the shot before he'll find cover behind the mud wall encircling the compound. Rolling my head to ease out the stiffness in my neck, I adjust my left foot to shift off of a sharp rock that is making my leg numb, and put my eye to the rifle again—there's movement. My pulse quickens as the mud hut door opens.

Here we go. A tall, dark, bearded figure with a red turban exits the compound with two bodyguards. The target always wears a red turban, the local mullahs wear white. *Gotcha*. I slow my breathing, swing the crosshairs onto the target's chest, release the safety, and ease my finger into the trigger housing. Suddenly, a cascade of small rocks tumbles from the ledge above me.

Instinctively I roll onto my back, pull the silenced pistol from my thigh holster and aim. A figure with a gun is leaning over the ledge, silhouetted against the moonlight. I fire a quick, silent shot and watch the figure drop.

Spinning back to the long gun, my heart now racing, I re-acquire the target. The red-turbaned Taliban emir of Deh Rawod is walking towards his Hilux pick-up, flanked by two bodyguards. Breathe in, breathe out, aim, smooth trigger pull. The 7.62mm heavy grain bullet rips through his chest and knocks the emir off his feet. The bodyguards leap for cover. One jumps behind the truck, the other runs for the door of the mud hut. I swing a bead on the one heading for the door and take him down with a shot to the right leg.

The wounded man lies there for a moment, then starts to crawl for the door, shouting for help. I set my sights on the door and wait for help to arrive. The door flies open and a short, fat, bearded figure steps out, blindly firing an AK-47 into the mountain above me. I let him take another step out of the doorway, then squeeze off a round. His head comes apart like a rotten melon.

There won't be any more Taliban charging out that door for a while. The injured bodyguard has made it through the front door. I give up on the bodyguard under the truck, drill a round into the truck engine, stand up, and sling the sniper rifle over my shoulder.

As I scramble up over the ledge above me, I see the figure slumped back against a large rock. I kick over the body to have a look and realize that something is terribly wrong. It's not a man, but a young girl, maybe 12 years old. A long shepherd staff lies at her side.

Two

I unlocked the Sea Wolf bookshop, the brass bells on the doorknob softly jingling and alerting Emilio, my full-time tenant. He stretched his front legs languidly and padded down the Old English row, sauntering past Milton, Percy and Shakespeare before rubbing against my leg and head-butting me. I'd taken him in one cold September day when Mrs. Johnson, proprietor of the Port Townsend Bakery next door, found him in the dumpster covered in powdered sugar. She pressed me in her maternal way, so I took the kitten—now a cat—who has become my night watchman, mouse catcher and moveable animal rug. I'll admit I'm not really a cat person, but Emilio is no trouble, and customers don't seem to mind his demands for attention. His only failing is that he drools like a dog with a wet, dripping tongue. Best thing about him, he likes an occasional thimble of whiskey.

I tossed my keys on the Indian mahogany captain's desk, pulled off my wet coat, checked Emilio's water and started up a batch of coffee as soft rain pelted the sidewalk. With a Starbucks across the street, not many customers bought my coffee, even if it was fifty cents a cup. I brewed it anyway—I liked the smell of coffee, and enjoyed sipping a cup as I made my rounds through the shop. I smiled to myself as I remembered my old platoon chief and his coffee. We were on a long zodiac transit in big seas with cold spray splashing over the bow and drenching us. I was literally freezing to death when I looked back and saw the chief balancing a cup of coffee in one hand and the outboard motor tiller in the other. He shook his head, yelled out over the noise of the engine and raging sea, "New guy, come here!" I scrambled to the back of the heaving rubber boat where he poured me a hot, steaming cup of black coffee—still the best thing I've ever tasted, even though half of it splashed all over me.

I liked to walk through the bookstore in the morning, and often got lost in thought as I passed my friends, the books. The shop was 20 feet wide and 40 feet deep. Two long rows of dark oak bookcases ran from front to back down the middle. Along the walls were two more sets of eight-foot-high bookcases. The floor was original weathered oak planking, rough in a few spots, but beautiful to the eye. I loved contemplating the weathered floor as I walked around the shop. *What history did these scratches and dents hide? A gunfight here, a sea chest dragged across the floor there, a spill of blood in the corner?*

My sea captain's desk sat to the right of the front door. Above it hung a small American flag that had flown in Iraq, along with pictures of SEAL Team mates all over the world. On the other side of the desk, near the windows, were a few old chairs and tables for customers to browse books or sit and sip coffee. There was also a small table that held the coffee pot and cups. The walls of the shop were eight-inch-wide stained spruce planks. They made the place look dark, but the wood grain was gorgeous and gave the room a feeling of warmth and history. Brass lamps hung from the ceiling, giving off a soft light and creating strange, oblique shadows. I was pretty sure I'd seen a raven and a wolf shadow-dancing on the walls.

Outside, the blue and white sign, *Sea Wolf Books,* hung above the windows. I'd named the store after my trawler, Sea Wolf. I'd lived aboard the Sea Wolf, now moored at the Port Townsend Marina, before I'd bought the parish house. It was a bit of a money pit, but I loved the old boat. Every man needs something other than a woman to dump his money into.

October brought the first rains of fall to Port Townsend. On Fridays, we get the tourist crowd that migrates up to our isolated town for the weekend, but by the end of summer they're all gone. This Thursday morning, other than a few weary souls slogging along the sidewalk in the drizzling rain, it was dead outside.

Suddenly there was movement in the back of the shop. I quietly pulled a 9mm Sig Sauer P226 from the bottom drawer of my desk and moved on my toes down the non-fiction row. At the end of the bookcases, I swung the pistol around the right corner and aimed. A pigeon was flapping in the corner. I sighed as I stashed the pistol in my belt at the small of my back. Emilio had played with the pigeon and chewed off a wing and most of the beak. Blood was splattered in the corner. I picked up the bird, twisted its neck and tossed it in the trash can outside. I have to remember to shut that high window before I leave for the day.

I returned to my desk, where my gaze inevitably wandered to pictures of SEAL Team friends on the wall behind me. I scanned the faces and places we'd been deployed, memories flooding in of good times and bad. I started to make a mental count of how many guys were now dead, deeply injured, divorced and how many had dropped completely off the grid, like myself.

I opened a small door in the bottom of my desk and took out a bottle of Glenfiddich single malt 12-year-old Scotch and a tall glass. When I first earned my Trident, the warfare insignia of the SEAL Teams, our Executive Officer, a tough and grizzled Vietnam vet, summoned me to his office. I knocked on his door and stepped in smartly when I heard his gravelly voice call out, "Enter!" I stood in front of his gray metal desk, expecting an ass-chewing for something. My eyes widened when he poured two very tall glasses of Glenfiddich. Handing me one, he toasted, "Welcome to the Teams." He stood there and watched me down the whole glass as if it was iced tea. Glenfiddich became my whiskey of choice after that.

I poured the smokey liquid into the glass, all the while arguing with myself about why I needed a drink at ten in the morning, knowing full well where it would end. A feeling inside was pushing for the drink to fill the dark void, make me forget. Another thought was arguing to put the golden poison away, but Glenfiddich won out. The first glass went down in two burning gulps.

The front door jingled and Mrs. Johnson stepped into my shop with a wicker basket in the crook of her fleshy arm. I set the bottle of whiskey on the floor out of her view. She was wearing a yellow flowery dress and a pink apron. Her long gray hair was tied in a bun and had traces of flour in it, making it look amusingly like a powdered donut. She and her late husband, Herb, had started the bakery next door after moving up from Seattle. She was a little too much into town gossip for my taste, but she had a big heart.

"I've brought you a little breakfast," she said kindly, lifting the lid on the basket and releasing the aroma of fresh baked blueberry muffins.

"Wow, those smell amazing. Thanks, Mrs. Johnson."

"No problem at all, Jack." She smiled, set the worn basket down, pulled out three large muffins and placed them on my desk with a napkin.

"Hyacinth is coming to Port Townsend this weekend, and I was wondering if you might like to join us for dinner this Saturday at the Belmont?" she asked, holding her tongs in the air in anticipation.

With a continuous supply of warm muffins in jeopardy, I couldn't help but answer, "Sure, that would be great." Mrs. Johnson had been going on about her daughter since I'd moved here last year and opened the bookstore. It didn't take her long to wheedle out of me that I'm divorced and currently single.

"Saturday at six?" she asked rhetorically as she smiled and waved on her way out the door, the aroma of blueberries wafting in her wake.

What had I gotten myself into? Mrs. Johnson was nice, but a bit overbearing. I had visions of her daughter as the type to try and organize your life and closets as soon as she met you. As it turned out, I couldn't have been more wrong.

I only had two customers all morning. The first, a young girl with black fingernails and spiky hair, asked if I had any used editions of *Harry Potter*. She looked disappointed when I told her that I only carry antique books. But when Emilio appeared around the corner, yawning and stretching, I knew I'd made a customer for life.

"Oh, what a beautiful cat!" She hit me with a volley of questions. "Can I pet him? What's his name? Is he friendly?"

"Emilio's friendly and will soak up all your time if you let him." The cat seemed to have a way with women. Maybe I could learn from him. When the bell on the front door rang, I left them to their love fest and returned to the front of the shop.

The man entering pushed the door open slowly, then looked around as if to make sure we were alone. He was an old salt, and wore rubber sailing boots, dirty blue overalls, and smelled like he was living rough.

"Do you have a maritime section?" His voice was scratchy with some New England in it. I could've sworn I'd seen him on the docks, but couldn't place him.

"Sure, right over here—anything special you're looking for?"

"Books on shipwrecks, especially here in the Straits of Juan de Fuca," he said, taking off his dirty ball cap.

"I don't think I have any books on shipwrecks, but you're welcome to look around."

I left him to it. He cocked his head to the right as he read the titles, touching the spines as if reading them with his fingertips. After he finished, he shuffled over to my desk, where I was eyeing the bottle of Glenfiddich on the floor.

"Could you find any books on shipwrecks in this area for me?" I wondered if his sails came all the way up the mast and figured this search would be a big waste of my time, but a customer is a customer.

"I'll see what I can do. Anything more specific than Puget Sound shipwrecks?"

He looked down for a minute, as if he was wondering whether he could trust me, then finally decided. "I'm looking for anything on HMS Hawthorn."

"Hawthorn, right," I said, jotting down the name on the pad I keep next to my keyboard. "Stop by tomorrow, I should know if there's anything around by then. Can I get a name and phone number?"

He held out a weathered hand. "Cap'n McMillan, but friends call me Cap. I don't have a phone, but I'll come by tomorrow," he said, heading for the door. The girl with the spiky hair set down Emilio, pulled out her cell phone and walked out ahead of him. Cap stopped at the threshold and looked me square in the eye. I had the eerie feeling he was searching my soul. He turned and the door clanged behind him.

I sent a query to an online book search site while wolfing down my second blueberry muffin. The rain had slowed to a soft gray drizzle. I sat back in my sea captain's chair, whistling for Emilio. He came bounding into my lap with an electric purr. The whiskey at my feet was begging for a second opening. I picked up the bottle, but something about that shipwreck intrigued me. I put the bottle back into its cubbyhole.

I recalled reading something about HMS Hawthorn during a visit to a museum in Seattle. I hit a search site and punched in HMS Hawthorn. A bazillion entries cascaded across my screen, but one on the third page caught my attention. A researcher from the Maritime History Department in the Royal British Columbia Museum had written a detailed description of the shipwreck.

Her Majesty's Ship Hawthorn was a 14-gun merchant ship destined to deliver a load of gold and goods to the Royal Trading Company in Victoria in 1840 in exchange for otter pelts. On September 17th, while tacking west near the mouth of the Strait of Juan de Fuca, she foundered in a storm, and all hands were lost. No one knew the exact location of the wreck, but a fur trapper named Jeremiah Benton working his traps on the southern side of the Strait claimed to have seen the ship go down. Benton kept a diary of his trapping days in the shadow of the Olympic Mountains and supposedly had included details about the shipwreck in his diary. The diary had been published by a small printing house in Seattle in the late 1800s, but no one had seen a copy of the actual diary since the early 1900s.

I closed up the bookstore at five o'clock and took my usual walk down Water Street to the Downtown Gym, leaving Emilio curled up on my desk. The Downtown Gym was my kind of place—cut-off sweats were common attire, and they didn't sell designer coffee and $10 smoothies in the lobby. They did have a beer vending machine behind the counter, where Old Tommy passed out tattered towels and dispensed advice on everything from chicken pox to the best crab bait.

I started into my Thursday routine, a circuit-training workout I'd perfected after twenty years in the SEAL Teams. After the fourth set, I noticed a striking brunette knocking out push-ups near the pull-up bar. I'd never seen her before, and this gym was all locals. I tried not to stare but she was a head-turner. She looked Middle Eastern or of Mediterranean descent, with olive-toned skin, raven hair, striking high cheekbones and a straight nose. I cranked out my fifth set of pull-ups. She sauntered up to me and asked if I was finished with the pull-up bar.

"Knock yourself out," I said casually, trying not to stare.

She smiled and jumped up to the bar, yanking out twelve clean pull-ups. My jaw dropped. I didn't know many women who could do twelve good pull-ups, especially when they were as top heavy as this brunette.

"Impressive," I said when she hopped down. "Where did you learn to do that?"

"The Army," she said with a shrug. "I was in for four years. I hated everything except the exercise. Now I'm addicted to working out."

14

Her voice had a hint of an exotic accent that I couldn't identify. She tucked a strand of her shoulder-length dark hair behind her ear. "Can you show me how you do those wall push-ups?" she asked.

Not shy, this one, I thought, perhaps a little cynically.

I demonstrated the technique of planting my hands nine inches from the wall while simultaneously kicking my feet up to land in a handstand position against the wall. She gave it a try and held the handstand against the wall but suddenly lost her balance while trying to do the vertical push-up. I grabbed her legs to keep her from falling over.

"Thanks," she said, standing up, and coming a little closer than necessary.

"No problem," I said nonchalantly, stepping back, as if catching beautiful women falling was a regular occurrence for me.

"I'm Linda," she said breathlessly, extending her hand, "Linda Tomkin."

"Jack," I replied, taking her long slender hand, "Jack Thibideaux."

"Listen, I'm here in town for the Maritime Festival this weekend," she said, running her fingers through her long, silky hair. "Would you like to have a cup of coffee with me this evening?"

"Sure, I know a good coffee shop around the corner," I said, wondering where this would lead.

After a quick shower, I waited in the lobby of the gym. Old Tommy gave me a sly wink when he saw Linda join me. She was wearing tight black pants that left little to the imagination.

Darkness sets in early in the fall in the Olympic Peninsula. We stepped outside into the cool, damp night. The rain had stopped and the streetlights flooded the wet pavement with soft yellow pools of light. We turned the corner and headed downtown to the Cup-O-Joe bistro, a local hangout named for its proprietor as well as its main offering. She strode confidently and decisively, her heels clicking rhythmically on the pavement.

Joe had been a Korean War Navy Corpsman and later became a diver. He'd been at Inchon with MacArthur as an 18-year-old kid. He came up to Port Townsend after the war to escape the dead and dying Marines and soldiers in his mind's eye and started the Cup-O-Joe. I met him at the VFW last year. We hit it off instantly as fellow escapees to this isolated town and Navy combat vets.

"Jack, my boy!" He waved us over to the empty corner table by the small wood-burning stove. Joe was a little shorter than me, maybe five-foot-six, but stocky and built like a tree trunk. He sported a crew cut atop his rather large head. His wiry forearms looked like coiled snakes. "How've you been, shipmate? Who is this lovely lady?" he asked, throwing a small towel over his wide shoulder.

"Joe, this is Linda Tomkin. You'll be sad to know she's former Army."

"I couldn't picture you in combat boots, my dear," Joe said with a twinkle. "What'll it be?"

"Two house coffees would be great Joe, thanks," I said.

As Joe delivered our steaming cups of coffee, Linda said, "Incredible," and gazed around the shop in awe. "It's like a museum or something." Joe collected decades worth of Navy memorabilia—pictures, plaques, old guns and swords were displayed on every wall. The propeller from a P51 Mustang graced the space above the coffee bar and a solid brass diving helmet was posted at the end of the bar.

"Lemme show you my favorite," Joe said, taking Linda gently by the arm and leading her to the far wall. He pointed to a faded plaque hand-carved out of monkeywood with a photo embedded in the corner. It was my DESERT STORM SEAL platoon. All the guys in the platoon had chipped in and had sixteen plaques made by local carvers in the Philippines on our way home from the Gulf War. I had little desire for my military memorabilia so I'd donated mine to Joe's coffee shop.

"Look at that young buck!" he said enthusiastically, pointing out my picture to Linda. She looked back at me with a strange smile, comparing me and my salty gray hair to the young man in the photo, ready for war and hell-raising. That smile made me feel uncomfortable for a second—there was something hungry below the surface.

"Joe shows that to everyone," I explained self-consciously when she came back and sat down. "He loves the SEALs. He was a Corpsman and supported the Underwater Demolition Teams in Korea, patched up many old Frogmen. He's kind of taken me in as the son he never had."

"He's nice," Linda said, sipping her coffee.

She seemed out of place attending our little maritime festival. I pictured her in a big city with shopping malls and nightlife. I was curious, "What brings you to Port Townsend?"

"I'm finishing my doctorate in Marine Biology at the University of Washington. I've come here to gather data for my dissertation on the decline of the Dungeness crab population in Puget Sound." She leaned forward in her chair. I noticed her necklace was shaped like a small crescent moon. It reminded me of the symbol I'd seen on top of mosques in the Middle East. "I've identified several factors leading to crab decline, but I need to correlate my information by looking at historical data on the Dungeness catch in various ports over time. I'm here to talk to some experts at the Maritime Festival."

I wondered why she had come specifically for the Maritime Festival. The experts she needed to talk to were always around. The Festival was just a big party.

"I'll interview these old fishermen and get what I need out of them," she said, sipping her coffee and training her gaze on me. I had a feeling she could get what she needed out of most men.

She leaned back in her chair, crossed her long, svelte legs and turned to me. "What do you do here?" she asked, leaning forward and looking directly into my eyes.

Her low-cut blouse was fogging my thinking. I looked away before I spoke. "I own a bookstore and a cat. They both keep me somewhat busy."

"A bookstore, hmm?" she asked with interest.

"Just a small antique bookshop. I bought it a year ago from a guy who retired to Phoenix. I enjoy books, so it's a good place to hang out and read."

"Well, I'm sure it's very nice." *Did I detect a hint of sarcasm?* "And how many people work here in Port Townsend?" she asked, looking at her cell phone with an apparent lack of interest in the answer.

"About half," I said, waiting to see if she picked up on my subtle joke.

"I'm looking for a place to stay tonight," she said, apropo of nothing and ignoring my joke. "Do you have any recommendations?"

Joe overheard the question from the coffee bar and gave me the thumbs up over her shoulder. There was a bed and breakfast near my bookstore, but I knew that could get complicated.

"I really don't know the best places to stay around here," I said only half-truthfully. "But there is a Visitor's Center just down the street that has all the local hotel information."

"Wonderful," she said, sounding annoyed and standing to leave. A little surprised at her sudden anxiousness to depart, I led her to the door, offering to walk her to the Visitor's Center.

"No, that's OK, thanks for the coffee."

As she stepped out the door strutting like a runway model, I had the feeling that there was more to Linda than she was letting on.

Joe came over and sat with me at the table. "Man, what a looker. Who is she?" he asked, watching through the window as she walked down the street.

"Some highfalutin PhD student at U.W. She came up to me in the gym and asked if I wanted to have coffee. No idea why, since she left so quickly."

"Gonna see her again, ya think?" asked Joe with what sounded like hope in his voice.

"I'm not her type, Joe. I bet she's a heartbreaker, all ambition and sharp heels. She kind of turned her nose up when I told her about my antique book shop."

"Listen, Jack, you're imagining this stuff. You need to find a woman—if not this Linda, then another one."

Joe was always trying to hook me up. He knew the divorce with Elena and my experience in Afghanistan had torn me up and made me wary of people and relationships. He was convinced that the right relationship would fix everything. I knew it wouldn't, even with Joe's 45-plus-year marriage to Jane as a shining example of what was possible.

"Just think about it, will ya, shipmate? Promise?" he asked, placing a paternal hand on my shoulder.

"All right, Joe, I promise," I said, not wanting to let him down. His heart was in the right place, but the last thing I wanted was to think about a relationship.

"That's my boy," Joe said, grinning ear to ear and slapping me on the back.

"How's Jane?" I asked hesitantly.

Jane was living in the Port Townsend assisted living facility. After 45 years of marriage to Joe, she had started to forget who he was. It hurt Joe somethin' awful, but last year he'd had no choice but to move her into the facility.

"She's doin' fine. I visit every night after work."

He didn't offer more and I didn't ask. I knew how much she meant to him and how deeply he missed her. After Korea, he'd told me he put Jane through hell as he dealt with the anger and shame of seeing so much death and being spared himself.

"Why don't you come over for dinner Sunday night?" he asked, looking older than usual.

"You got it, buddy, I'll bring the crab."

"Great, see ya then." He grabbed Linda's empty cup and headed back to the bar.

I slugged the dregs of my coffee and started the walk home, thinking about both Joe and Linda on the way. They were complete opposites, but there was something they both had in common. I couldn't put my finger on it, but then it popped into my head—pain. I was an expert in it, I should know.

THREE

— ❧ —

I lived a few short blocks from downtown Port Townsend, up on the northern bluff of the city overlooking the Strait of Juan de Fuca. After I retired from the Navy and divorced, I saved enough to buy a Victorian home that needed a lot of work. The house sat next to the Episcopal Church and at one time was the original rectory. It had been neglected over the years and finally the Church had decided to sell it. It retained a lot of charm, including beautiful moldings, oak floors and a stained-glass window of Saint John in the hallway entrance. I bought the house, planning to renovate it, but so far hadn't done much. I was pretty sure ghosts roamed the hallways.

I walked up Parish Street, passing rows of ornate Victorian mansions. The sidewalk was wet and a cold northern wind sliced into me. I shivered and leaned into the gusts. That was the only problem about living on this bluff, you caught the icy north wind full force. On the way up the hill, through the window of a quaint home I saw a man and woman sitting down to have dinner together, and it made me think about the gaping hole in my life.

I turned on the news, sat down at my wobbly Goodwill card table and dug into cold, leftover spaghetti. A 16-inch TV perched on a Navy foot locker in the corner filled the stark room with the sounds of two talking heads. I flicked it off and stared at the white, cracking walls as thoughts of the day drifted through my head. The encounter with Linda puzzled me—she was definitely not the type to work out at the Downtown Gym. The clientele were all locals and I'd never seen a woman dressed like her there. I wondered why she had chosen to approach me out of all the people working out. Now that I thought about it, she seemed to have made a beeline straight for me. I've been in gyms all my life and in my experience, people generally want to be left alone and work out by themselves, especially women. There was something about Linda that seemed odd, but I decided to let it go.

I fired up a kettle of hot water and brewed a strong cup of Irish tea. The tea reminded me of a funny incident when I was training with the Australian Special Air Service in the Queensland outback. The two Aussie special forces soldiers I was working with asked me if I wanted to stop and have a brew. I said, "Jeez boys, I don't drink when I'm working." They looked at each other and laughed, then unpacked a small kettle and started to brew a pot of tea. Stupid American.

I poured a chaser of Tullamore Dew whiskey into my tea, figuring the two Irish would go well together. The wind was straining against the old house so I went out back to assess the situation. Dark clouds were swirling rapidly across the sky as if in a race to flee a terrible storm. I settled into my old rocker, watching the lights of freighters making their way up the Strait to deposit goods at the ports of Seattle and Tacoma. I loved this view of the Strait, especially at night. I'd be happy to live in a tent on this lot if I could keep the view. The slow-moving freighters reflected my slow-moving life. After a dynamic career in the SEAL Teams, operating all over the world, I had retreated to this place alone, where I was going nowhere slowly. I needed solace and a reset in my life. I'd never pictured myself alone and haunted at the end of my Navy career.

The cracks in my life had been obvious to others but I'd been too busy and ambitious to care. I'd jumped on every opportunity to deploy overseas, consumed with the War on Terrorism. The changes in myself and the effects on my wife had crept up slowly. Now I could see that for years Elena had been giving me signals that she wasn't happy being the wife of a Navy SEAL who was gone all the time and who bottled up stress during his infrequent visits home. I didn't know how to deal with her emotions—I was born to be a SEAL and loved everything about it. I figured she'd eventually get over it. I realized too late that I was a better operator than a husband.

After the incident in Afghanistan, things went from bad to worse. I came home, but was in a deep pain spiral. She'd put up with the night sweats, bad dreams and drinking before, but I was more distant and withdrawn than ever. She pleaded with me to retire from the Navy... to start over. That scared me, so instead I deployed overseas again; probably not my smartest move. I volunteered for an assignment as an advisor in Africa and while I was gone she packed up and left for good. Ironically, after the divorce, on top of the incident in Afghanistan, I no longer had the motivation to continue in the Navy. I submitted my retirement request and made the escape here to Port Townsend.

A flood of bad memories of Afghanistan plundered my mind like a Mongol army. The white walls began to close in on me. A roiling undercurrent of dark emotions, depression and mental pain surged through my heart and soul like some demon animal. The devilish beast was so real, it had a name and a face: The Black Dog. *How do I wipe my memory clean? How do I end the pain and guilt? How do I erase the memory of innocent blood on my hands?* These were the howling thoughts that went through my mind over and over again.

"*You've gotta stop re-living the past, Jack,*" I scolded myself aloud. "*It's over man, get a life!*" I wanted to get a new life, but the past wouldn't pull its teeth out of me. A slippery thought slid in. *Where's your pistol? You can end all this pain right now. Do it.* I wavered, but stepped back from the abyss. I'd seen suicide up close, including that of my best friend. The damage done to those left behind was devastating. I'd tried to clean it up, but it was too big a mess. I'd always told myself it was a selfish act—ya kill yourself to stop the pain, but you end up transferring the pain to others. *Of course, if I isolate myself, there'll be fewer people to hurt,* I thought.

It wasn't late, but I decided to go to bed and read before falling asleep. I turned the lights off downstairs and walked up the creaky oak steps to my small, dark bedroom. I propped up the pillows in my futon bed and pulled an old brown leather book off the 40mm ammo can that served as my nightstand. I'd been re-reading Shakespeare's plays and I was halfway through *Hamlet, Prince of Denmark*. I read a few pages, but the dreariness of the three witches under the cold, dank Danish night made me feel even more miserable. I set the book down and reached under the bed for my deployment journal, the log of all of my deployments and incidents that had happened to me during my career. Towards the back of the journal was the section on my last tour in Afghanistan. I opened it at a random place and read, "I'm packing up my kit for redeployment. The Commander here is sending me home after the incident with the girl. He doesn't know whether to pin a medal on me or refer me to court martial. I really don't give a shit either way. I can't get those piercing blue eyes out of my head."

A sliver of moon shone through the cold window, bathing the room in a gentle white light. The wind had eased, and I could almost hear the weary Puget Sound freighter captains breathing sighs of relief. Good spirits moved silently through the house. I envied them—unlike me, they seemed to always be happy.

FOUR

I kneel over the young Afghan girl. She's wearing a green wool tunic with hand-stitched embroidery around the neck, heavy pants and leather sandals. Deep blue eyes stare back at me. There's no emotion in her soft, dirty face, just those penetrating eyes. I pull the gunshot triage kit from my belt and struggle to open it, cursing as my trembling hands fumble with a plug to seal the wound in her shoulder. I cover the bullet hole and gauze plug with a patch impregnated with a chemical that stops the bleeding. She mumbles softly. The goats are baying at each other, wondering what to do without their shepherd. Thoughts of my niece playing in the green grass with her fox terrier puppy cross my mind as I finish dressing the girl's wound. A salty tear falls from my cheek into the loose powdery dirt. *What kind of animal shoots an innocent kid?* I brush the hair from her face and pour water from my canteen into her mouth. She swallows slowly, but she's beginning to shake, the symptoms of shock are coming on.

My orders are clear, but the situation has changed. If I leave her here, she'll bleed out or be dragged off by an animal. If I take her to the village where I shot the Mullah, the Taliban will find out and kill me. Suddenly I don't want to be in this damn war anymore.

An unexpected feeling comes over me. I heave her onto my shoulder like a sack of potatoes. Something inside of me breaks and gives way, like a dirty glacier calving into the clear blue sea to reveal a pristine ice wall. A new sense of purpose forms in my gut like a budding crystal.

I start the slow climb down the backside of the mountain, tears rolling down my green and black camouflaged face into the bloody Afghan soil. I scramble down cliffs, navigating by the GPS on my wrist and the map in my pouch pocket. After an hour I set the girl down under a small cedar tree. Above me, the peak looms, a dark foreboding menace as the moon rises above the valley. The wind tears through my uniform, chilling me to the core. The girl is breathing, slowly. Suddenly there are voices above me. It's hard to tell how far away they are, as sound travels easier at night. My thumb slips the safety off my rifle. I wait, fully alert, ready to spring into action.

The voices drift away after twenty minutes. I hoist the girl over my shoulder again. She weighs about 60 pounds, but feels light. My mind is clear for the first time in a long while. I'm going to miss the extraction window but I'm not going to leave her. I realize what I have to do—it's about more than making amends. It's making things right, no matter the cost.

FIVE

Friday morning broke clear and crisp. The strong winds and rain of the night before had blown out, replaced by a rare blue sky and light easterly breeze. To feel the sun in full shine in October was splendid. I could even see the snowy peaks of Mt. Baker to the northwest. The darkness of last night had faded like mist, if only for a time.

I headed down the hill to the bookstore thinking about the upcoming day. After closing the shop this afternoon, I'd take the skiff out crabbing. That would be something to look forward to. The Black Dog wouldn't hound me today.

The sleepy little town was alive with activity. Merchants and organizers were getting ready for the Maritime Festival, which officially kicked off tonight. There was a buzz about the streets as city workers hung banners, blocked off parking and cleaned sidewalks and alleys. The ornate Victorian buildings I passed hinted at the former greatness of little Port Townsend. It had once been a thriving seaport at the mouth of the Puget Sound. Many thought that the "City of Dreams" would be the major seaport in the Northwest, but Seattle and Tacoma overtook it. Port Townsend was relegated to an isolated time capsule, perfect for those, like me, who needed to slow down, get away from people and start a new life.

I waved to Mrs. Johnson as I passed her bakery. The smell of fresh baked goodies wafted out from under the door. It was undoubtedly a better advertisement than her weathered old bakery sign. I unlocked the bookstore with a jingle of keys and whistled for Emilio. He scooted out from under a chair with half a mouse in his mouth. He was eating it like corn on the cob. I coaxed it from his mouth by the tail and tossed it in the trash can on the sidewalk outside, compensating him for his hunting efforts with a fresh bowl of food and water.

I brewed up a pot of coffee using Joe's special roast, Dark Mud. It was terribly strong, but I'd acquired the taste for strong coffee in the Navy. I poured myself a steaming cup, sat at my desk and fired up the laptop to check email. While the electrons were warming up, I gazed out the window onto Water Street. Despite the lift in my mood that the fine weather had brought on, The Black Dog was digging holes in my psyche just below the surface. I'd been out of the Navy and living here in Port Townsend for over a year now, but still felt a lingering darkness, a heavy feeling in my heart and a tangible sense of hopelessness. *Would it ever go away?* I wondered.

Mrs. Johnson appeared in the doorway with a basket of muffins on her pink arm, interrupting my morose musings. "Good morning, Jack. I've brought you oatmeal bran muffins today." She set the basket on my desk, pulled a napkin from her pocket and placed two big brown muffins on the napkin. They smelled delicious.

"Why thanks, Mrs. Johnson. You know I love those."

"Everybody does — they're my best sellers. Don't forget dinner tomorrow. Hyacinth is excited to meet you."

"I'm looking forward to meeting her too." Not exactly a lie. I was curious about her daughter, suspecting that under her mother's overbearing thumb she was either the rebellious type or as meek as a mouse.

"Six o' clock then, dear. We'll see you then."

"Thanks for the muffins, Mrs. Johnson!" I called after her as she stepped out the door.

My computer finally came to life and I logged on to check my email. Most of it was spam, but there was a response from the online antique book search. A vendor in British Columbia had a book in his collection printed in 1910 titled *Shipwrecks of the Strait of Juan de Fuca*. The email stated that the book contained a short section on the sinking of HMS Hawthorn, was in fair condition and for sale for $35. I bookmarked the email so I could show it to Cap if he came by the store today.

The door jingled and I looked up to see Linda Tomkin standing in the doorway. She was wearing red sunglasses that looked to me like high-end eyewear, brown stiletto-heeled leather boots and a short plaid skirt. She wore a red vest over a black silk blouse that accentuated her hourglass figure. She looked more ready to stroll down a fashion runway than attend a maritime festival. Her dark eyes reminded me of the women's eyes I had seen behind the black veil in the Middle East—both mysterious and alluring at the same time.

"I saw the Sea Wolf bookstore sign and figured this might be your bookshop," she said with a coy smile. Her high heels made a metallic clicking sound on the wood floor that corresponded with my increased heart rate. She wandered around, assessing the shop, as if she was hunting for a bargain at a department store.

Emilio poked his mottled gray head out from under a chair to scope out the new visitor. "Is this your famous cat?" she asked, squatting down to greet him. As I was trying not to gape at her shapely legs, Emilio cautiously crept up to her, then circled back to the protection of his chair before she could pet him. I'd never seen him do that with a customer but have always heard that cats have an instinct about people. Linda followed him to try and pet him, but I intervened before Emilio took a bite out of her.

"He's the only cat I know that licks like a dog and he just ate a mouse for breakfast, so you might want to avoid him this morning," I cautioned.

"Oh, how gross!" she shuddered and stood up quickly, spooking the cat, who dashed under my desk for protection.

Wow, smart first line Jack. You freaked her out within the first minute. I tried to recover, avoiding staring at her long legs. "So, you're off to the festival to gather crab data?"

"Yes, that shouldn't take all day though. I was hoping to have some fun, too. What are you doing after you close the bookshop today?" she asked with a smile that had just enough mischief behind it to make you wonder what kind of fun she had in mind.

"I'm planning on taking my skiff out and pulling up a few crab traps. Would you like to come along?"

"Jack, I'm studying crab data," she said, sounding a little exasperated. "I think I get enough of them," she clarified, swinging her large purse over her shoulder.

"Suit yourself, it's nice on the bay at sunset."

"Why don't you meet me after your little crabbing expedition down at Union Pier near the grandstand? I hear there's a good Irish band playing tonight."

I had a gut feeling that I should pass, but my primal desire won out. *Why not?* "Sure, I'll swing by about 7:30 or 8:00, after I finish crabbing and cleaning up."

"Fine, see you then. I better get down to the festival. Ciao," she waved her bangled wrist at me and sauntered out the door.

That woman has an agenda, said my inner voice. She was beautiful, unabashed, annoying, smart, aggressive and very attractive, but underneath it all, I sensed a coldness. I'd met too many fanatical men and women not to recognize that. Hell, I'd been fanatical in my own pursuit of being the best SEAL operator I could possibly be—I knew all about cold, hard living.

SIX

— ※ —

I spent the morning organizing bookshelves and trying to find a logical location for the boxes of books I'd scrounged at estate sales and swap meets. I loved to skim through the books before I placed them on the shelves. It wasn't a very efficient practice, but I enjoyed the feel of the old books and couldn't help cracking their covers to search for some ancient wisdom or a handwritten note. The books I loved best I kept on a small shelf behind my desk. I didn't intend to sell them, but for the right buyer I'd let them go.

I wasn't a very effective bookseller—barely making enough to pay the shop's modest lease and utility bills. But I wasn't that interested in making a ton of money. Not that I had anything against money; it was just the compromises you had to make along the way that disagreed with me. Hard work didn't bother me, but wasting my time on work that had no meaning was not a fair trade for my life. I was content to live on my Navy pension, which was shared with my ex-wife, along with some moderate investments we'd made over the years. Maybe someday the bookstore would make decent money, but probably not while I was running it.

At eleven o'clock, ol' Cap strolled in wearing a Greek fisherman's hat that made him look younger, despite his gray beard. He looked at me and smiled without saying a word and sat down at one of the small tables by the window. I sat down with him and explained that I'd found a book online that contained descriptions of the sinking of the Hawthorn. His eyes lit up when I told him that I could get it in two days via FedEx. I explained there was no guarantee that it contained all that much information on the Hawthorn itself, but he was undeterred and asked me to order it for him. He pulled a grimy wad of small bills out of his pants pocket. I told him not to bother until I'd actually received the book.

He sat at the table staring out the window as if lost in his thoughts, as I went back to my computer and placed the order. I had a feeling that Cap was alone in this world, much like me. "Hey Cap, how about some lunch? My treat."

His face lit up like a lighthouse, "Splendid idea, young man. We should grab a bite before the festival crowds clog the town."

"Where do you like to eat around here, Cap?"

"Jay's Crab Shack has the freshest seafood. Jay's father used to work on my boat," he said with a hint of pride, as he slowly got to his feet.

"I'd like to hear more about that," I said enthusiastically as I locked up the bookstore. I liked Jay's too - the food and the service were good, and it was close to the bookstore.

The waitress led us past rusty crab traps and white buoys adorning the walls to a polished pinewood table. Jay, the owner, noticed us and headed over. He was a small, wiry man with hair down to his shoulders and tattoos on his forearms. He'd seen me here a few times during lunch, but we'd never met.

"How ya doin', Cap?" he asked. Then he extended his hand to me, "I'm Jay."

"Jack Thibideaux, nice to meet you. I own the bookstore down the street." I stood up and shook his vice-like grip.

"It's good to see someone is keeping the bookstore going," he said. "Too many shops are goin' outta business with all the online sellers."

Jay turned to Cap. "Haven't seen ya in a while, Cap. Were ya on a trip or somethin'?"

Cap shrugged as if he didn't want to talk about it, but said, "I was outta town on some personal business."

Jay looked like he wanted to ask more, but let it go. "I'm sorry about your boat, Cap. That was a real shame," he said sincerely.

Cap looked down at his hands for a moment and I noticed a twitch in his face. He looked at me before responding, "Thanks Jay, lots of good memories went down with that boat." He was shaking his head dejectedly.

Jay turned to me but motioned to Cap, "Cap won't talk about it, but he saved my dad's life on that boat. A crab trap came loose during a storm and knocked my dad overboard. Cap was piloting the boat and didn't notice he was gone. When he realized what had happened, he turned the boat around in huge swells and searched for my dad until he found him, unconscious and almost dead in the freezing water. He rigged a quick hoist, jumped in and hauled him aboard. The doc said Dad woulda died of hypothermia in another five minutes."

I looked at Cap with newfound respect. It's easy to forget that many of the old men around us were once heroes. He said modestly, "Anyone woulda done the same for their crew."

"Aw, they mighta tried, but only a captain with your skill coulda pulled it off at night in a storm," Jay said forcefully. "Your money's no good here, order whatever you want." With a nod to me, he headed back to the kitchen.

The place was starting to fill up with tourists and festival goers. I let Cap order first. He went for the Dungeness crab special and I ordered the same. Much bigger than the East Coast Blue crab, a single Dungy could make a meal. The plates came fast and hot. I started to crack the claws and make a good mess. "Cap, how did you end up in Port Townsend with a crab boat?" I asked.

He took a sip of frothy beer and looked out the window reflectively, as if watching his past sail by. "I always wanted to become a fisherman. It was in my blood. My father was a cod fisherman on the Banks. The fishing industry was having a hard time in Massachusetts, but the salmon trade was booming in the Northwest. I decided to move to Port Townsend in 1978 and start over. I took the earnings from my merchant seaman travels and bought a salmon trawler."

"You were a merchant seaman too?"

"Yep, for 15 years I sailed on freighters from the eastern seaboard to all points east." He beamed with pride as he told his story.

"What was fishing like here back in 1978?" I asked.

"Those were good days. Salmon was plentiful—I caught a lot of fish. I was able to buy a bigger boat and keep a crew of six men employed." I could see the pride he felt as the memories came back to him.

"But you lost your boat?" I asked hesitantly, alluding to Jay's earlier comment.

He paused and took a deep breath, as if he wasn't sure he wanted to talk about it. "Three years ago, I was approached by Jim Tripper. He runs the Port Townsend Boat Works and owns his own salmon fishing fleet. He wanted me to sell 'im my boat and salmon quota."

I'd seen Jim Tipper around the marina, but hadn't met the guy.

"At first, he made a lowball offer, which I didn't even respond to. A month later I was fined for an environmental infraction because of oil supposedly leaking from my boat."

"Supposedly?"

"Wasn't my boat. Someone had spread oil around my hull at the waterline to make it look like it was leaking. After that, Tripper came to see me again. He insinuated that I would have more troubles if I didn't sell out to 'im."

"Did you tell the police?"

"No, I told him to suck eggs. One night three weeks later my boat caught fire, burned and sank while tied to the pier. The fire department investigated but couldn't identify the source of the fire. I knew what'd happened though. Tripper burned my boat," he stated, staring at me with fury in his eyes.

I recognized the pain in his face. "What happened then? Was it insured?"

"Oh, I got a small insurance payout, but it wasn't enough to replace the boat or my fishing gear. I still had my salmon quota, but no boat to fish with. I went to confront Tripper. He kept avoiding me but I finally caught up with him in his office."

"And?" I asked, on the edge of my seat.

Cap took a big gulp from his beer mug before speaking. "He'd destroyed my boat and I told him so. He shoved me out of his office, and said if I ever came back to the docks something bad would happen to me."

"*Then* did you go to the police?" I asked incredulously, developing a clearer picture of Jim Tripper.

"Naw, I knew he'd deny everything and get away with it."

I shook my head in shared dismay at the shocking injustice. "So what did you do when you couldn't fish anymore?" I asked quietly.

A pained look came across his face. He took another swig of beer. "I'm not proud of it, but that meeting with Tripper and the destruction of my boat sent me to a bad place. I lost everything I'd worked for my whole life. Truth is, I lost the will to live. I lived on the streets of Bremerton for almost two years. Tripper took everything from me. I've met a lot of bad men in my travels around the world, but never one as greedy as Tripper."

"Jeez Cap, I'm really sorry to hear all that," I said, feeling genuine sympathy for the guy and no small amount of disgust for Tripper.

The pain practically seeped out of Cap's pores. He gazed out the window and spoke as if talking to someone else. "I used to go into the library in Bremerton to keep warm in the rain and cold. I'd sit in a little leather chair in a corner and stare out the window at the tall dark cedars. In the spring I watched the flowers bloom from a chair beside that window. The librarian let me sit there every day, and after a few months, she started bringing me books. She never said anything, just left a book for me on the chair every day. Eventually I started reading them. Ya know what, Jack? Those books were like rungs on a ladder that helped me climb out of the pit I was in."

"Well, Cap, it sure looks like you did that. You're back here and you look good." I knew the pain of loss, but homelessness was another level of despair.

He started to peel the label off his beer. I could tell there was more he wanted to say, so I waited. Eventually he looked up at me, "I have a hard time trusting people after what Tripper did to me, but I have a hunch I can trust you, Jack."

It's no small thing to hold someone's trust—I've dropped it before, and it felt like a glass shattering.

Cap continued, leaning in closer, "I haven't told this to anyone, but a year ago I started reading about shipwrecks and came across the story of HMS Hawthorn. The librarian helped me research shipwrecks and I discovered that very few of them are ever salvaged. That's when the idea came to me that I could salvage the gold and get my fishing boat back."

Cap's eyes lit up and his voice was filled with passion and life as he talked about the shipwreck. I felt sorry for the old guy, knowing the chance of finding, much less salvaging a wreck like that was a huge long shot. He'd obviously latched onto this idea as a rope to pull himself out of the pit of despair. Who was I to tell him that the rope led nowhere?

Suddenly I remembered the trapper's journal. "Cap, I forgot to tell you something I found out about HMS Hawthorn." He looked at me eagerly. "I was searching online for information about the wreck and found a researcher at the Royal British Columbia Museum who said a trapper, Jeremiah Benton, had left a journal that supposedly described the sinking of the Hawthorn. Apparently, Benton saw the ship go down in a storm from the southern shore, where he was hunting, and described it in his journal."

"Jack, you've found the key! This is the clue I've been looking for!" Cap exclaimed with what I thought was irrational enthusiasm. "You'll find it for me, won't you? I mean you're an antique book dealer; you must know where to find this trapper's journal, yeah?"

I didn't want to let the old guy down and crush his dreams but I also didn't want to give him false hope. "The journal was published in very limited quantities around the turn of the century, Cap, and as far as anyone knows, it's been lost. No promises, but I'll do my best to find a copy. There are a lot of places to search, so maybe we'll get lucky."

That wisp of hope was enough to put a permanent smile on Cap's face. Even if it led to nothing, I wanted to help the old guy get his mojo back. If I was honest with myself, part of me, deep down, felt very much like Cap—lost in the darkness and loneliness of this world. Like him, I felt betrayed, by my own ambitions, my mistakes and the incident in Afghanistan. Seeing his hope, even if it was the wildest of long shots, gave me the feeling that I could have my own hopes, that I could pull myself out of the tailspin I felt I was in.

SEVEN

Cap and I parted with a handshake and I strolled back to the bookstore. I thought about the courage it had taken for Cap to jump into the sea at night and save Jay's father. Behind every man was a defining moment—surely that was Cap's moment. The sun was still out and a warm light breeze sparked a memory of walking on the beach with my ex-wife. It wasn't a real memory, but a fusion of past memories with my long-gone wishes for a happy future, forming a fanciful vision of what could have been.

I unlocked the bookstore to find Emilio laying on my desk in a sphinx pose with his paws on my keyboard. I rubbed the little beast, revving up his purr motor. "How come you're so happy to see me today?" I felt the pull of that Glenfiddich in my desk, but I had a mission—I wanted to get a line on that trapper's diary.

My usual used book sources wouldn't be able to locate a book as obscure as an out of print copy of the trapper's diary, but I had an idea. A friend of mine from the SEAL Teams had become a professor of history. He used to carry paperback history books in his cargo pocket on missions. I remembered him reading Herodotus while we were in the back of a C-130 getting ready for a night freefall jump. He was reading with a red lens flashlight just before we plunged out the back of the plane into total darkness. I ran into him briefly at the SEAL reunion last year, where we exchanged emails. I shot him an email asking if he had any ideas about how to find a copy of the old journal.

At four-thirty, I locked up and headed down to Union Pier and my skiff. Festival-goers were beginning to converge on the wharf, but it wasn't too crowded yet. My skiff was a classic design—horizontal, lapstrake planking, built by students at the Port Townsend Wooden Boat School. It was a great rowing and very seaworthy craft. Just seeing the little blue boat bobbing in the green bay water made me smile.

I pitched a bag of rank chicken necks into the bilge and pulled away from the pier with long strokes. Even if there were no crab in my traps, I loved to row out into the bay. The lofty bow on the skiff protected me from spray and the keel kept her steady in a beam sea. *This will be my workout today,* I thought, as my shoulders and arms felt the steady resistance of the cool green water. The breeze wafted the odor of rotting chicken necks up to my nose, bringing with it the memory of standing next to a burn pit in Iraq—a pile of old tires and an eviscerated dog with a black tongue were smoldering as if it was a rotten funeral pyre. I shuddered as the horrible smell came back to me. I had stood next to that burn pit wishing I was in a place like Port Townsend. Now part of me wished I was back in Iraq, in the fight, back to a time and place where I had clarity of purpose and a mission.

My first crab trap was 400 yards from the mouth of the harbor. I easily reached it in twenty minutes. The line down to the trap left slimy sea grass on my cold hands as I pulled up the wire cage from the deep. Four or five Dungies were scuttling around in the rusty trap. I double-checked their size with my measuring tool to ensure they were bigger than the legal limit. Putting two males in a wet canvas sack, I tossed the females and too-small males back. *A good start on dinner.*

I pulled chicken necks from my bait bag, baited up the pot and let it sink into the blue-green depth. A few hungry gulls landed nearby, hoping to horn in on a free dinner. I looked north as the little skiff rocked and saw the small orange buoys of my remaining three traps about 200 yards apart from each other. Looking over my shoulder, I started to pull toward the next trap, but halfway there I stopped. It hit me—rowing this skiff was a metaphor for my life now. I'm constantly focused on the past while plowing blindly into the future.

Three traps and an hour later, five dinner-size crabs were clicking and snapping at each other in the wet canvas bag. As I rowed back to the harbor, the sun set over the bay in a crimson orange burst of color, turning the water a brilliant purple and red. I stopped rowing for a minute and just let the skiff drift in the calm of the bay. My senses came alive. Until now, I hadn't noticed the gentle rocking of the skiff, the sound of the seagulls screeching above, the briny smell of the bay water. *There are a lot of beautiful things in this world, Jack. You need to start paying attention.*

I walked up the hill with the crabs snapping at each other in the bag and tossed them on ice when I reached home. After a shower and a microwave burrito I looked at myself in the mirror. A day's worth of black stubble covered my face under a faded ball cap. I'd thrown on a pair of weathered blue jeans and a plain Polo shirt, certainly not a fashion statement to match Linda Tomkin. For a second, I thought about changing into something nicer but then said aloud, "To hell with that." The stars were out in force and it was a beautiful crisp evening as I walked down to Union Pier.

Weaving behind the throng of spectators and partygoers to avoid the crowd, I stopped in front of a mobile coffee van to scan the bleachers for Linda. She was sitting with her arms wrapped around her legs, listening to the band towards the bottom of the bleachers. I bought a couple of cups of steaming coffee and poured a small bottle of whiskey into mine. I had to climb steps up the backside of the bleacher and then walk down to her from behind. As I got close, I realized she was on her cell phone and didn't see me behind her.

"Hello there," I called out over the rhythm of the Celtic drums. She immediately put the phone away. A flash of what looked like anger crossed her face, but she quickly caught herself and offered that trademark beaming smile that would stop any man's heart.

"This band is great, come sit next to me, it's cold out here. Oh lovely—coffee."

I knew how to take orders so I sat down next to her. The heat coming off her short skirt and long, crossed legs was enough to make me warm.

"How was crabbing?" she asked.

"Wonderful. I pulled up five keepers. The sunset was beautiful, too. A great way to end the day. You should try it sometime." I couldn't see her stepping into the skiff in those sleek golden sandals. "How did your crab research go?" I asked, taking a gulp of my spiked coffee.

"Excellent. I met a bunch of old crabbers who shared all kinds of data with me," she said.

The young Irish singer on stage had a beautiful voice. She drummed on the bodhran while gracefully dancing across the stage. A few spectators arose and began to dance in front of the stage.

"Come dance with me," Linda coaxed, as she stood up and grabbed my arm.

I'm a terrible dancer, but I figured I could blend into the crowd. I stood there dumbfounded as she danced around me, her enticing moves resembling those of a belly dancer. She was light on her feet and it felt like she was putting a spell on me. She became one with the music; spinning, tapping, swaying and twirling to the mournful sounds. In the end, all I could do was stand there gazing at her, tapping my foot.

I was mesmerized. Her long hair bouncing, her short skirt swaying, her come-hither smile—it was all overwhelming. I felt myself slip into a familiar place, like holding my breath under a pounding wave and looking up to see the blue ocean silently roll over me. I didn't know how this night was going to end, but I knew I didn't want to be alone with The Black Dog. Didn't want to go home, stare at the white walls and let the dark past kick my ass again.

Linda sensed something in me—a weakness maybe, a dark door, an opportunity. She pulled me close and whispered, "Take me home with you." I thought, or at least hoped, she was expressing compassion, or maybe even attraction, but I really had no idea what her motivation was.

The light from the moon shone through the bedroom window onto Linda's bare back as she slept. I glanced at my watch and saw it was 5:00 a.m. The night cascaded into conscious thought: Linda's mesmerizing solo dance, slow dancing together, walking up to my house and open-ing the door, three more shots of whiskey, passionate kissing, Linda dropping her clothes on my living room floor and a wild flurry of love-making. I had a headache and a soul ache. The room was boxing me in and I had to get out.

Slipping on my clothes, I quietly stepped outside. It was chilly and the moon was about to set. Up hill a few blocks was a 24-hour diner. The place was empty except for a young girl with mermaid tattoos on her neck wiping the counters. I ordered coffee and stared into the dark liquid as if it was going to tell my future. Somehow I knew my life was about to change. I always had a sixth sense for these things. It had saved me many times in dangerous situations. Now it gently slipped into my consciousness. Something was about to happen, but no detail accompanied the feeling. *Maybe it was Linda? Maybe she would be the change in my life.*

I ordered a cup of coffee to go for Linda and walked back to the house. She was gone. There was a note on the ammo box nightstand saying that she needed to run some important errands. I expected to feel something - anger, sadness, joy, but I felt nothing. One thing struck me as odd—she hadn't asked anything about my past. I was wearing a SEAL Team ball cap and she must have seen the pictures behind my desk at the bookshop. Usually that generates at least a couple of questions from people who were in the military, and even from most civilians. *Interesting.*

EIGHT

— ❖ —

U nder the cover of a twisted pine tree I check the girl's ragged wound using my red lens flashlight to avoid detection. The bandaging has stopped most of the bleeding, and she's in and out of consciousness. I roll up her tattered sleeve, find a thin vein on her left forearm, clean her arm with an alcohol pad, insert a needle into the vein and plug in my one bag of IV saline solution. After tying it off to an overhead branch, I twist the valve open and let the life-saving fluid drip into her.

I flip on my radio and unfold the antenna. "Firebase Trident, this is Jackal, over. Firebase Trident, this is Jackal, over." Nothing but static. I check the radio to make sure I'm on the right channel and see a big dent in the side of the case. I must've smashed it against a rock. *There goes my lifeline.* I fold the antenna and stow the radio in the bottom of my pack, then check on the girl. The IV bag is almost empty; I let it finish dripping. The girl awakens and stares at me with cloudy blue, uncomprehending eyes. I gently remove the needle and bury it alongside the empty IV bag in the damp soil.

I'm at a final crossroads. I can either make my way east around the mountain to the secondary extraction site and hope to get radio contact to coordinate an alternate extraction, or scrap that plan and work my way down the mountain to the nearest US military firebase. I'm on the opposite side of the mountain from the extraction site. I've been forced to patrol to this side to avoid contact with the Taliban. It would be shorter to work my way around the mountain to the extraction site, but the chance of running into a band of Taliban searching for the infidel who killed their Mullah is high.

My gut tells me to take the girl down the mountain, my rational mind screams to leave her and head to the secondary extraction site. I realize the consequences of my gut feeling: my career, maybe my life will be over. A thought hits me like a sledgehammer: *The girl is more important than my career or my life. I've lived long enough, she's still young.* I know now that I will not leave the girl behind.

I decide to go with my gut: head down the west side of the mountain, hike across the valley, and walk into a firebase. The Taliban won't expect me to do this, and if there's one thing that has saved my bacon over the years, it's that I know not to be predictable.

The other tactic that has kept me alive is to move only at night. I can move fast during the day, but the Taliban can move faster. This is their home turf. They can see me move from miles away and surround me before I have a chance to escape.

We've got about two hours of darkness left. I search for a good hide site and find a thicket of dense brush that will work well. I carry the girl to the edge of the bushes, set her down in the dirt, lay down on my stomach and pull her onto my back, then crawl through the thicket along a narrow animal trail. I stop and pull branches behind me to hide the entrance. A good tracker would find us, but no one else would detect us in this site. I set the girl down and wrap my Gore-Tex jacket around her. She makes a little sound that I can't understand. I move a few feet from her and sit against a rock with the rifle in my lap. *I will take her down the mountain to a field hospital. This is my responsibility. Nothing else matters.*

NINE

——— ✦ ———

I kept the bookshop open till noon on Saturday. After locking up for the day, I headed to the marina to make an inspection of my boat. Sea Wolf was a 1979 42-foot trawler, powered by twin 120-horsepower Ford Lehman diesels. Her interior was a beautiful dark red teak. There was a master stateroom aft with a head and shower, and two small staterooms forward, along with another head. In the center of the boat was the galley and dinette, along with the navigation station and interior helm. She was old and slow, making ten knots tops, but she was seaworthy and surprisingly fuel-efficient. She'd carried me through many storm-tossed seas.

I checked the bilges, which were dry, and pulled the engine dipsticks to inspect the oil level. She started with a satisfying rumble. The dual engines idled as I inspected the dock lines and fenders. Chasing a seagull off the mast, I made a mental note to get one of those fake owls that are supposed to scare away birds. As Sea Wolf's diesels came up to operating temperature, I sat in the open cockpit aft and enjoyed the afternoon breeze coming down the bay into the marina. *I could just pull in the dock lines, head out of here and start a new life... again. I'd find an uninhabited bay surrounded by dark trees and live off the land, hunting and fishing.* But my sense of responsibility called BS on that option, although I realized my escape to Port Townsend was the first off ramp on the road to isolation. There were always more remote turns I could take if things really went south.

Walking back to the parking lot, I passed a 40-foot Hunter sailboat on the pier and saw the telltale bubbles of a diver in the water. On the other side of the boat I spotted the dive cart of my Aussie friend Steve Cooley. Steve had landed in Port Townsend about the same time as me. His marriage, much like mine, had gone sour, though for different reasons. He'd worked as a commercial diver in Australia before he and his wife started a dive school in the Middle East. It was tough getting started in business in the Arab world. When they hit financial hard times, Michelle left him, so Steve packed up his dive school business and came to Seattle to work in the diving salvage business. Eventually he drifted up to Port Townsend and started his own hull cleaning and underwater repair business. We met on the docks and became fast friends.

I yanked on the yellow umbilical air hose a couple of times and he came to the surface, his black wetsuit hood and bushy mustache making him look very much like a sea lion. The water up here never warms to more than the high fifties. Without a wetsuit, a diver would reach hypothermia in 15-20 minutes. That's why boating was dangerous in these frigid waters; if you accidentally go over the side, you quickly become too cold to save yourself. It took some extra gumption to dive in this region.

Steve pulled himself up onto the pier. "G'day mate!" he greeted, as he shook the water off his shock of long red hair. "Checking up on the old Sea Wolf, eh?"

"Yeah, I haven't been aboard her in a week. Everything looks good," I said.

He stood up, "I checked your zincs yesterday, they were 25% gone. I'll change them out at 50%."

"How did the bottom look?" I asked.

"Smooth, mate—the barnies don't like your new paint flavor," he joked. "I didn't even have to swipe it with a sponge."

I laughed. I'd mixed powdered cayenne pepper in the bottom paint to keep the barnacles off: a trick Steve had taught me.

"Glad my tip is working," he said, throwing on a hoodie. "How 'bout a beer tonight?" he asked as he packed up his dive cart.

"I'd love to, but I've got a dinner date."

With a sly smile and raised eyebrows he asked, "New love in your life then?"

"No, I promised Mrs. Johnson I'd go to dinner with her and meet her daughter."

"Good luck with that, Jack," Steve said with a smirk.

The thing I love about Steve is that he's a straight shooter, no pretenses. He used to be one of the top commercial divers in Australia, and now he scrubs boat hulls in Port Townsend. He didn't let his ego get away from him when he was making big bucks offshore diving, and he doesn't feel bad about his current work. He's one of those rare souls who's been able to separate his ego from his work.

A lot of SEALs I knew had a tough time making that separation, me included. Our identity gets wrapped up in being a Navy SEAL. When we're no longer in the SEAL community we have a hard time finding ourselves, sorting out who we really are outside of the Teams. I thought it wouldn't be a problem for me. I was wrong.

I used to counsel the young guys in the Teams, telling them to find themselves beyond the SEAL Teams. One day they wouldn't be in the Teams anymore and they needed to have a solid sense of their own worth separate from the all-consuming life in the Teams. The intensity and deep brotherhood of the SEALs made it a hard thing to do.

Steve started stowing his gear on the dive cart and threw on a heavy wool sweater. I turned to go, then stopped and looked back at Steve. "Hey Steve, what do you know about Jim Tripper?"

He paused, thought for a moment, then said, "There was this diver who worked for Tripper. We dove together in Seattle a few years ago." He looked down and shook his head with regret. "He drowned in this harbor last year when he got tangled on the bottom. I took up a collection for his widow from guys in the maritime industry around here. I went to see Tripper for a donation but he wouldn't give a dime. That's the kind of guy he is." Steve gulped water from a Nalgene bottle and shook his head with obvious disgust. "Don't tell me he's a mate of yours?"

"No, I'm just trying to get a read on the guy. I've heard some things," I said, thinking of Cap's boat story.

"Yeah, well believe what you've heard, Jack," Steve said as he finished rolling up his air hose.

"Thanks for the heads-up," I said, nodding. "We'll have that beer soon, yeah?"

As I headed up the pier to my truck, I thought about what Cap and Steve had told me about Tripper. I've dealt with a lot of twisted, evil men in my career, but just plain greed was something I rarely encountered.

TEN

⸺ ◦ ⸺

At 6:15 I walked into the restaurant and checked out the place. Wherever I go, I like to arrive early to scan the environment with a tactical eye before I sit down. I'd rather choose my own seat with a view of the entry points and exits than have someone choose a seat for me where I would be boxed in. I picked out a booth next to the window overlooking the Puget Sound that gave me a clear view of the rest of the tables and the only entrance. No one could approach the table without being easily seen by me.

The Belmont had a nice view of the bay framed by tall pines. The restaurant served homestyle American food at a decent price. Shelves holding books and knick-knacks were mounted on the walls. I guess it was supposed to make you feel at home. Seemed more like a fake museum to me.

Mrs. Johnson and her daughter stepped through the front door at 6:35. Mrs. Johnson wore a flowery Laura Ashley dress with a matching green scarf. Her daughter wore tan slacks and a plain blue blouse. Mrs. Johnson was talking and waving her arms in her usual exuberant manner. Her daughter walked slightly behind with her head lowered, as if trying not to be recognized. She looked up and spotted me waving from the booth and motioned to her mother, who was talking to the hostess. As they strolled down the aisle, I watched Hyacinth's face—she looked embarrassed, almost reluctantly following her mother. She was shorter than Mrs. Johnson, about five-foot-five, with shoulder length, wind-tossed blonde hair. She had the stride of an athlete and my first impression was that she looked like a long-distance runner. As they approached, her eyes locked on mine, and then the tiniest smile rose like a sunrise from the corners of her mouth.

"Jack! So good to see you," Mrs. Johnson exclaimed as if she hadn't seen me for a year. "I want you to meet my daughter Hyacinth."

I moved out from the booth, stood up and extended a handshake. Her hand was small, but strong. "I go by Cindy, actually. Mom just doesn't like that name," she explained with a chagrined expression.

First hint of rebellion. She certainly didn't seem like a copy of her mother. I gestured for them to sit opposite me in the booth. I was deathly afraid that Mrs. Johnson would try to sit next to me. I don't like anyone to block my escape from a seat, plus I knew I wouldn't be able to handle her chattering away into my ear. Luckily, she scooted into the inside seat across from me, next to the window, and her daughter sat directly across from me. Now that I could see her up close, Cindy looked about ten years younger than me, without the lines on her face that I carried. "It's the miles, not the years," a Master Chief had once reassured me when we were joking about our bodies prematurely aging.

Cindy had cream-colored skin and high cheekbones. Beautiful deep blue eyes stared intently at me without blinking. I sensed she was trying to figure out the weathered-looking, 40-something, wiry guy in jeans and polo shirt who owned a bookstore next to her mother's bakery. She was very attractive and I returned her stare and added a smile. My first impression told me that those soft blue eyes were the windows to a compassionate person.

After the waitress had taken our order, Cindy broke the ice with, "Where are you from Jack?" Her voice carried a bit of a West Coast accent.

"I grew up in Louisiana... in a foster family." People don't often ask more about my background after that bit of news. "I joined the Navy when I was 17. I wanted to see the world." That's the story I've come to tell myself. It cuts a little too deep to think that I joined the Navy to find family and prove myself worthy. "How about you?" I asked her.

"I grew up in Seattle, majored in education in college and became a teacher after graduating. Now I work overseas. So how long have you been here in Port Townsend, Jack?" she asked.

I hesitated before answering, thinking about a way I could steer the conversation away from my past. I tried to redirect back to Cindy, "I've been here about a year now. What do you do overseas?" Mrs. Johnson shook her head slightly and looked down at her hands. I got the feeling she wasn't happy with Cindy's work.

"I work for a non-profit called Teachers Care. We build and operate schools in Pakistan on the Afghanistan border in remote, poverty-stricken areas. I'm the Director of Teacher Development. I oversee curriculum and teacher training in those countries. We use the trimester system so I get about a month off three times a year. That's how I'm here visiting mom."

Fascinated, I said, "Wow, that sounds like tough work. How did you end up working in Pakistan?"

"I was teaching at this elite private school in Seattle; you know, the kind where the parents complain if the kid gets an A-minus and mothers pick up their kids in Porsches or BMWs. Lots of dot-com money."

"Yeah, I know the type," I nodded.

"After a few years I felt like I wasn't making a difference, like what I was doing didn't really matter." She gazed down at the table, thinking about her past. "We had a guest speaker talk about teaching girls in Central Asia, in places where they're often not even allowed to attend school. Suddenly I felt like my training could serve a greater purpose. I did some research, sent in my resume and they hired me."

I thought about the courage and dedication it took to leave a known, comfortable job and head off to a danger zone to help kids who had a dark and uncertain future. I looked at her with newfound respect. "What's it like teaching kids over there?" I asked, thinking of the girl in Afghanistan, who I doubted was even allowed to attend school.

She thought for a moment, then answered, "Once you strip away money and material things, kids are all pretty much the same. They haven't absorbed all the aspects of their culture yet, so they're very open. For example, children aren't naturally racist, right? That has to be drilled into them." She spoke with a passion and enthusiasm that I used to feel. I was impressed. It might have been the freckles on her nose or the dedication she had for a worthy but dangerous cause. Actually, I was more than impressed.

Mrs. Johnson was beaming as Cindy spoke. Cindy noticed her mom nodding her head in approval and said, "Mom, tell Jack how you sponsor some of the girls in our school."

"Oh, well, it's not much," Mrs. Johnson blushed, but I do enjoy making sure those poor girls have proper school supplies. It doesn't cost much really." She reached into her handbag and brought out a postcard-sized photo and pushed it across the table to me. "Here are some of the girls with their new backpacks," she said with obvious pride, looking up at me.

I picked up the card. Four girls were standing next to a battered metal building, each one hugging a pink or blue backpack as if it was a treasured gift. My gut tightened as I thought of a little blue-eyed Afghan girl who should be in a picture like this with her own new, pink backpack. I laid the photo back on the table, "Yeah, those are lovely, Mrs. Johnson," I said, trying to keep my voice steady.

"I make a special gingerbread cookie," she said. "All of the proceeds from the sale of that one cookie go towards those girls. I've raised over $3,000 so far." I made a mental note to buy a batch of those next week. I saw there was clearly more to both of these women than what appeared on the surface.

"How long have you owned the bakery, Mrs. Johnson?" I asked, trying to piece together how she ended up in Port Townsend.

"It's been three years now," she said. My husband Herb and I worked as accountants in Seattle. He passed away three years ago and I moved up here to do something I always wanted to do—own a bakery." I don't know why I hadn't asked Mrs. J about this before tonight. I felt like a schmuck, mooching off her free muffins all this time, engrossed with my own problems. I should have known this.

"So why Port Townsend?" I asked her. It seemed like everyone I met retreated here for one reason or another.

Cindy answered for her mother, "My parents used to bring me here for the 4th of July when I was a girl. We hiked, collected seashells, walked the beach, bought ice cream and watched the fireworks. It was wonderful."

I saw Mrs. Johnson's face light up with a memory. "Do you remember when your father danced with Bigfoot?" she asked, turning to Cindy with a smile. They both started laughing. I waited for the backstory, envious of their happy memories.

Cindy explained, "Down at a concert in the park, someone dressed as Bigfoot started dancing in front of the stage. We were in the front row, so Bigfoot grabbed Dad's hand and he stood up and did the Macarena with Bigfoot!"

"To answer your question, Jack," Mrs. Johnson said, trying to stop laughing. "We had so many good memories here in Port Townsend that I decided to start my bakery here."

That's funny, I thought, *I moved here to get away from my memories.*

While Mrs. Johnson told the story of how she came up with her first recipes, I stole a glance at Cindy, who returned my gaze with a smile and a knowing shake of her head. She seemed to know her mother could drive people crazy with her syrupy sweetness and non-stop talking. I returned her smile but suddenly felt like the walls were closing in on me. If I had to listen to another one of Mrs. Johnson's recipe stories, my head might explode.

Dinner arrived, bringing a short period of blessed silence as we dug in. I ordered the hamburger, Mrs. Johnson had the pasta and Cindy ordered a salad. As we ate, I noticed a rough-looking character walk in and start to yell at someone in the foyer. He was wearing a biker's jacket and sported piercings in his ears and nose. I stopped eating and watched him take a seat, clearly making the staff and customers uncomfortable. My mind short-circuited to the Galidari Hotel in Sri

Lanka. LTTE terrorists ran a car bomb into the hotel I was staying at and followed up with suicide bombers in the lobby as people tried to escape. Few people knew how brutal that civil war had been. Cindy noticed the hardening of my jaw and the faraway look and turned her head to see what I was watching, then turned back to me.

"Is something wrong, Jack?" she asked with obvious concern, setting her fork down.

"No, I'm fine," I lied, forcing myself back to the present.

The twinkling lights of ships steaming down the Sound were visible in the clear night through the darkened window. I envisioned myself heading off on one of those freighters to a foreign port without a care. I glanced at Cindy and her eyebrows were raised as if she was reading my mind, wondering why I wanted to be somewhere else while I was supposed to be here with her.

After dinner we walked along the bluff overlooking the Sound. The cool onshore breeze was gusting, swaying the tall, dark pines. "I'll have to excuse myself, dear," Mrs. Johnson said with what sounded like faux regret. "The wind is too much for my hair." I was sure she'd planned the exit so her daughter and I could be alone together.

Cindy and I started walking slowly back to town. "I want to apologize for my mother. She's always trying to set me up," she said, sounding a bit exasperated.

"No problem, your mom's sweet. I'm not sure I could live without her regular delivery of muffins at this point," I joked. I thought for a moment, then added, "You're not what I expected when I envisioned her daughter."

"Whadda you mean?" she asked, turning to look at me.

"You know, your mom's so talkative and bubbly and you seem... well... sort of quiet and reserved." She nodded in agreement, seemingly approving of my analysis.

Beams from the streetlights were dancing off the wet pavement as we walked back to town. "Did you go to Evergreen State?" I asked. She had donned a green parka with a small emblem of the school on the front. Evergreen was known as a kind of free-thinking hippie school.

"Yeah, I graduated ten years ago. It was a great education."

"Really?" I sounded too surprised and hoped she wasn't offended. "What did you study?"

"The paradox of progress," she answered, zipping up her parka against the wind.

"Wow, that's a unique major," I said, instantly regretting my tone.

She gave me a look like, "Hey jackass, it's a great school."

We walked through the darkened downtown area, the shuttered shops reflecting the quiet of the street, then through a residential neighborhood dotted with small, turn-of-the-century homes trying to hold on to their former glory.

I didn't want to pry into her life, but I figured we were getting to know each other so maybe I'd ask her something more personal now that her mother was gone. "Have you ever been married?"

Walking alongside me in perfect rhythm, she turned her head to look at my eyes, before staring straight ahead, "No I haven't. My career right now would be tough on a relationship. I'm gone up to 8 months at a time. My work with those girls is so important right now." She paused before adding, "I'm not so blind as to believe that someone else couldn't do my job," she said, "But I'm really good at this and we're making a difference over there... ya know what I mean?"

"Cindy, believe me, I know exactly what you mean."

"How did you get started with bookselling?" she asked with genuine curiosity in her voice.

"It's kind of a long, sad story." *Why the hell did I say that? Pathetic!*

"I'd really be interested in hearing it, Jack," she said quietly, stopping and looking at me pointedly.

I paused for a moment and looked into her face, suddenly feeling I could trust her. I told her the short version of my career, marriage, divorce, retirement from the Navy and how I'd found myself in Port Townsend.

Cindy listened with her eyes more than her ears. I'd started out with the surface facts, as if I was talking to a newspaper reporter. She nodded at each turn of my story, as if fully digesting every decision I'd made. There's a need in all of us, I think, that yearns to be understood on more than a surface level and I felt like I could open up to her... at least a bit.

"There's something else..." I stopped and looked directly into her eyes. I'd been thinking about those girls all night in the photo Mrs. Johnson had showed me. "I shot a girl in Afghanistan." I don't know why I told her—it just came out, like the guy who says to a new friend, "By the way, I'm an alcoholic." I couldn't hide the pain in my voice; it was a confession that felt horrible, yet freeing at the same time.

She turned to me and said, "I can't imagine what that was like, Jack, but I'm sure it was an accident." I looked at her. *What could I say?* I stopped talking and we walked on in silence.

We arrived at her mother's home, where Cindy stopped in the driveway and took my hand in hers. It was warm. "Listen Jack, I'm glad I met you. I hope I'll see you again."

"Me too," I blurted out a little too fast. She quietly opened the door, turned around and gave me a soft smile. I started to walk home, already feeling the darkness seeping into the corners of my mind.

Zipping up my coat against the cool evening breeze, I walked up Water Street, passing a few souls who were out and about. The Black Dog had been waiting for me, slinking around one of these corners, knowing that I'd soon be alone. An impulse came to try and fend off the impending darkness. I turned into the VFW building as if pulled by a hidden magnet. Except for a tall vet with long dark hair seated at the end of the bar nursing a Budweiser, I had the place to myself. I liked to drink alone when I was wrestling with the Black Dog. I talked to myself and the mangy beast, sometimes out loud—behavior that usually freaked people out.

"Double rum on the rocks," I said to the bartender as I took a seat. The girl behind the bar had the Sailor Jerry look with faux red hair and nautical tattoos on her arms, but looked too young to be working at a VFW. I was used to seeing old wives or girlfriends of veterans behind the bar. They were pretty good at reading vets.

The Black Dog awoke when I'd told Cindy about the girl in Afghanistan. I ran my hands down my face as if that could wipe away the grief, threw back the double rum then ordered another. After my third, visions from the day cascaded in my mind like a jerky black and white movie reel. I saw Cap on his fishing boat, full of life and vigor, hauling in a dripping line of sleek silver salmon, Jim Tripper counting pieces of gold on a table while men around him were eating chunks of rotten black bread, Cindy walking through a knee-high field of green, her blonde hair blowing in the wind. Her back was to me, but she stopped, turned her head and smiled. I saw a young girl with a dirty face and blazing blue eyes staring at me, as if to ask, "Why?" I mouthed, "I'm sorry, I'm sorry, I'm so sorry," and was reaching for my fourth drink when the vet from the other end of the bar came over and sat down next to me.

"You all right, bud?" he asked. "You were talkin' to yourself."

I turned on my barstool to get a better look at him. He was tall, maybe six foot, with shoulder-length black hair and high cheekbones. I glanced down and saw a prosthetic leg protruding from his pants. Deep scars on his face looked like burn marks. I'd seen injuries just like that before.

"Yeah, I'm OK, thanks," I said.

"I'm Micah," he said, his voice deep, as he extended his hand.

"Jack," I reached out my hand with all the respect I could muster. "IED blast?"

He nodded, "Army convoy driver in Iraq."

I knew he wouldn't share unless it was with someone he trusted. I took another chance. "I was in the SEAL Teams in Iraq and Afghanistan."

He nodded, then his face hardened into a look that brothers-in-arms would recognize as the game face right before you go over the wire into bad guy territory. "I was drivin' a humvee in Baghdad, moving VIPs outside the Green Zone," he began, staring into his beer. "We were hit by an EFP. It killed the other three in the vehicle but only took my leg." An EFP was a type of shape charge that sent molten steel at speeds up to 2000 meters per second through anything. It cut through vehicles like cheese.

I respected that he'd said it "only took my leg," as if that was a minor thing he could live without. Convoy driver had to be the hardest job in Iraq and Afghanistan. They were targets every time they left a compound. Al Qaeda in Iraq, ISIS and the Taliban in Afghanistan were always waiting for them and planning attacks. I glanced again at his torn up face and instantly felt like a self-absorbed jerk for letting my troubles get the best of me when others had taken harder hits.

"I mostly flew in helicopters to missions in Iraq," I offered.

He took a sip of beer, then spoke quietly, "I was dead for a few minutes but they brought me back somehow. I've had 17 surgeries." It sounded like the confession of a dying man. I could tell he must have been burned pretty bad and endured painful skin grafts.

"The Army discharged me and I came back here to my home," he said, taking another pull on his Budweiser.

"Makah Tribe?" I took a guess.

"Yes, they're my people," he said, clearly proud of his heritage.

"Do you live here in Port Townsend?" I asked.

"No, on the Makah Reservation. I come to Port Townsend once a week to take my niece to therapy."

I shouldn't have asked, but the rum made me impolite, "Therapy for what?"

"My older brother Jerry neglects her and beats her when he gets drunk, so I take her to therapy once a week. It's the least I can do."

"Jeez man, I'm sorry to hear that. How old is she?" I asked.

"Ten," he replied with anger and sadness in his voice.

My gut tightened. "Where is she now?" Again, none of my business, but I asked anyway.

"I have a cousin in town who has a daughter. I drop her off so they can play together when we're in town."

I picked up my fourth double rum, but set it down again. "I own a small bookstore on Water Street. Why don't you bring your niece around? I'll pick out some books for her."

He looked at me and nodded appreciatively. "She'd like that. She loves to read. I'll take you up on that," he said enthusiastically. It was the first time I'd seen him smile.

"Hey, I appreciate you checking on me," I added.

"That's what soldiers do, right? Look out for each other."

"I was in the Navy, but I have a lot of respect for soldiers. To you, soldier," I toasted, raising my drink so he could clink his bottle against my glass."

"Does your brother work on the reservation?" I asked.

"He does random jobs all over. He just started working for some guy named Tripper here in Port Townsend. I'm not sure what he does, but Jerry's not good for anything except muscle and intimidation."

"I've heard bad things about Tripper. Sounds like those two have a lot in common," I said.

Micah finished his beer, then turned to me. "Well, Jack, I've got a long drive back to the rez tonight, so I need to roll."

I stood up and shook his hand, "Alright Micah, good to meet you. Bring your niece by, I'd like to meet her. What's her name, by the way?"

He started toward the exit then turned around and said, "Sarah," before disappearing out the door.

I sat there and thought about Micah's niece. *Who would abuse a ten-year-old girl? Micah's brother had to be some kind of twisted lowlife.* But then thoughts of that young girl in Afghanistan hit me in the gut like a baseball bat and I could hardly breathe for a second.

The young bartender tapped me on the shoulder, "Hey, you OK?"

I snapped back. "I'm fine, thanks," I lied. I laid a wad of cash on the bar and walked out into the night. The stars were hidden under a dark, cloudy sky. I tucked my hands into my jacket and trudged home. *This fucking life is miserable.* The Black Dog trotting next to me lifted his head into the air and nodded in agreement—he smelled his prey.

ELEVEN

— ✳ —

I check the girl's pulse—weak but steady. The outer bandage is holding, but seeping blood. I lift her head, pour dollops of water down her throat. She takes a sip, coughs and slowly opens one eye. I expect to see hatred, but all I see is a piercing blue eye looking back at me. It's dusk, and the wind has died down to a light breeze. Dark clouds drift across the moon, but there's still ambient light. "I'm gonna get you help," I whisper forcefully, more for myself than for her.

I take a drink and check my watch; 1800—eleven hours until twilight. I gently hoist the girl to my shoulder, holding her with my left hand and carrying the rifle in my right. I look up before heading out; the sky is full of stars, the clouds have moved on. I stare for a minute into that infinite space, then start trudging down the mountain.

The treacherous rocky terraces and ledges are giving way to tall pines and softer soil. The paths are still steep but there's better footing. Looking up for a second, I trip on an exposed root in the dark and fall to my knees so I won't drop the girl. A sharp rock below the pine needles cuts into my left knee. I'm frozen there in pain for what seems like an eternity. The physical pain throbs and opens the dungeon door to emotional pain. For the first time, I think, *I'm not going to make it.* But as quickly as that comes, I think, *I have to make it. I won't stop,*

I won't quit. The confidence within, born of training, experience and pluck quiets the physical pain. *This is much bigger than my puny life. I have a young life to save.* I get up off my knees, stop feeling sorry for myself, wrap a bandana around my wound and continue down the mountain.

The air warms as I descend and I'm sweating now. We rest next to a large granite rock on the side of the valley. I pull a water bottle from my pack and pour a few sips into the girl's mouth, then take a swig myself. Pulling out my red lens flashlight I look into her eyes—she's barely conscious but stares at me wordlessly. I wonder what she's thinking. Her eyes close, I shake her and she opens them again. "I'm going to get you some help. I'm going to get you off this mountain. Hang in there!" She doesn't understand, of course.

I pull out my laminated map of the area. It's a 1-50,000 scale, so the detail is not great. I locate our current position based on my GPS track, then scan the map looking for the best route and destination. The map shows a small village in a valley at the base of this mountain about thirty kilometers from here. I circle it on the map.

TWELVE

—— ◦ ——

S unday morning broke clear and crisp. I was sitting on my back
porch sipping tea, when I heard church bells ring up the hill.
The bells took me back to the last funeral I had attended for a SEAL
friend. Several of his team mates, all those who were not overseas at the
time, had stood after the solemn graveside service, and lined up next
to his shiny coffin. One at a time, we each removed the Trident on our
chest and slammed the sharp tacks on the back into his coffin. After it
was complete, thirty or so golden eagles clutching a pistol and trident
adorned the casket of our brother. He would be going six feet under,
but not without the sacred symbol of his blood clan.

Later that afternoon, I put the Dungies I'd caught in a cooler with
ice and headed down to Joe's house on the southeast side of town. He
lived in a squat 1950s brick rambler in a quiet residential neighborhood.

On his doorstep, Joe hugged me and enthusiastically slapped me
on the back. I wasn't a hugger, but with Joe it felt natural. He was
the friendliest person I knew, with a positive outlook on life that was
always refreshing. Unlike his coffee bar, Joe's home was uncluttered,
almost spartan. That was Jane's Scandinavian influence. Joe boiled
up the Dungies while I put together a salad. A football game on the

71

TV in the living room provided comforting background sounds and a warmth came over me—this was the first time in weeks I'd felt a sense of home.

It was a warm day, so we sat outside on a redwood picnic table in the backyard, cracked Dungy shells, washed them down with Rainier beer and watched the clouds float by in a rare blue Pacific Northwest sky. Joe was one of the few people in the world who I could really talk to about combat experiences and life.

"Joe, how long did you have bad memories after Korea?" I asked hesitantly.

He looked up and was quiet for a moment. "Still do, my friend."

"Are you serious? Fifty years later and you still have nightmares?" I asked, knowing I wouldn't be able to hang on that long.

"It's like this," Joe began thoughtfully, as he sipped his beer, "Those events were so intense that they were seared into our lives like a tattoo. Every time a guy sees the tattoo of his crazy ex-girlfriend on his chest in the morning mirror, he remembers the bad times. It's a reminder of pain in his life. He can cover it up, but it's still part of him. It's like that with what we've been through, Jack—it's a part of us forever. These events'll drag us back to a past burned into our soul with blood. You have to learn to put them in a box in the corner of your mind so they don't take over." He looked closely at me, sounding a little worried, and asked, "You still havin' bad thoughts about Afghanistan?"

I took a big gulp of beer and thought about what Joe said before answering. I'd spent so many years covering up every injury, pain and even weakness I'd felt that I had a hard time being honest about my real life, even with Joe. I decided I couldn't tell him about the Black Dog... yet.

"Yeah, they play like a record in my head. I wish there was a way to let it all go—get it out of my mind, especially at night."

His face softened, "Yeah, I know, buddy, God knows I've tried—lemme tell you what doesn't work: booze. I've seen, I dunno how many vets crawl into a bottle to sanitize their heads and they end up swallowing a pistol."

My gut tightened. After heavy drinking, I'd thought a time or two about taking a shortcut to the next life, if there was one. Joe was looking straight at me, probably trying to get a read on how committed I was to this life, and the scrutiny was uncomfortable. I drained my beer and deflected it with a question back to Joe. "So how do you put thoughts and feelings into a box?"

"Let's do the dishes," he said. We carried the plates into the uncluttered kitchen and over to his big stainless sink. He filled one side with hot soapy water and started to scrub each dish, then passed it to me for rinsing. He turned to me as he handed over the pot for the Dungies, "This is how I put my thoughts and feelings in a box."

"By doing dishes?" I asked with a smirk, mystified at where he was going.

He didn't react to my sarcasm. "By focusing on the task at hand, Jack. In my mind, all kinds of thoughts and feelings are constantly coming up. Some are happy memories, like Jane and me on a canoe trip, some are terrible, like the blood spurting out of a Marine's neck while I try to plug the shrapnel wound. The bad memories used to take up all the room in my head—they'd push out the good thoughts and leave me filled with depression and guilt for days on end. But I've learned to put my energy and focus on the task at hand, instead of on the demons. When I do that, they end up in that little box in the corner of my mind. They'll probably never go away, but they've become smaller over time and they find their way out of that box less often. You get me?" I wasn't sure I did, but I knew I wanted to.

Once we'd finished the dishes, we went back outside to watch the sunset. The brilliant orange ball of life and light drifted down through tall cedars, streams of orange and red filtering back to us like a laser show.

"So what else have you been up to besides chasing away beautiful women?" he asked, trying to brighten my mood.

"I'm not chasing them away, they just don't fit with my current lifestyle—owner of an old bookstore and a cat that drools." I regretted the self-pity as soon as I'd said it.

"It's not about the bookstore, Jack, or the cat—you know that. You've built a wall around yourself with bricks of guilt, shame and pain."

That's why I both loved and hated talking to Joe—he could get to the truth, but the truth cut like a knife. I didn't respond, just sipped my Rainier and looked back at his wise and weathered old face, a face I respected and admired. I pulled back from the dark void of truth.

Joe stood up with his back to me, ran his hands through his short, thinning hair, then turned back to face me. "A good woman can help you through this messy life, Jack. You can't do it alone. Even when I was a ghost of a soul, Jane saw me as lovable. I don't know how she did it." He paused as pain flashed across his face. "I was a terrible husband after the war. I'd lose my temper over any little thing, descend into these dark bouts of depression and drinking. I put her through hell, but she wouldn't give up on me, even when I was giving up on myself." His love for her was written all over his face.

It was clear why it hurt him so much to see her in the nursing home. After a moment, I stood up to leave and Joe put his hand on my shoulder. "Just be open to the possibility of being happy one day, OK, Jack? Maybe not today, maybe not tomorrow, just don't give up, shipmate." As I left, he hugged me and this time I hugged him back.

THIRTEEN

━━ ◆ ━━

C limbing down the mountain at night with the girl on my shoulder is taking all my energy. My feet feel like they're encased in cement. I try to keep her on my left shoulder so my shooting arm is free, but every few hundred yards my left arm goes numb. I find a soft patch of pine needles at the base of a pile of rocks and set her down so I can rest. The night sky goes on forever. I lean against the rock pile and check the girl's pulse; it's weak, like a bird's footstep in the snow. Her breathing is shallow, too. I pull my poncho out of my backpack and cover her with it. I stop and listen—voices carry on the wind above me. I unsheath the six-inch dagger on my hip and hold it in my lap. The noise of a shot here would bring all hell down on us.

The moon peeks over the jagged ridgeline, casting a dull light around us. I hide under a rock overhang and listen for sounds. After two hours, I doze off, then suddenly awaken, aware that something is moving near me. I hold my breath and peek around the corner of the rock overhang. The moonlight slices through the trees, casting dark shadows. Footsteps above me are coming down the mountain. I move to a crouching position, like a tiger preparing for an ambush. My heart is banging like a pump being pushed to the limit. This is it—heart pounding silence for five minutes. A shadowy figure emerges six feet to my left looking down the hillside, an AK-47 slung over his shoulder. He doesn't see me. Instinct takes over, the animal in me springs. My left hand reaches from behind his head to cover his mouth as I plunge the knife into his chest and feel the blade hit bone, deflect, tear into tissue and stick into his spine. He screams into my hand and tries to lunge away, but I trip him with a wrestling move. My hand comes off his mouth when we hit the ground. He tries to yell but nothing comes out but a spew of blood and air. His eyes are wild with fear and hatred. A last ripple of strength roars through his body as he pushes back against death but I hold tight and finally he lies still. He looks at me with pure hatred then fades into eternity. Blood is dripping from my hands and down my sleeves.

FOURTEEN

—:—

After punishing myself at the gym, I headed to the bookstore. Emilio greeted me, clearly upset by his empty bowl, so I threw some kibble in it. There was an email from Jerry Hill, my ex-SEAL Team professor friend. He'd done some research for me on the trapper's journal and discovered that there had been a few printings over the years, but he didn't know where to find them. He suggested I search the archives of the Royal British Columbia Museum in Victoria. They had a large collection of historical files on trappers and hunters from that era. I sent a quick reply thanking him.

Linda walked in around noon. I looked up from my desk and felt a magnetic pull on my moral compass. She was dressed in all black with a leather skirt, silk blouse and what looked like 4-inch heels. She walked up to me, set her purse down and leaned forward on my desk. My view at that point was at least PG-13, if not R. She was wearing the gold necklace shaped like a crescent moon I'd seen her wearing before.

"So Jack," she said in a sultry voice, "I haven't seen you since the night of the festival. What've you been doing? Are you avoiding me?"

A torrent of thoughts rolled through my head—everything from taking her to the back of my shop and introducing her to D.H. Lawrence to reaching under the desk for my pistol. What stuck with me, though, was that Linda was more than a PhD student—a lot more.

"I've been busy, Linda. The antique bookstore business is cut-throat," I joked.

She threw her head back with a snort and stood up. "How about taking me to lunch since you've been ignoring me?" she said with a fake pout.

"Sure, why not." I knew I was playing with fire but she was hard to resist.

We walked a few blocks to an Irish pub, The Green Fields. She ordered a Caesar salad and I got a bowl of steaming Irish stew and a pint of Harp lager.

I was feeling awkward about our one night stand. *Did she want more? Did I want more?* "I had a good time the other night." I regretted saying it as soon as the words came out of my mouth. It reminded me of graffiti on a bathroom stall: "For a good time call Sally."

Thankfully, Linda had this way of expertly changing the subject when it suited her. She ignored my comment and asked, "What have you been up to besides selling books?"

"I met an old fisherman who thinks he can find a sunken treasure," I said to entertain her.

"Really? Tell me about it," she leaned forward, sounding very interested.

"It's far-fetched, but he thinks he can find and salvage a sunken ship in the Strait that was reportedly carrying gold to trade for furs in the 1800s. It's a pipe dream but the ol' guy looked like he really needed some hope, so I told him I'd do a little research, that's all."

"You're a sentimentalist, Jack. What's the old guy's name?" she asked, sitting up a little straighter.

"He goes by Cap. He was a sea captain and then a fisherman here in Port Townsend."

The waitress stopped by our table carrying a load of dirty plates and asked if we needed anything else. "I'll take a Boilermaker," I said. She looked confused. "That's a shot of whiskey in a beer," I said, trying not to sound condescending.

The conversation drifted back to Cap and his gold salvaging dream.

"Why does Cap think there's sunken treasure out there?" Linda asked, sipping her white wine and leaving dark pink lipstick on the rim.

"Part of me thinks he just needs something to hang on to, like a life raft."

"And the other part?" she asked, as if she already knew the answer.

"Well... it's not impossible that a ship full of gold is out there, but the chance of finding it is nearly zero." I had to admit to myself that I hoped the chances were a lot better than zilch.

"Where's the ship supposed to be located?" Linda asked with obvious curiosity about the lost gold idea.

"That's the problem. There are no accurate descriptions of where it sank. I have a friend, a professor of history, who told me I might find an out-of-print trapper's journal at the Royal British Columbia Museum that could shed some light on the shipwreck."

Our food came and I dove in like a starving prisoner. "Are you thinking about going all the way to British Columbia to chase down a journal that probably doesn't exist for a guy you hardly know?" she asked before putting a forkful of salad in her mouth. It was a logical question, but a question that also revealed something about Linda.

"I dunno. You're right to think it's probably a wild goose chase." I didn't tell her that I was becoming interested in the wreck myself. She'd think I was as crazy as Cap.

The young waitress brought my Boilermaker in a tall glass. I downed a third of it in two gulps. Linda was looking even more attractive. I was tempted to ask her over for a drink tonight, but thoughts of Cindy glided into my mind like a dove circling my conscience. It was like deciding between Oreo cookies or spinach salad for dinner. The cookies were an immediate rush but left you feeling like shit after gorging on the whole pack. I blame that Boilermaker for pushing me over the edge to make a bad decision. I took another shot of liquid courage to ask her out when suddenly her phone rang. She picked up and quickly stepped outside to take the call. Either she was being polite, or didn't want me to overhear the phone call.

She returned and said she had an appointment. We parted ways and I headed back to the bookstore, feeling as empty as ever. I walked to the small bathroom in the back of the shop and looked at myself in the mirror. "You almost asked her out for a date, dumbass," I said out loud. Gray eyes the color of a weathered Navy ship that had been on too many deployments stared back at me, framed by crow's feet that were etched on my face by years of operating in the sand, salt and sea. *If it hadn't been for that phone call, you might have been entangled with her tonight. Get a grip, man. What would Cindy think?* Suddenly, it mattered very much what Cindy thought of me. I punched the weak bastard in the mirror, cracking the glass into a spider web and bloodying my right hand. The pain felt good... cleansing.

Suddenly Emilio appeared between my legs, rubbing his mottled neck on my boot. I reached down and picked up the little guy. "Sorry buddy, I didn't mean to scare you." He licked my busted knuckles with a wet sandpaper tongue as I strolled back to the front of the shop. I set him down near my desk, wrapped a rag around my knuckles and pulled out a long piece of string I kept in the desk drawer... his favorite toy. I threw the end of the string over the front edge of my desk, like a fly-fishing cast. As usual, he attacked the end of the string with vigor. It was better than fishing... I caught a catfish every cast.

It was a slow afternoon. Emilio fell asleep under my desk. I decided to go next door and talk to Mrs. Johnson. I had newfound respect for Mrs. J after dinner the other night. Most people tended to avoid older folks, probably afraid of seeing what they would eventually become. Not me. When I was young, a Pearl Harbor survivor and his wife, Jim and Carol, kind of became foster grandparents for me. I saw these little, bent people sitting in their living room, sipping chamomile tea, but there was another incredible story behind it all. Bob had been aboard the USS Nevada when it was attacked at Pearl Harbor. A bomb from a Japanese plane flew through the porthole of his workspace, killing everyone but him. He was gone for three years during World War II. And Carol had worked on some secret project during the war. They taught me that behind every supposed frail person might be an incredible story of survival and courage. I had judged Cindy's mom by her appearance and forgotten that lesson.

I locked up the shop and walked next door. Mrs. Johnson was in the back mixing dough. She saw me step inside the empty bakery and came up front, wiping her hands on a wet towel.

"Jack, what a treat... is there anything I can get you?" She always brought goodies to my bookstore so I hardly ever came to her shop.

"Hey Mrs. Johnson... I just thought I'd stop by, see how you're doing," I said, noticing the gingerbread cookies for sale in the glass case. "And I'll take a dozen of those cookies for the Afghan girls," I said, pointing at the case.

She picked up the cookies with tongs and put them in a brown paper sack. "That'll be $12, Jack," she said, handing me the sack.

I gave her a fifty. She started to make change but I said, "Use it for the girls, Mrs. Johnson." She looked at me for a moment, unsure what to do, then smiled and placed the fifty in an envelope underneath her register.

"Have a seat, Jack, let me get you a hot chocolate?"

"No, I'm good," I said, raising my hand and taking a seat at the small wooden table near the front of her store. She looked a little concerned, since I had never been to her shop just for a chat. She slid across from me into the small chair, hands in her lap, with uncharacteristic silence. The ball was in my court.

I cleared my throat awkwardly, not sure how to begin. "Well, uh... at dinner the other night... uh... when Cindy told me she worked in Afghanistan and Pakistan I saw you make a face, like maybe you didn't approve. I dunno, maybe I was wrong, it was just an impression I had." I was glad I'd gotten it out, but now I wondered if I should've asked Cindy instead of her mother. A flash of pain crossed her face. I couldn't tell if she didn't like my question or there was something else bothering her.

She tucked a few strands of loose hair behind her ear, then spoke, "I'm so proud of her, Jack. I mean, what she does for those girls is amazing." She closed her eyes and rubbed her forehead, "But I'm so worried about her," she said, almost pleading to me. "It's a dangerous place and there are factions over there that don't want girls to have an education... you know what I mean? I love what she does, but I'm still her mother, right? I can't stop worrying about her."

I was wracking my brain for something to say, something to ease her worry. But I knew how dangerous the border between Pakistan and Afghanistan could be, especially for a Western woman. "Cindy seems passionate about her work there... and I sense how important it is to her that girls in those repressive countries have access to education. But I know it's dangerous and I can't blame you for worrying, Mrs. Johnson."

She sighed resignedly. "Well, maybe she'll find a reason to stay here instead of going back," she said with a suggestive wink, and laughed. "Well, Jack, I'd better get back to my oven. Do me a favor," she said, patting my arm before she stood, "Don't mention that we spoke. She knows that I worry about her... I don't want her to know how much."

"You got it, Mrs. Johnson. I'll see ya tomorrow." I left her to her baking and stepped out into the cool evening. A strong breeze whipped the leaves around my feet into a frenzy as I walked home.

FIFTEEN

— ❖ —

T he next morning, when I arrived at the bookstore, a FedEx box was leaning against the front door. I fumbled with my keys and opened the door while reading the return address. It was from the online bookseller I'd contacted. Emilio greeted me as I settled into my desk and sliced open the box with curiosity: *Shipwrecks of the Strait of Juan de Fuca*. I flipped through the index until I found the listing for HMS Hawthorn. There were a few pages on the purpose of the voyage and the background of the captain and owners. At the end of the section there was a drawing and diagram of the ship. Suddenly the wreck became more than a wild idea—here it was in black and white: wood, iron, hemp, sailcloth and sailors. It was real and alive.

The author confirmed that the Hawthorn had sailed with a cargo of gold to be used to purchase otter pelts for trade back in Europe. She'd left Victoria on September 17th, 1840, heading due west out the Strait en route to trade with the villages, outposts and settlements on the western side of Vancouver Island. An unexpected storm blew in from the north, the ship lost steerage and was wrecked on the south side of the Strait in what is now Washington State. There was no more detail on the actual location of the wreck. However, the chapter contained a crude, hand-drawn map of the Strait with a little drawing of a sunken ship marking the estimated position of where HMS Hawthorn was believed to have sunk. I stood up and paced around the shop, my mind going a mile a minute. "Old Cap might only be half-crazy," I said to Emilio, who watched from one of the visitor chairs near the window.

As I was strolling absently around the bookshelves, deep in thought, I noticed a tall, dark-haired man pacing up and down outside my shop. He was talking to himself and clenching and unclenching his fists. I walked over to my desk where I had the pistol in a drawer and sat down, keeping an eye on him. He pushed the door open forcefully and stood at the threshold in a rage. Emilio immediately sensed danger and high-tailed it to the back of the shop to hide under a shelf. The man was tall, maybe 6 foot 2, wearing a flannel shirt, jeans, work boots and a nasty-looking Bowie knife on his right hip. He had long, greasy hair down to his shoulders. He saw me sitting at my desk, but scanned the rest of the store with his dark eyes. I figured he was making sure we were alone.

He walked closer to my desk and stood with his feet apart, "My daughter told me you wanted to see her. You better stay away from her, creep," he said with a deep voice. It hit me that this must be Micah's brother, Jerry.

I remained seated, figuring I'd first try to defuse the situation. If I had to stand up, I wouldn't be shaking his hand and showing him gardening books. "So you're Micah's brother?" No response. "I invited Micah to bring his niece here so she could pick out some books. You know... *reading*?"

"I told you to stay away from my daughter," he nearly spat the words out. He took a few steps closer to my desk and I saw his right hand fiddling with the Bowie knife.

I thought I'd throw him a curveball, see how he reacts. "I heard you work for Jim Tripper."

His eyes narrowed, "None of your fucking business," he hissed.

The angry animal in me was rising up. I slid the Sig behind my back in case things got real ugly and stood up, calmly walked over to Jerry and stopped about two feet from him. I figured he wasn't used to people getting in his face, and maybe it would throw him off his game of intimidation. He was taller and heavier than me, but after 20 years as a Navy SEAL, I'd taken down more than my share of big men.

"Are you afraid of books, Jerry?" I asked with feigned innocence, staring up at him. He looked puzzled. "Are you afraid your daughter might gain some knowledge, find out what she loves, realize what a real father is supposed to be like?"

I was ready for him to reach for that Bowie knife; instead he threw a giant swing at me but telegraphed it well. I ducked under the hay-maker, moved quickly behind his back and threw a rear-naked choke hold on him from behind, cinching it down and dropping the big man to his knees. I was bent over behind him, still on my feet and slowly increasing the pressure. He had about ten seconds before he passed out when I eased off the pressure. "Drop that knife on the floor," I ordered calmly.

He reached for the knife, and I tightened the pressure to let him know I'd choke him out if he tried anything. He pulled the knife from the big scabbard and dropped it to the floor with a clank. I eased off the pressure and let him go, then kicked the knife back towards my desk. He stood up on wobbly legs. "You'll be paying for that," he threatened in a raspy voice, clutching his throat.

"Well, you know where I'll be, so come on by anytime, Jerry."

He stormed out of the shop, looked back at me with a menacing grimace, then disappeared around the corner.

I walked through the bookshop aisles to let my heartrate calm down. As the adrenaline ebbed, a dark current took its place. I felt some of my humanity had drained out when I'd resorted to violence. But guys like Jerry didn't understand anything but force. I saw that with the Taliban in Afghanistan. You can't reason with that mentality—they only understand power.

Books have always helped me forget my troubles, for a time. I pulled Ernest Hemingway's *A Farewell to Arms* off the shelf behind my desk. I had always admired Hemingway's tales. He'd been in war, lost his wives and lovers and wrote eloquently of adventure and human nature. It always bothered me that such a talented writer could blow his own head off with a shotgun. *Was I capable of that?*

I opened it at random to Book II:

She put a thermometer in my mouth.

"The Italians put it under the arm," I said.

"Don't talk."

When she took the thermometer out she read it and then shook it.

"What's the temperature?"

"You're not supposed to know that."

"Tell me what it is."

"It's almost normal."

"I never have any fever. My legs are full of old iron too."

"What do you mean?"

"They're full of trench mortar fragments, old screws and bed-springs and things."

She shook her head and smiled.

"If you had any foreign bodies in your legs they would set up an inflammation and you'd have fever."

"All right," I said. "We'll see what comes out."

She went out of the room and came back with the old nurse of the early morning. Together they made the bed with me in it. That was new to me and an admirable proceeding."

I tossed Jerry's knife on the desk and took out the bottle of single malt, pouring myself a glass of liquid painkiller. But then the door to the shop jingled open and Cindy walked in. Her shoulder-length blonde hair was tied in a ponytail. She wore a jean jacket, black wool skirt and white flats. She looked at me, then the whiskey on my desk and back to me again. I felt like hiding the whiskey.

I stood and moved in front of the desk because I definitely didn't want to explain the giant Bowie knife. "Hey, Cindy! I thought you were leaving town?"

"I've decided to take some time off. I haven't had a vacation in over a year and could use a break before my next trip back to Pakistan." My heart skipped a beat at the thought that she might be around for a while.

"What do you do for fun in this town, Jack?" she asked with a mischievous smile.

"I could take you crabbing. It's beautiful out on the bay," I said, figuring that would be a harmless first date. As it turned out, I got the harmless part wrong, but I was eager to show her what I did with my spare time.

"I think I'd enjoy that. I've never been crabbing." I watched her eyes drift to the Bowie knife on my desk but she didn't say anything.

I took a chance, "How about this afternoon at five, after I close up?"

She hesitated for a moment, then smiled and said, "Sure, that sounds great. Do I need to bring anything?"

"Do you have a windbreaker and some rubber boots?"

"Sure, OK," she nodded. "I've got some shopping to do now, so I'll see you later."

I watched her leave, feeling strangely excited for our crabbing trip. She hadn't said anything about the whiskey, either. I looked down at the glass of smoky Glenfiddich and poured it back into the bottle.

Sixteen

⸺ ◆ ⸺

I needed to get out of the shop and walk. I checked to make sure Emilio was OK after his fright, then hung a "Will return in a few minutes," sign on the window and locked the store, a cool breeze from the north greeting me as I stepped onto the sidewalk. Tucking my hands in my pockets, I meandered down the street, staring down at the sidewalk, deep in thought. *Why had I put the whiskey down when Cindy came into the shop?* That puzzled me.

My feet took a random turn down a residential street. The fall orange, brown and red colors were striking and leaves danced at my feet. A shabby brick house with a huge elm tree on the corner was holding a yard sale. I always take a peek at yard sales, hunting for antique books for my stock. The homeowner pointed me to a couple of beat-up cardboard boxes in the back of the garage. I sorted through the first box with no luck. The second box yielded a good find—a second edition of Joseph Conrad's *Heart of Darkness.* I paid ten dollars for it and walked back to town, enjoying the break in the clouds and the late season warmth.

Back in the bookstore, I cracked open *Heart of Darkness.* A previous reader had highlighted some passages. I thumbed through the novel scanning them. On page 27 I found this, "*There is a taint of death, a flavour of mortality in lies—which is exactly what I hate and detest in the world—what I want to forget. It makes me miserable and sick, like biting something rotten would do."* I thought about how lies of any kind made me feel rotten too, then I thought about Linda and Cindy. *Was I lying to Cindy by not telling her about Linda? Was I lying to myself about my physical attraction to Linda?*

The door jingled and it occurred to me that my little bookshop was getting a lot of visitors lately. Micah and his niece walked in. I doubt either of them knew that Jerry had paid me a visit earlier, because they seemed quite content together. She looked small for ten. Two long brown ponytails framed her round face. Her striking blue-green eyes scanned the bookstore before settling on me.

"Micah, Sarah! Welcome to my bookstore!" I smiled and rushed over to greet them. "Hi Sarah. I'm Jack. Your uncle told me he'd bring you by." She nodded but said nothing. "I hear you like to read?" I asked. Another shy and wordless nod. I started to wonder if she could speak. "What kind of books do you like?" I tried. She shrugged. I didn't know her reading level, but I had an idea.

"Micah, there's some coffee in the pot," I offered. "I'm gonna take Sarah down this aisle for a minute." Micah nodded appreciatively and poured himself a cup of lukewarm coffee, taking a seat by the window. "Sarah, I wanna show you a book I loved when I was your age."

Sarah looked nervously at Micah, but he gave her a reassuring nod and she followed me to the children's section. Emilio had appeared and was eyeing us with interest. Sarah smiled sweetly at him as he came closer. I pulled down a copy of Maurice Sendak's classic, *Where the Wild Things Are.* "Have you ever read this?" I asked, handing her the book. She shook her head. "You're gonna love this. Wanna sit?"

We sat on the floor together, leaning against the bookshelf behind us. Emilio approached Sarah and nestled on her lap as I started reading, *"The night Max wore his wolf suit and made mischief of one kind and another his mother called him 'WILD THING!' and Max said 'I'LL EAT YOU UP!'"*

Sarah smiled, engrossed in the fantastical pictures as she petted Emilio. I handed her the book. "You read the rest, I'm gonna go talk to your uncle." She nodded enthusiastically, and that became the best part of my entire week.

I walked to the front of the store, poured myself a cup of stale coffee and sat down next to Micah. "Can she talk? She hasn't said a word."

"Yeah, she's just really shy," he said, clearly used to the question.

"Hey, I get it." I hesitated to tell Micah about the encounter with his brother, but figured he needed to know. "By the way, your brother came by the bookstore earlier today."

Micah straightened up in his chair, shaking his head. "What happened?" he asked with a worried look. He knew Jerry had not come by for a social call.

"He threatened me, tried to get physical," I shrugged. I didn't want to share all the ugly details. I knew Micah had enough on his plate.

He sat back as if he'd had the wind knocked out of him. "I don't know what to do, Jack, he's a terrible father, but he can't stand anybody doing anything good for Sarah." He took his hat off and ran his hands through his long dark hair in frustration.

It was hard enough to see this guy with a missing leg and scars on his face. To see him in anguish over the mistreatment of such a sweet young girl was awful. "Listen Micah, you're doing right by her. She's gonna be OK," I said with all the conviction I could muster.

"Yeah, but I can't be around her all the time," he said, slumping in his chair, defeated.

I looked over my shoulder at Sarah. She was sitting on the floor, her lips moving as she quietly read aloud to Emilio, who was apparently enrapt.

I didn't know how Micah would react, but I reached over and put my hand on his shoulder and said, "Soldier, look down that aisle. Your mission is to protect that girl. You got that?"

He looked up at me and I saw the face of a soldier ready to do his duty in spite of the fear of failure. I'd seen that same look a hundred times in other men.

"Yeah, I got it, Jack. Thanks." He seemed calmer and more determined.

"You can drop her off here anytime. If I can help in any way, you let me know, OK?"

"I'll do that, Jack," he said, looking visibly more confident now.

I walked over to Sarah, who was sitting cross-legged in the aisle reading aloud, with Emilio quietly purring as his head lay on her leg. I sat down across from her. She read the last line of the book, oblivious to my presence.

"*Max stepped into his private boat and waved goodbye and sailed back over a year and in and out of weeks and through a day and into the night of his very own room where he found his supper waiting for him—and it was still hot.*" A satisfied smile flitted across her innocent face for the second time that day and then she looked up and noticed me there.

"You keep it, Sarah. Here's another one you might enjoy," I said, handing her a copy of *The Swiss Family Robinson*. You get your uncle to take you back here so you can pick out another one when you're done with this one. Would you like that?"

She smiled almost imperceptibly and nodded, then kissed Emilio, stood up and walked over to Micah, carrying the books under her arm. Micah took her other hand and mouthed *thank you* as they walked out. Sarah looked over her shoulder at me as she left. It was a look I'd seen before.

SEVENTEEN

E milio was pouncing on shadows near the front windows as I locked up for the night. A breeze at my back swirled golden leaves around my feet as I walked home. After changing into rubber boots and a wool sweater for crabbing, I headed down to the marina to meet Cindy. She was standing on the pier and I couldn't help but smile when I saw her wearing yellow rain boots and a blue poncho, her blonde hair blowing in the wind.

"Hey, Cindy, you beat me here."

"It was a nice afternoon, I came early and took a walk on the beach looking for seashells."

I noticed the wet sand on her boots. She had something in her hand, "Find anything interesting?" I asked.

"A few clam shells, but look at these," she said happily. She reached into her coat pocket and pulled out a handful of broken glass shards that had been polished smooth by the sand and wave action. There were blue, green, red and root beer-colored pieces in the palm of her small white hand. They looked like precious sea jewels.

"Aren't they beautiful?" she asked.

They were. I'd never noticed. I held out my hand and she placed a translucent turquoise shard in my palm. I held it up to the pale sun and the light shining through it looked like gentle waves on a Caribbean beach.

"Those are amazing, Cindy. I walk this beach all the time, but never noticed the gems right under my feet. You have an eye for beautiful things." *I used to take pleasure in small things like that. What happened to that view of the world?*

I reached out to give her the piece of glass back. She coiled my fingers around it. "You keep it, Jack," she said as the wind blew her hair wildly.

"Are you ready for some crabbing?" I asked as I put the shard in my pocket for safe keeping.

"Sure!"

I walked her down the pier to my ten-foot skiff and helped her aboard, pulled the oars out of their locks and dropped the blades into the cool green sea with a splash. I rowed out of the harbor towards my first trap. She sat in the back of the skiff enjoying the late afternoon views of the bay. The lines on the moored sailboats clanging against the masts made a musical twang as we cleared the mouth of the harbor.

"How was your day in the bookstore?" she asked, her hand trailing in the cool bay water, leaving a small foamy wake.

"It was a strange day," I admitted. I told her how I'd met Micah at the VFW and found out he'd lost a leg and been torn up by an IED in Iraq. "He lives on the Makah reservation, but he was in town to bring his niece Sarah to counseling. His brother Jerry abuses the girl."

"Oh no, how awful. What kind of abuse?" she asked.

"Neglect and an occasional drunk beating," I said, my heart rate increasing as I thought of Jerry.

Cindy shook her head, "The poor girl."

I stopped rowing for a moment. The skiff rocked gently in the bay.

"Her father came by the shop this morning and threatened me for offering to let her pick out a book."

She pulled her dripping hand from the water and placed both hands in her lap like a schoolteacher interrogating a 7th grade spitball sniper. "And what did you do?" she asked quietly but with obvious worry.

"Well, I don't think he's gonna be a customer of mine," I joked, pulling on the oars and ducking my head so she couldn't get a read on me. From the look that flashed across her face, she seemed to be wondering if I'd buried Jerry in a shallow ditch.

"I defused the situation," I told her. Not a lie, strictly speaking. "Anyway," I continued, trying to change the subject, "Micah brought Sarah by this afternoon. She's a sweet girl, but she didn't talk. She did read out loud, though."

"Maybe she's nervous around new people," Cindy suggested.

"I hope that's all it is. She's ten years old," I said, the girl in Afghanistan immediately springing to my mind.

I put my back into the oars, heading to the first trap. Drifting up to the buoy, I tied it off the bow of the skiff, put on gloves and started to pull up the slimy trap line hand over hand. I didn't expect much since I'd just checked them.

Cindy was a good listener—it was easy to bounce ideas off her. "Oh yeah, ya know, two days ago I met an old sea captain and crab fisherman named Cap who thinks he can salvage a 19th century wreck out in the Strait. I've been helping him search for information on it." Cindy took her eyes off a lone pelican floating in the bay and looked up at me with interest.

"His boat burned at the pier, so he lost his livelihood and seems to have lost his way in life." Oddly enough, I really wanted to know what this woman I'd just met thought about all of this. "This search for the wreck seems like a wisp of hope he's holding onto. He's a decent old guy, but I don't know if he understands what a long shot it is to find a sunken ship in the Strait."

"Maybe so, but as you said, Jack, this might be the last thread of hope he's holding onto, right? If you tell him it's a pipe dream, where does that leave him? You don't want to leave him without that thread of hope, do you?"

When she said "thread of hope," it triggered a flashback to a passage I'd written when I was trying to make sense of my best friend's suicide. After he killed himself I went to a dark place, trying to figure out what I could have done to prevent it.

People who kill themselves believe they have no threads of hope holding them to this world, so they take fate into their own hands. More often than not, there are strong invisible threads enveloping them, but they don't feel these threads.

I thought my best friend had many threads holding him to this earth, when in the end he may have only had one. I hadn't weaved my thread strong enough. One dark day that last thread snapped and he blew out of this world on sorrowful winds.

Cindy leaned toward me in the skiff, squinting her eyes against the late afternoon sun. "Jack, what are you thinking? You were staring out at the water and muttering to yourself."

"I'm sorry, I was just remembering something."

"Anything you'd like to share?" she asked softly.

"Not today," I shook my head.

The crab trap was empty. I lowered it back into the blue sea, cast off from the buoy and headed to the next trap.

Over the lapping of waves against the sturdy hull, Cindy offered, "Cap probably just wants his life back, wants to be a sea captain or fisherman again. It's a terrible thing to lose your way of life." *Didn't I know it.*

"Maybe if there was a way to get him another boat?" she asked hopefully.

"It would take a lot of money to make that happen," I said, wondering if a new boat would even bring back his old life.

"Yeah, I guess you're right," she nodded.

"Do you think I'm stringing the guy along with false hopes by gathering information on the wreck?" I asked, eager to hear her opinion.

She cocked her head slightly and gave me a wry smile. "Haven't you ever chased a dream, knowing deep down you'd never catch it? But you needed to keep moving forward anyway? Somehow you sensed that the journey was the real prize, not the end result?"

I thought again about the incident in Afghanistan. "I guess I know what you mean."

"For Cap, I bet it's more about the journey, the process. About bringing passion back into his life, something to live for, don't you think? If you've done what you can to help him and there's a dead end, I bet he'll be OK. I don't know if it would be right to cut off his dreams before they have a chance to unfold naturally, Jack, would it?" For a second, I thought she was talking about me instead of Cap.

"How come you're so wise?" I asked with a sly smile. The sun was setting behind me. The last rays of red and purple beamed onto her soft face as I rowed back to the harbor.

"Would you be interested in taking a trip to Victoria with me? I need to chase down a lead I found about a trapper's journal that may have more clues about the location of the wreck." It was kind of like asking her on a date, but not as risky or personal.

"I do love the tall trees and roses in British Columbia," she mused. "I'd love to go, as long as we can take a walk to enjoy them," she said with a broad smile.

"Absolutely. How about the day after tomorrow? That would give me a chance to line up the logistics."

"Sure, that'll work fine," she said with enthusiasm.

"I'll get us two rooms at a bed and breakfast." After the bombing in Sri Lanka, I avoided hotels, so I hoped that was acceptable to her.

"Sounds lovely," she beamed.

We moored up to the last buoy after taking in two good keepers from the previous trap. Pulling up the heavy trap from 50 feet below felt good on my back and arms. I lifted the slimy trap into the bottom of the skiff. Two good size Dungies were clicking and hissing in the trap.

"Can I try and pick one up and put it in the bag?" Cindy asked with endearing excitement.

"Of course, just grab them from behind quickly, don't hesitate."

I dumped the trap so the Dungies were in the bottom of the boat and easier for Cindy to grab. She reached for the first one, but hesitated, so the big Dungy spun and clipped her finger, drawing blood. She yelped in pain.

"Motherfucker!" I screamed, grabbing the crab and violently ripping his claws off and throwing them overboard.

"Jack, it's OK! I'm not hurt. Calm down," she said, staring at me, clearly alarmed by my outburst.

I ran my hands through my hair in frustration. "I'm sorry, I didn't want you to get hurt."

"It's just a small cut, I'll be fine." She looked at me with a slightly shocked expression. I figured I'd just blown the whole relationship.

As I rowed back to the pier, *What an idiot!* kept playing over and over in my head. Cindy was watching the sunset and pointing out fish jumping all around us at dusk. Back at the marina we said goodbye and planned to meet on Wednesday for the trip to the museum in British Columbia.

I walked home in silence, The Black Dog nipping at my heels. *What is wrong with you, man? Why did you lose it in front of her?* I opened my door, grabbed a bottle of Glenfiddich, went out back to my porch overlooking the Strait and sat in the old rocker. The sky was dark gray, hiding the maroon sunset to the west. *Two acts of violence in one day. I'm losing control,* I thought, as I took two long pulls on the whiskey bottle. *At least Cindy is still going to BC with me. I've got one day to get my act together.*

EIGHTEEN

I awoke early, lying in bed as the light crept into my room, chasing away the darkness. I didn't get up, just wanted to lay there and forget the world. A heaviness in my soul held me down like a weight on my chest. Part of it was undoubtedly the whiskey from last night. *I've got to get up, keep moving forward.*

I brewed a pot of coffee and padded around the kitchen, looking out the window at the gray sea. Small white caps were dancing on the slate water as the wind blew from the west down the Strait. *Another day, one foot in front of the other, people (and a cat) depend on me. I can do this.*

I opened the bookstore and called out for Emilo. He was sleeping on the bottom shelf in my naval history section. Maybe *The Influence of Seapower upon History* by Mahan had put him to sleep, like it did me. He didn't move as I approached him. "Hey buddy, wake up, have some breakfast." He gave me a big yawn, jumped off the shelf and padded towards his food bowl.

I reserved a two-bedroom bed and breakfast in Victoria for Wednesday, then set about organizing books. I remembered what Joe had told me about focusing on what you are doing as a way to keep the demons in the box. This would be a good task that I could use to shut down my relentlessly noisy mind. Focus on the job at hand—pick a book out of the box from the yard sale, feel its weight, flip it open to make sure it's in good shape, find the right home for it on the shelf. After placing it on the shelf, I ran my fingers down the books on either side to make sure nothing was out of place. I picked up a copy out of a dirty plastic bin of *Trustee from the Toolroom* by Nevil Shute. I loved Shute's storytelling and the mechanical and aeronautical angles to his stories. This one went behind the desk for my personal collection.

After an hour of organizing, my mind started to wander like a dog left off leash in a vacant lot. Nasty thoughts of Afghanistan got a toe in the door when I picked up Kipling's story of Afghanistan, *The Man Who Would Be King*. That toe in the door of my mental gate opened to a flood of bloody, dark thoughts—images of a friend who'd been blown to bits when his vehicle hit an IED, visions of a guy who had been shot in the face. I'd visited him in the field hospital and wondered how he was still alive. *Why is my mind always trying to screw me over?*

At 10:00 a.m., Cap walked into the shop wearing dirty blue jeans and a bulky fisherman's sweater. He looked like he'd slept in his clothes. His voice was like a wire brush on rusty steel, "So Jack, have you heard anything from your booksellers?" I reached behind my desk and brought out *Shipwrecks of the Strait of Juan de Fuca*. His whole face lit up when I handed him the book. He put out his weathered hands as if I was giving him communion.

"There's a good description of the ship in there, as well as a rough sketch of where she sank." You would have thought I'd handed him a bag of gold. He carefully turned the pages. "So this is enough to go find her, right?" he asked with a sea bag full of enthusiasm. I remembered what Cindy had said about not being a hope-crusher.

"This is a start, but we have no idea where she actually went down." I debated not telling him about my impending trip to BC, but in the end figured he deserved any hope I could give him, and I knew he'd be pleased to hear that I was committed to helping him. I scooted my chair a little closer to him, "I've got good news, Cap. I'm going to the Royal British Columbia Museum tomorrow to try and track down more information. No promises, but I might get lucky." His eyes became watery, and he wiped a tear from his cheek with the back of his hand.

It was getting stuffy in the bookshop. The sun was peeking out behind cotAnthony clouds. "Let's take a walk to the Cup O' Joe," I suggested. Joe and Cap were about the same age. I had an idea that Joe might befriend Cap—they were both dealing with loss, after all.

We walked in silence, enjoying the rare, late afternoon sunshine. When I opened the door, Jim Tripper and Jerry were seated at a table in the corner and were in deep conversation. Tripper had his back to me. Jerry looked up at me with dead eyes. I looked at Cap. He'd seen Tripper and the ol' guy was grinding his teeth and clenching his fists.

I was sizing up the situation as I guided Cap to the coffee bar and away from Tripper. We took seats at the bar, and I glanced furtively over my shoulder. Tripper stood up, walked out the door and drove away in a black SUV. Cap relaxed when he saw Tripper leave. Jerry, however, remained in his seat, glaring at me.

Joe finished ringing up a customer at the cash register, then walked over to us. I motioned for Joe to lean in so I could speak to him quietly. "You see the big fella behind me near the window?" I asked. Joe looked up discreetly and nodded. "If he heads in my direction, gimme a signal, yeah?" He nodded knowingly.

"Joe, have you met Cap?" I asked so Cap could hear.

"I've seen you around town," Joe said, speaking directly to Cap. "But we've never met."

Cap held out his hand, "Friends call me Cap."

Joe shook his hand, then asked, "What'll it be, boys?"

"How about two cups of your mud?" I asked. Joe was about to fetch our coffee, but Cap, gazing around the room, said, "I like your nautical equipment. I was a mariner and fisherman. This place feels like home."

"I was in the Navy myself," said Joe, as the corners of Cap's mouth rose to form a smile. I was gratified to see it, and figured he'd have a lot in common with Joe.

I glanced over my shoulder to see that Jerry was still glaring at me from where he sat. I started to think through the options if Jerry confronted me here, and none of them were good.

Joe returned with two steaming cups of coffee. He turned to Cap, "Just this morning a guy was in here telling me about his Lund fishing boat. He claimed it was the best for crabbing. I'm thinking I might try one out." I knew Joe had no intention of buying a boat with Jane in the hospital, and appreciated what he was doing. We briefly made eye contact before Cap took the bait and ran with it.

Cap animatedly discussed fishing boats with Joe. "I prefer a downeast style, semi-displacement hull craft. They originally came from Maine. They have a strong, high bow and can carry a lot of weight. The open cockpit in the back allows you to move around and attend to all your fishing equipment nicely."

Suddenly, Joe nodded pointedly to me so I spun around in my barstool. Jerry was walking up to me. I decided to stay seated and try to de-escalate the encounter. He stopped about six feet away. He looked taller than I remembered, and spoke with a low, menacing voice, "Let's go outside into the alley and settle some things."

When really pushed, an energy surged through me like lightning, and I was capable of bad things... very bad things. Every fiber of my being told me to stand up, take this guy out back and unleash the wild animal. But I didn't. Instead, I turned back to the coffee bar and took a sip of coffee. Joe and Cap, eyes wide, were staring at Jerry and wondering what to do.

I looked at Joe. He'd let me know what was going on behind me. After a few tense moments, Jerry walked out the door. I turned in my seat to face him as he left. "You and I are not done here, Jack. You better watch your back," he hissed as he slammed the door and stomped out.

Joe and Cap both looked stunned. "What was that about?" asked Cap. I sipped my dark roast to settle my nerves, then told them about Micah, Sarah, and the encounter with Jerry at the bookstore.

"You're making some good friends here in town," Joe quipped, trying to lighten the mood as he wiped down the bar.

"Yeah, I'm a regular social magnet," I said sarcastically.

I needed to get back to the shop, so I paid for the coffees and gave Joe a big thumbs up thank you over Cap's shoulder as I walked out the door. He nodded with a knowing smile. Cap and Joe resumed talking about fishing boats as I left.

I spent the afternoon trying to regain control of my off the leash mind. I kept thinking, *How many bad men do I have to deal with*? I opened a tattered, damp box that smelled musty and moldy. I'd grabbed this one at a garage sale south of town, thinking I might be able to salvage a few of the books. Most of them were damp and smelled of dead mice, but there was a pocket-sized, half leather-bound copy of Shakespeare's Sonnets that was in good shape. Opening it at random, I fell upon Sonnet 50. The last line seemed like a tagline for my life today: *My grief lies onward, and my joy behind.*

The light faded outside, as shadows danced in the windows. I locked up the bookshop and walked home, feeling The Black Dog trailing nearby. I took a turn into the VFW, hoping to lose it for a while.

There were two old vets at the end of the bar wearing red Marine Corps ball caps, nursing Bud Lites and watching a game on the TV above the bar. I avoided them and sat at the opposite end. The older woman working the bar greeted me. She was the wife of a vet who had died last spring. I'd been a member of the rifle detail at his funeral because he'd been a Navy Vietnam veteran.

"What'll it be, Jack?" she asked kindly.

"I'll take three shots of tequila."

She raised her eyebrows and cocked her head, looking at me for a long second, then asked what kind of tequila I wanted.

"Whatever you got is fine."

She lined up the clear cactus funk in front of me with a slice of lime for each. I threw the first one back, letting the hot burn reset my head. The last line of that sonnet bubbled to the surface, *My grief lies onward, and my joy behind.* I tossed the second shot back and the sonnet's foreboding warning floated in my thoughts like a bloated dead fish.

A woman about my age wearing a green sweater and form-fitting jeans sat down two stools away from me. She had long, thick black hair with gray streaks and a beautiful face that was heavily made up. I noticed a wedding ring on her hand.

Throwing down my third shot, I stole a glance at her. "I like your style," she said with a Midwest accent. The bartender asked what she wanted to drink. "Same as him, three tequila shots." *This could get interesting.*

"My husband lost the battle with his demons. I can see you're fighting your own," she said nonchalantly, throwing back her first shot.

I turned to her, "What does that mean, he lost the battle with his demons?" I knew exactly what she meant but I wanted her to say it. I was aggravated by her soothsaying—she was interrupting my daily self-loathing.

"You know what I mean," she said. "The Black Dog took him down."

"How do you know about The Black Dog?" I spun my barstool around to face her.

"I recognize it," she said with a smirk. "He hounded my husband for twelve years. I saw The Black Dog waiting outside when I came in here. Now I know he was waiting for you." She turned back to the bar and threw back another shot.

"Jeez, are you some kind of witch or mind reader?" I was getting pissed, but also curious.

She faced me and said, "No, I can just read the history of people. They wear it like a tattered coat. I can see it."

"You mean like an aura, like I have an invisible radiance telegraphing my every thought?" I asked with no small degree of snark.

She paused for a moment, then said, "No, not like that. Everyone has a history, and I can see a lot of it in their faces." She cocked her head slightly and looked at me, waiting for my reaction.

Intrigued, I spoke with more anger in my voice than I'd meant to, "OK, so what's my history, since you're so good at reading people's faces?"

She didn't react, just stared at me for what seemed like a long time. "I can tell that you've suffered great loss, that you're feeling guilty about a lot of things, that you're on the edge, that The Black Dog is close."

"Lady, I don't know what you're talking about," I lied. "I don't have any problems."

She threw back her last shot and turned to me with knowing eyes. "You can deny it, but it's plain to see, you're struggling to make it through each day."

I grimaced as if I'd bitten into a lemon, "That sounds like the description of most men I know: struggling to make it through the day." I waved the bartender over for another round.

"Whaddid ya do in the service?" she asked. I hated that word "service." It made me feel like I was in the Peace Corps.

"I was in Naval Special Warfare," I explained, rattling off the innocuous term that meant nothing to most people.

"You mean the SEAL Teams?" she asked. The only way she'd know that was if she was a Navy spouse or former Navy herself.

I tapped my shot glass on the bar so the bartender moved down and poured another shot for me, shaking her head with disapproval.

"Yeah, the SEAL Teams," I confirmed.

"You must really miss that," she said earnestly.

"Hemingway wrote, *the value we have as human beings is our ability to take risks.* So yeah, my value as a human being is not what it used to be," I shared in a slightly snide tone. I tossed back my fourth shot. "I do miss the Teams and my brothers—they were my family."

We sat in silence for a moment before I asked, "What did your husband do?"

"He was Navy Intelligence—interrogated Al Qaeda operatives overseas after 9/11. The things he heard and saw got under his skin."

"Yeah, I can relate to seeing evil," I said, thinking of the Al Qaeda detainees I had come across. Definitely not model citizens. I added, "Sorry for your loss."

"Thanks. Ya know, women are much better at handling stress than men. Men just bottle things up and drink themselves to death. Women find more constructive ways to deal with stress," she said, toying with her glass.

"Yeah? So what ways do women use besides drinking tequila?" I asked in a sarcastic tone that I immediately regretted.

"Well, in general, women talk out their problems with friends and are more willing to seek help. Personally, I've learned how to live in the now. I've lived in the past and the future my whole life, hoping and dreaming for better things and wishing I could change the past or the future. I've learned to let all that go. I just live in the now."

"I'm Sheila, by the way," she added, extending her hand. She had long fingers and perfectly manicured nails.

"Jack, Jack Thibideaux. Nice to meet you."

I thought about what she said about living in the past and future. It made a lot of sense, and kind of meshed with Joe's advice to focus on the task at hand. I've spent most of my mental time in the past and future, without a lot of good to show for it.

"What brings you to Port Townsend?" she asked.

I couldn't tell her that I was trying to escape my past and start a new life, "I own the antique bookshop on Main Street. I've been here a year. How 'bout you?"

"I own the beauty shop on Third Avenue," she smiled. "Cheers to small business owners," she said, raising her glass and throwing back yet another shot.

I got up and moved next to her. "You're the real small business owner because you employ people, I just employ a cat."

She laughed at my self-deprecating comment and we talked for another hour about Navy life and how we'd both ended up in Port Townsend. At 9 p.m. she finished her last drink and stood up, "I've gotta get home. It's been nice talking with you, Jack."

I wanted to talk more with her—we had a lot in common. I stood up and said, "It was great to talk to you, Sheila, and to get my fortune read. I hope to see you again."

She smiled and threw her purse over her shoulder as she walked out. "It's a small town, Jack, you can't avoid me," she joked. I was conditioned in the Navy never to sleep with another man's wife, but a widow was different. The real reason I went home alone was Cindy. We were heading to British Columbia tomorrow and I was thinking about her.

In my bed, the room spun and thoughts of the day drifted through my head like pop flares over a target. I felt good about taking Cap to meet Joe, but the encounter with Jerry was a pit in my stomach. I was sure it would end in violence; I just didn't know how yet. I thought about Sheila. It would be nice to have a female friend, even though she'd tried to read my mind. Maybe it'd be like having the sister I'd never had.

I dreamed of Sheila's husband, seeing him walk into their backyard in his Navy dress uniform, leather shoes shined, cap on straight, a Beretta M9 in his hand. He looked up at the starry night one last time and closed his eyes. Suddenly he remembered the puppy he'd had as a kid licking his hand. The shot dropped him face down onto the inlaid brick patio. A dark pool formed around his head, his other hand unclenched, and a wedding ring rolled out, spun and came to a final stop.

Nineteen

—※—

I rub my hands in the dirt, trying to wipe off the sticky blood of the Taliban fighter. They'll come looking for him soon. I drag his body to a small cliff and roll it over the edge. It bounces twice and comes to a stop with a quiet thud. That will keep them busy searching for a few hours, giving me time to get ahead of them. Pulling my map out, I check the distance and bearing to that village—almost due west. I peel back the patch on the girl's shoulder to check her wound. There's discoloration and smell—infection is setting in. I have to get her medical help. I clean up the hide site and sling her over my shoulder, heading down the mountain and checking my bearing every 30 minutes.

Walking downhill with her is crushing my legs. It's still dark, but the pale crescent moon is starting to rise above the peaks behind us. I come across a dry river bed and decide to take it. The bushes around the river bed provide good concealment and it meanders roughly to the west. The sand must've been wet in the last few days, it makes a crunching sound like soft saltine crackers under my boots. I come across a small rock ledge that would be a waterfall during monsoon season. I set the girl on the top of the ledge and scramble down the left side, then reach up and pull her onto my shoulder before gently carrying her down the rocks. I continue making my way down the west flowing river bed.

The sand is easier on my knees when I fall or have to set the girl down. I'm leaving tracks in the sand, but I can make better time in this river bed and I have to get ahead of those fighters. The moonlight illuminates my path, a light breeze blows at my back. My mind is as clear and focused as it has ever been, with no thoughts of the past or future. I'm completely immersed in every detail of saving this girl.

At four in the morning, I spot a small cave entrance twenty yards above the river bed. It'll be difficult to carry the girl up the rocky embankment to the cave, but it looks like a good hide site and defensible position. After slipping and scrambling on loose scree, I make it to the top. The cave is five feet high and about fifteen feet deep. Scanning the back of the cave with my red lens flashlight, I find the dirty white bones of a small animal, but everything else looks safe. I move a pile of sharp rocks off the ground towards the rear of the cave to make a soft place to lay the girl down. Checking her pulse, I listen for breathing. Her pulse is slow but readable, breath is shallow. I hold up her head and pour a teaspoon of water into her mouth. She tries to drink, but it spills out the side of her mouth. One blue eye opens slightly and stares at me for a few seconds before closing. After getting her settled, I move to the mouth of the cave and find a seat against the side of the rocky wall about four feet into the cave. I'm concealed from anyone looking up into the opening from the river bed but I can see down the valley. I rest the rifle on my lap. The canyon wall across from me is dark, but above it stars are hidden behind black clouds. Dawn will be here soon. It's cold and the wind is picking up. I have to get some rest. I do a quick mental calculation; I haven't eaten in 36 hours, have half a quart of water left, but I can filter more if I can find a stream. I figure we have one to two more nights of walking to reach the village. The girl is in and out of consciousness, but alive. Fear seeps up my spine like a rotting disease. Something swells up deeper within me, an unnamed force, a primordial feeling—my whole life has led to this. I'll get this girl down the mountain and nothing will stop me. I see and feel my own death but for the first time in my life, it doesn't matter. I fall asleep as the tall Bhutan Pines stand a steadfast watch in the forbidden valley.

TWENTY

A raven cawing outside my window woke me early in the morning. My head was groggy from cheap tequila and terrible memories of the girl in Afghanistan. I remembered what Sheila had said about living in the now. I was ready to try anything to beat back The Black Dog. I started by making some fresh coffee and focusing on the process, pouring the correct amount of beans in a simple hand grinder and turning the grinder handle to release the rich, nutty aroma of the coffee beans. Pouring the beans into a small glass French press, I heated water in a kettle on the stovetop and poured it over the beans. I savored the smell of the coffee as I poured a hot steaming cup.

I'd heard the term *mindfulness* thrown around. I had no idea what it meant, but if it could help me break away from The Black Dog, I was all for it.

The microwave burrito tasted like salsa on cardboard, but I ate it anyway. I packed for the trip to BC and tossed an overnight bag into my faded white 1992 Toyota pickup truck. She's like me, getting old but refuses to quit. I was scheduled to meet Cindy at 9 a.m. at the Cup O' Joe before we headed out to the museum in Victoria. I smiled as I thought about spending the day driving with her through the tall green forests on the way to Port Angeles. I was looking forward to getting to know her better.

I arrived early and ordered my second cup of the day while chatting with Joe. Two young skateboarders with shaggy hair were laughing at some video on their phone and a young woman in a business suit was working on a laptop in the corner. Other than that, the place was empty. Joe told me Cap had stayed yesterday for another hour to talk about boats and might be back today, which was good news.

"How's Jane?" I asked, a little afraid of the answer.

Joe looked down at the cup he was drying. "She didn't get outta bed yesterday, Jack. That's a first, so I'm not sure what's going on."

"What about when you went to see her?" I asked, sipping my coffee.

"I held her hand, and she smiled, but that was about it."

"I'm really sorry, Joe." I couldn't imagine what he was going through.

The door to the coffee shop swung open and Cindy walked in wearing a black puffy jacket, a Native American print skirt and tall brown boots. She was dragging a roll-aboard suitcase. I was relieved to see that she'd shown up after witnessing me blow a gasket while crabbing yesterday.

"Cindy, you look ready for the road," I said in greeting, swiveling in my bar stool.

"Hey, Jack, Hi Joe. Can I get a cup of coffee before we head out?"

"Got it right here for ya, honey," said Joe as he poured her a hot cup and set it on the coffee bar.

"So Jack, what does the trip look like this morning?" she asked as she sat next to me. She smelled like lilacs.

"Well, we have about a 4-5 hour transit. We'll head out around Discovery Bay, pass through Sequim and catch the ferry at Port Angeles. There's a good clam chowder house in Port Angeles if you're up for it?"

"Oh, that would be lovely. Do you think we'll see an Orca on the ferry?"

"I think they're too big to get on the ferry."

She laughed at the unexpected humor and almost spit out her coffee, "Ha ha, Jack, you're too funny."

Her soft blue eyes were captivating and her smile reminded me of the feeling I'd had opening Christmas presents as a kid. She finished her coffee and we loaded up her bag for the trip.

The scenery was spectacular as we drove west along the lush and rocky coast. The temperate rainforest of the Olympic Peninsula is overwhelmingly beautiful. The tall Sitka spruce and western hemlock dominated the landscape, with lush ferns and moss providing thick green and blue undergrowth. We caught occasional views of the Strait of Juan de Fuca off to our right, and with a break in the clouds we could see across the Strait to Canada. The sun peeked out between high clouds and shone beams through the dense forest like white lightsabers. Cindy was fiddling with the radio dial, but only getting static.

"At dinner the other night, your mom said your dad died three years ago. What happened, if you don't mind my asking?" I was curious why she and her mom didn't talk much about it.

Cindy looked out the passenger window before speaking. "My dad was the most positive influence in my life. He was an unstoppable force for good; worked with homeless children, was a dedicated father and husband, and the kindest man I've known. He was my mentor." She turned to look straight at me. "He died in a nursing home three years ago after a long bout with early onset dementia. It was very hard on my mother and me."

"Oh geez, I'm sorry to hear that, Cindy," I said, feeling her sadness. Just then two deer darted across the road in front of us, breaking the tension of the moment. "Wow, did you see that big buck?" I exclaimed. "I would hate to hit him with this truck—it would cave in the whole front."

We stopped for two delicious bowls of chowder in Port Angeles then caught the 1:30 p.m. ferry to Victoria. After parking the car in the belly of the ferry, we climbed to the upper deck to enjoy the fresh air and view. Small white-capped swells rolled in from the west, hitting the ferry broadside and causing a gentle rocking of the large ship. The sun was shining beams of brilliant light onto the slate-colored water. Cindy stood next to me at the rail as we watched seagulls circle the boat. Her cheeks were flushed from the cold air.

"This is so beautiful," she observed, waving her arm across the horizon.

"Yeah, I love the sea. It's peaceful and majestic at the same time. I guess that's why I have a boat, even though it's a money pit."

"You mean your skiff?" she asked, zipping her jacket up against the wind.

"No, I have a 42-foot trawler I keep at the marina. We'll have to go out for a cruise sometime."

"That would be fun," she said, her hair blowing across her eyes. "Do you ever dive off your boat?"

"Not since I moved to Port Townsend, but I dove a lot in the SEAL Teams."

"I'm a certified diver, too," she shared, surprising me. "I took a course when I was on vacation in Hawaii five years ago and fell in love with it. I take dive vacations and work on different dive certifications when I come back from Pakistan each year. It's like another world underwater. I love it," she beamed.

"That's awesome," I said. I was becoming more and more intrigued with this woman. Not only was she a teacher in one of the most dangerous parts of the world, she was also passionate about one of the most dangerous sports in the world. Clearly, she was tougher than she looked, which was appealing to me.

"You're full of surprises, Cindy. Next you're gonna tell me you have five thousand parachute jumps."

She laughed, "Oh no, I like to keep close to the ground if I have a choice."

We reached the port, cleared customs and drove into Victoria to find our bed and breakfast inn. After a couple of wrong turns, we pulled into the driveway of a light green clapboard home with a tall roof and white brick chimney. A young Chinese woman wearing a red skirt and black pumps showed us to our rooms and told us that breakfast was served from 7-8 a.m. A cat that looked like Emilio's twin was perched on a window sill, soaking up the sun. I thought of Emilio, who'd really grown on me, and hoped he was catching all the mice he could eat, though I had also asked Joe to check up on him.

We decided to drive to the museum right away, since we had a few hours before they closed. After finding a parking spot, we were directed to the archive administrator, who could give us permission to look in the archives. A woman in a fuzzy sweater scrutinized us through horn-rimmed glasses perched on her long nose. She explained that the archives were closed to the general public, but they did allow access to researchers and educators. I knew this and had discussed it with Cindy ahead of time. She joked that I was merely using her for her ID card, but she knew better and was happy to help. She produced her teacher identification card and after studying it closely, the woman gave us access to the archives.

"We're looking for a journal from the 1800s written by a trapper named Jeremiah Benton that could shed light on a shipwreck that occurred in 1840 near the coast of Washington State," I explained to the woman.

The administrator removed her glasses and looked at us like we were wacko American treasure hunters. She waved two bony fingers and we followed her through a massive file room. "This row contains the files and documents from the mid-1800s," she said, turning back toward us. There were huge drawers that pulled out of eight-foot-high rolling file cabinets. "I don't think you'll find what you're looking for, though," she warned. "We don't hold many journals." She left us to it, reminding us that they close promptly at 5 p.m.

We stood next to each other in the massive hallway of files. The room was cold, probably to preserve the files. The fading afternoon light was streaming through high windows. Fluorescent lights buzzed above our heads sounding like hopped-up moths. There were no tables, so we had to hold the files and look through them. "Well, we could start with 1840 and later, since the shipwreck was supposed to have happened in September 1840, right?" Cindy suggested.

I took September 1840 and Cindy started with October. The documents within each file weren't organized by any category, so we had to pull out each one and scan it. There were transcripts of trading companies, copies of land deeds, records of town and city administrations and every other document related to life in the Pacific Northwest in the mid-1800s. It took us an hour and a half to get through one month each. At 5:00 the archive administrator appeared at the end of the row like a gulag security guard. She didn't say anything, but the message was clear—time was up. We followed her silently to the exit. We hadn't seen anything like a trapper's journal. I had a bad feeling we were wasting our time.

It was dark as we wound through the lush streets and roundabouts of Victoria. Ornate lamp posts holding large baskets of flowers flooded the sidewalks with soft yellow light, reminding me of London.

We stopped for dinner at a sleek modern restaurant that specializes in local salmon grilled on cedar planks. The view of the bay from our table was dazzling—red, green and white lights of boats navigating the harbor reflected a kaleidoscope of color on the inky black water. I ordered a bottle of Spanish Tempranillo as we waited for the salmon. The sommelier brought the bottle, expertly popped the cork and poured us each a glass of the fragrant red wine. Cindy was fascinated with the view of the bay and stared at it with a beautiful smile. The delight on her face as she watched the dance of light and color on the dark water moved me. She seemed to have an endless curiosity about everything around her. I'd forgotten what that was like, but as I watched her, I saw the world through her eyes. A feeling of peace washed over me like a warm wave. For a few, brief seconds, my mind was silent and there was nothing but peace in my heart.

She turned to me, "What is it, Jack? You're staring at me."

"I'm sorry, I haven't felt like this in a long time," I shared, sounding more vulnerable than I meant to.

"Felt like what?" she asked softly, curiosity written on her face.

I looked at her compassionate blue eyes. She was leaning forward in her seat, her soft blonde hair tied in the back with a blue scrunchie. Knowing there was no turning back now, I replied, "My life's a struggle every day, I can't really explain it. I haven't felt at peace for so long that I forgot what it feels like. But just now, when I was watching you stare out the window... I dunno... I felt something like peace come over me."

Cindy took a deep breath as if getting ready to jump off a high dive into a pool. "Jack, is your struggle related to that incident in Afghanistan that you told me about? The one with the girl?" It was obvious she'd been trying to process that since I'd told her about it. *Why hadn't I just kept my mouth shut?*

The truth was I didn't know the actual source of the darkness in me, but I knew the incident with the girl was a large part of it. I looked out the window at the horizon, reminded of what Nietzsche said, 'The strength of a person's spirit would then be measured by how much 'truth' he could tolerate.' I wasn't sure if either of us could tolerate that much truth right now.

She reached across the table and placed her hand gently on my arm. It was a small gesture, but it meant much more. Her deep blue eyes reflected the glow of the harbor. Right then I knew that she wouldn't judge me for what had happened to that Afghan girl. I judged myself every day. That was more than enough.

I felt a tear in the corner of my eye. I wasn't used to that kind of touch; the touch that transcends words, the touch of empathy and understanding. A touch that doesn't want anything, but simply listens and gives.

"Jack, it's OK," Cindy breathed, as I swiped at the tear with the back of my hand, trying to hold back the flood. "Jack... look at me." I lifted my gaze from my hands. She was leaning in, her head slightly cocked and her eyes laser-focusing on me, "You don't have to tell me anything. I just want you to know that I'm here for you, OK?"

"Thanks, Cindy," I said quietly, pulling my arm back into my lap. If I left it in her warm hand any longer, I might tell her truths she wasn't ready for... things I wasn't ready for myself. She sat back, still gazing at me intently. *Probably trying to figure out what kind of a nut she was with.* I was spent, had nothing more to say. Luckily that was the moment our server brought our salmon plates. A silence hung in the air like a wet wool blanket as we ate dinner then headed back to our B&B.

TWENTY-ONE

— : —

I woke early, dressed and headed downstairs to the small dining area in the Inn. The woman who'd shown us to our rooms was cooking breakfast in a kitchen nook off the dining room. I could smell bacon sizzling. There was a carafe of coffee on a small table by the window. I poured a cup and looked out the bay window at the misty morning. I thought about last night and regretted telling Cindy about what haunted me. But I had to admit it felt good to let someone know that I wasn't hitting on all cylinders. My boss once told me, "Don't be the last one holding a secret." Just then Cindy practically bounded down the stairs, wearing black tights and a gray wool dress. Her ensemble was elegant, but not overdone; very attractive.

"Well, good morning, ready to dig through a pile of moldy old files?" I greeted.

"Have you eaten already? I'm starving," she said with a grin. I was relieved she didn't want to talk about last night. I was embarrassed. I couldn't recall ever crying in front of a woman.

"Of course not. I was waiting for you!" I teased. "Don't worry, it's still cooking." Just then, the woman in the kitchen appeared with two plates of eggs, bacon, toast and sliced tomatoes. Cindy slid the tomatoes delicately to the side of her plate. "I like tomatoes, but not for breakfast," she shared.

"Yeah, it's an English thing," I said, scarfing down the eggs.

"So what do you think our chances are today?" she asked.

I took a sip of coffee, thought about it, and said, "I would say slim. I didn't see anything even resembling a trapper's journal yesterday. I hope we're not wasting our time."

"We're not wasting our time, Jack," she said emphatically. "If we don't find the journal, you'll still have done everything you could to help Cap. I'm sure he'll be grateful that you went to this much trouble for him."

I usually think in terms of mission failure or success—if we didn't find the journal, I would consider it a failure. But Cindy's perspective was more nuanced; a view of the world I was beginning to appreciate.

The archives opened at 9:00 a.m., and we were there waiting when the administrator opened the door. We had come up with a plan on the drive to the museum: I would take November 1840 and Cindy would take December. Whoever finished first would move on to the next month. We jumped right in and started our search. Not only were the document contents themselves varied, but they came in a wide variety of physical forms. There were loose, yellowing papers, ledgers of accounts, and handmade books that were quarter-bound, half-bound or fully-bound with leather. It was tedious work to decipher what each one was. A book full of numbers was the easiest to blow through—it was usually a business ledger. The documents full of handwriting were the most challenging, since we had to skim the contents to figure out if anything resembled a trapper's journal.

We punched through lunch. My eyes were about to give out when I found a pink cardboard marker in the middle of the 1841 file folder. On the pink marker was written the word, *Benton*. Cindy was working the next row over so I yelled out, "Hey, I think I have something!" She rushed over and we flipped through the file together but there was no trapper's journal. The pink marker looked to be a placeholder.

"Let's ask the administrator," Cindy suggested.

"Good idea."

We went to the front desk with the file. The administrator was looking at a computer screen with her back to us, so Cindy spoke up, "Excuse me, Miss? We found a marker in this file with the word *Benton* written on it. We're looking for a journal from a trapper named Benton. Do you know what this pink marker means, by any chance?"

The woman spun in her chair and stared at us. "You're not allowed to take a complete file from the archive room," she scolded through tight lips.

"We didn't know, we're very sorry," Cindy said in a soothing voice.

The woman stood up, looked at the marker, then walked over to another table and began to search through a pile of folders and books. After a few minutes, she pulled a small leather book out from a large stack and showed it to us.

It was titled, *My Time as a Trapper* by J. Benton. We both tried to contain our excitement, but were amazed that we were staring at exactly what we'd come for but hadn't fully expected to find. It was hard to decipher the writing, but there was no doubt that it was the trapper's journal we'd been searching for. There were dates on each page corresponding to a journal entry from the author. He hadn't written every day, but we could see that he'd made entries every 2-3 days from early 1839 through mid-1841.

"Why is this not in the file?" I asked, wildly curious to know how the very thing we'd been searching for happened to be out here at the front desk.

"A woman came in yesterday, searched the archives and made copies of this. When you said you were looking for a journal, I didn't put two and two together. The documents on this table have been checked out but haven't yet been returned to the archives yet," she explained.

"Can you tell me about the woman?" I asked. I had a bad hunch.

"Well, she said she was a PhD student from Washington. Tall, dark hair, olive skin, Mediterranean features."

Linda—she'd played me like a fiddle. I didn't want to tell Cindy about Linda for a variety of reasons, so I just played it cool. "OK, thank you. Can we get a copy of this book?" I asked, changing the subject.

The administrator let us use a special copy machine that took pictures of each page without damaging the paper. We gathered up our copies and rushed back to the port to catch the 3:30 ferry back to Port Angeles. Luckily, we beat the afternoon traffic and secured one of the last spots on the ferry. It was cold and spitting rain outside as we huddled in the coffee shop on the main deck during the transit. While Cindy was trying to read the journal from the beginning for context, I found the page for September 17, 1840. Sure enough, Jeremiah Benton had made an entry that day. He wrote,

"Whilst hunting hart and searching for signs of otters off Kydaka Point, I witnessed a thing that I shall not soon forget. I was above the coast on a rocky outcropping spying for signs of otters off the coast with my glass, when I saw a large ship making its way westward down the strait. It were

a windy and blustery day with waves as large as a small cabin coming from the north. As I continued to watch the ship, she began to lose steerage as she was drifting from the middle of the channel towards the south. The winds were mighty and shifting about. I saw the ship pass by me heading west, but drifting too close to shore. I had a feeling, God forbid, that she would founder. As sure as I am here today, she drifted to the south and went down a mile off the next prominent point west, northwest of me. I gathered up my musket and pack and walked the five miles to the point to look for any survivors, but heaven help me I saw none. I camped that night off the point with a big fire so wayward seamen should see my fire and be guided to safety, but alas I saw no souls."

The cold rain was lashing the ferry as we huddled in the sterile stainless steel and vinyl coffee shop. We finally had time to talk about our findings. My coffee cup almost slid off the table as the big ship rocked in the westerly swell. Cindy was holding a hot chocolate with both hands in the booth seat next to me, where she sat with her legs curled under her. I was able to get a WiFi signal, and pulled up a map of the Strait of Juan de Fuca on my phone.

"Cindy, look at this. If Benton was at Kydaka Point and saw the ship go down west, northwest at the next prominent point, that would be here near Shipwreck Point," I pointed out to her. That also aligned with the general description of the wreck described in the book on shipwrecks in the Strait that I'd found for Cap.

I downloaded a nautical chart for that area. "Check this out," I said excitedly. She scooted next to me. "You can see on this nautical chart where Shipwreck Point is located. You can also see that the gradient of the coast drops off into very deep water. If the shipwreck was a mile from the coast, by my rough calculation it would be in 100 feet of water!"

"That's not too deep, is it?" she asked. "I did a bounce dive to 120 feet once in training."

"The problem is we can't stay down at 100 feet very long doing search or salvage work with compressed air."

She grinned, "I noticed you said *we* can't stay down very long, Jack. It sounds like you've already made up your mind to give it a try, huh?" I hate when women read my mind, it must be an easy read.

"Whaddaya make of the woman who found the journal before we did?" Cindy asked. "That's a pretty strange coincidence, don't you think?"

I knew she would ask about that. "I'll be right back," I said, standing and heading to the bathroom as if it was an emergency. I needed time to think before I answered her. I couldn't lie to Cindy, but didn't want to tell her about Linda. I looked at myself in the mirror and dark eyes stared back at me. *I'll tell her the truth,* I decided.

I walked down the passageway and came up behind Cindy at the booth as the ferry gently swayed under me. She was talking on her cell phone. I slid in and heard her say, "I should be home for dinner, Mom. OK, see you then."

"Everything good with your mother?" It was a lucky opportunity to change the subject.

"Yes, she's fine, she was just wondering if I'd be home for dinner." She didn't ask any more about Linda so I'd dodged a bullet... for now.

We crept off the ferry and drove back to Port Townsend in a gray slurry of rain and sleet. "So what are you planning to tell Cap?" asked Cindy as we approached the outskirts of Port Townsend.

That was a tough question. Cap tended to get overly hopeful about positive news, but the trapper's journal had definitely narrowed down the search. It was still a huge area to cover for divers, plus the depths and currents made diving in that area very hazardous. "I dunno, I'll have to sleep on it. What do you think?"

She gazed out the wet window for a moment before speaking, "Whatever you decide, Jack, I'll support you. I'm glad you made the effort to find the journal—not many people would have done that for someone they'd just met."

I realized then that I wasn't the saint Cindy thought I was. I needed to climb out of a deep, dark hole and Cap's crazy shipwreck idea had caught my attention. It was giving me a focus that I badly needed. *Was I hijacking his plans for my own needs?*

TWENTY-TWO

E milio was stretched across my desk, doing a good job of dusting it as his tail swept back and forth. I was nibbling on a poppy seed muffin that Mrs. Johnson had brought over earlier that morning. She'd told me, as if sharing a secret, that Cindy had had a good time with me in British Columbia. I smiled and nodded, and simply said I was happy to hear that, hoping she would make a quick exit and not want to engage in one of her long conversations. I needed to think.

I still hadn't figured out what to tell Cap. I tried to organize boxes of books, but my mind was focused on that shipwreck. *Let's just say the wreck is in the general location the trapper described and not too deep,* I reasoned. *If that was true, why hadn't someone else tried to salvage it years ago? If there was gold involved, that would bring out all the crazies looking for a quick strike. Maybe they hadn't known about the trapper's journal?* I surmised. *If the only description of the wreck was somewhere off Shipwreck Point, that would be hundreds of square miles of searching. The information in Benton's journal had narrowed it down considerably.* I had to admit it was theoretically possible that the wreck could be found, with some luck. I was becoming excited about the opportunity to put a team together and do something difficult and interesting. I went with my gut. I'd tell Cap about Benton's journal and offer to lead an initial search for the wreck with the caveat that we had to have a defined end point. The search couldn't last forever. If we didn't find any evidence of the wreck after a week, we'd have to call it off. We didn't have rich backers who would let us go on and on until we found something.

At 11:30 Linda blew into the shop with a waft of high-dollar perfume trailing behind her. This woman knew how to dress, and it sure wasn't like any PhD student, especially one studying crab populations. Today's ensemble was a tight-fitting blue wool dress with a plunging neckline, a hem that stopped mid-thigh, and black high heels.

"Jack, where've you been?" she immediately sang out with feigned curiosity. "I haven't seen you for a few days. D'you wanna have lunch? It's on me."

I said yes without answering her first question. I wanted to see what I could find out without letting on that I knew she'd scammed information out of me and beat me to the museum to find the trapper's journal. She was one step ahead of me, but I planned on catching up.

She picked out a swanky new restaurant that was full of modern art, stainless steel and glass. The menu listed exotic vegetables I'd never heard of and I couldn't find any meat on the menu. "It's vegan," she gushed. There was a fake hamburger, but I went with the pasta.

"So what have you been up to the last couple of days?" I probed, after some cursory small talk. I was eager to hear how she would answer.

She set her fork down, reached into her handbag and brought out a manilla envelope. "You remember how you told me about that trapper's journal? You said a friend of yours told you there might be more information at the Royal British Columbia Museum?"

I set my drink down, trying to look nonchalant. My mind was racing for an answer. "Sure, I remember."

"I like doing research, and I wanted to surprise you, so I went up there the day before yesterday, and guess what?" she beamed. "I found the journal." She handed me the manilla envelope.

I didn't know what to say, literally. Obviously, I didn't want to tell her that Cindy and I had found the journal yesterday. *Was Linda nicer than I thought, or was there something else going on here? Maybe I should have given her the benefit of the doubt?* I just couldn't tell with her. I had a deep suspicion that she was a master of hiding her intentions. I said, "Wow, that was such a nice thing to do, Linda. Thank you." I flagged the waitress for a drink to give me time to think.

I opened the copy of the journal and scanned the pages. Linda was watching me closely. I found the entry from September 17, 1840 with Benton's description of the wreck. I glanced at Linda, who had a look of anticipation on her face. I silently read the entry, but there was something off about it. I needed to compare this entry to the one Cindy and I had copied. I carefully slid it back into the envelope, nodding.

"So now you have information to give to your friend, right? Maybe it's enough to start a search," she batted her lashes at me expectantly. I stared at her—she had a beautiful face, but just below the surface I sensed something else that I couldn't put my finger on. Something dark.

"So, Jack, you think it actually exists and can be found?" she asked, putting her elbow on the table and her chin in her hand.

"Well, it's a huge area from a diving perspective, even with the trapper's information. I'm not sure, but I might give it a try and see if I can at least give Cap a little closure."

She laughed a little mockingly. "Jack," she shook her head, "you really are a sentimentalist, aren't you?" Her dark eyes were boring into me, the long eyelashes making me woozy.

"I've really gotta get back to the shop, Linda. I've got lots to do." I needed to get away from her—she was like Kryptonite. "Thanks again for this," I motioned to the envelope.

"OK, how 'bout drinks tonight?"

My pulse skipped a beat. "I have other plans, unfortunately. Rain check?" I asked as dismissively as I could manage, thinking about Cindy. She looked at me with what I first thought was disappointment, but as I was walking out the door, I realized it seemed more like disdain.

TWENTY-THREE

B ack at the bookstore I pulled out the copy of the journal that Cindy and I had found and flipped to the entry describing the wreck. Setting the two copies side by side, I carefully read each. I was right. In our copy, Benton said he was hunting off Kydaka Point and saw the wreck go down off the next prominent point west, northwest of his location. In the copy from Linda, the trapper said he was hunting on the coast and saw the wreck go down off Kydaka Point. It was a subtle change, and one not everyone would catch, but it resulted in a difference of five miles. A five mile difference underwater for a diver in cold, murky water was like a thousand mile difference on land.

I looked at the handwriting between the two journal entries and noticed subtle differences. I could barely see them, but someone had skillfully rewritten the description in the entry that Linda had given me. *What was going on? Had Linda made the changes? Had someone at the museum made the changes? Was someone else out for the gold?*

Cap walked into the shop right before closing. This time he took off his hat as if he was walking into church. His white hair was slicked back over his ears, making him look younger.

"Cap! I've been hoping I'd see you today." I stood and went over to greet him.

"Yes, hello, Jack. I had planned to come in this morning but my arthritis was acting up. So tell me... what did you find in British Columbia?" He moved slowly to the window to sit at the table as Emilio came out from the back to greet him.

I didn't want to oversell our findings to Cap, but I said, "My friend Cindy and I did find the trapper's journal."

"Oh, that's wonderful!" he exclaimed. "And? What does it say?" The hope in his eyes was almost painful.

I made a copy of the page where Benton describes the shipwreck and handed it to Cap. After reading it, he looked up at me with a grin. "Shipwreck Point—that should narrow it down!"

I had a sailing book with nautical charts of the Strait of Juan de Fuca. I pulled it from the shelf and opened it on the table in front of Cap, turning to the section covering Shipwreck Point.

"Here's Shipwreck Point," I pointed out.

"Been fishin' there many times," he said, nodding. He moved his hand slowly across the chart like he was caressing a lover.

"Then you know that the bottom drops off steeply into hundreds of feet of water near the coast," I pointed to the area right off Shipwreck Point. "If the wreck is more to the north, it would be in deeper water than most divers can access. Plus, there are strong currents through that area that run up to three knots at maximum tidal ebb and flow. Any diving would have to be done around slack water each day."

Cap ran his hands through his hair and scratched his white stubble while considering his words. Finally, he said, "Son, it sounds like you know more about this business than a bookstore owner should know."

I smirked and sat down before speaking. "To be honest, Cap, I was in the Navy. I've done a lot of diving in difficult conditions."

He looked directly at me and his eyes shone. "Listen, Jack, I have this feeling. You're the one to help me. Not only did you find the key that tells us where to look, but I think you're the right person to help me find it *and* the treasure. I just feel it. Fate led me here.."

I had to be careful about what I said next. I looked down and sighed, and then said quietly, "OK, Cap, so I'm not a professional salvage expert, but I do own a boat and know a few divers. We would need to get a lot of specialized equipment together if we were gonna attempt this."

"That's not a problem, son, I can find the money."

"Cap, I'm not worried about the money. I just want you to understand that this is a dangerous and risky mission with very little chance of finding anything." I regretted saying that as soon as it came out.

Cap's face clouded over and his eyes looked down at his wiry hands. Then I thought about what Cindy would say and I continued, "Cap, listen, we're gonna give it a try, OK? Who knows, maybe we'll get very lucky and find something. But you've got to understand that a search can'tgo on indefinitely, yeah? People have lives and work. We can probably search for about a week, but if we don't find anything by then, we'll have to call it off. Fair enough? Can you live with that?"

The gratified smile returned to his lined and weary face. He stood up, put his cap back on his head and reached out to shake my hand. His leathery hand was trembling when I took it. "I can live with that, Jack. You've done right by me so far and I feel good about our chances. You let me know how much you need to get that equipment and those divers together."

"OK Cap, will do," I said, suddenly feeling a swell of anticipation and excitement about this little adventure that had found me.

Cap looked me in the eye and then headed out the door.

But almost as quickly I thought, *Man, what have I committed to? What if I get somebody hurt out there? What if we don't find anything and Cap can't let it go? What if the conditions prove too difficult?*

I recalled a passage I'd written when I was facing a tough decision in the Navy. I'd been given the choice of two sets of assignments—one would lead to a dangerous assignment overseas, the other would allow me more time at home with my wife: *Inertia is the enemy. The very subtle feeling to take the soft or easy path leads to a wasted life.* I chose the hard path.

TWENTY-FOUR

— ❋ —

I closed the bookstore and buttoned my jacket against the cool northern wind. I decided to stop by the VFW on the way home. *Maybe that mind-reader woman would be there again. What was her name? Shirley... no Sheila.* As luck would have it, I walked in to see her sitting by herself at the left end of the bar. She was wearing a black silk blouse, with light slacks and heels, as if she'd just gotten off work in an office. Her long, gray-streaked hair was tied with a brown ribbon that looked good on her. I sat next to her.

"Well, well," she said, turning towards me with a wry smile.

"What're ya drinking?" I asked.

"Today is my Irish day—Tullamore Dew Irish Whiskey," she lifted a shot glass and toasted me.

"I'm an international drinker myself. I'll drink to the Irish." I flagged the young bartender and ordered a shot of Tullamore Dew on ice.

"Here's to the Irish," she said with a smile and we clinked glasses. "Ya know, I've gotta say, you have a glow about you tonight," she said as she looked me up and down like she was examining a specimen in a lab.

Oh here we go again, I thought. "Oh, yeah, what kinda glow?"

"Well, either you're in love, you've found your purpose in life or you've been exposed to radiation."

I snorted, maybe my first good laugh in a long while. "You read it right, I was standing too close to the microwave this morning when my burrito burned. I've been lighting up the room everywhere I go today."

She laughed and smiled—it was easy to talk to her. I told her about Cindy, describing this amazing woman who had given up teaching rich kids to teach impoverished girls in Pakistan and who was also a scuba diver. I said she was smart and kind but also strong and had a sense of humor. I guess I was gushing a little bit, and didn't realize it.

"Yep, you're in love, Jack," Sheila informed me with one of her knowing winks. "I knew I was right."

"No... she's too young for me, she has a whole career ahead of her. She'll be running her institution in a few years. I'm just a bit player in her life. She's a good friend, that's all." I guess I was trying that line on for size but didn't like the way it fit at all.

"Oh, c'mon Jack, you light up when you talk about her," said Sheila confidently as she took another sip of her dark Irish whiskey. "So, how about a nightcap?" she asked.

I didn't want to spend the night with Sheila. She was attractive and funny but my life didn't need any more complications at this point. On the other hand, she'd been great to talk to and was a Navy wife who'd lost her husband to suicide. I was sure she was very lonely.

"I can come by for one drink and then I'll have to get home."

"OK," she nodded, "One drink it is."

Her house was a little cottage four blocks east of the VFW, with a small, well-kept English garden behind a short, black wrought iron fence. The house had a high-peaked roof and sat on a narrow lot, sandwiched between two larger modern homes. The front door was bright green but the rest of the house was painted a soft blue. Window boxes held vivid blue and yellow flowers. The place clearly had a woman's touch.

Her living room was small but comfy. Several pieces of Native American art adorned the walls; a painting hung above the fireplace of a hunter in full stride on a bareback painted pony chasing a bison. Her furniture fit well with the small house and made me realize how crappy my stuff was. A soft leather couch sat in front of the fireplace with a matching armchair to the right. On the left was what looked like a handmade bar carved out of wood. Her late husband probably had it made in Asia somewhere when he was overseas. Behind the bar was a mirror with shelves full of liquor bottles. She started a small gas fire that took the chill out of the room. I stood there awkwardly, not sure where to sit.

She kicked off her heels and commanded, "Make yourself comfortable, Jack. What'll you have to drink?"

"I'll stick with the Irish if you have any."

She poured us both a glass of Tullamore Dew on ice and sat down on the couch next to me. *Maybe I should have taken the chair.*

"So tell me about your husband." I said suddenly. "When did he pass away?"

"Alex didn't pass away, he killed himself," she said with admirable frankness, taking a long sip of her drink.

I could sense her grief. I shouldn't have asked, but unfortunately it's a subject I have experience with. I took a sip of whiskey. "OK, so how did he kill himself?"

She rolled her head like she was preparing to enter a dark mental place. "Pistol to the head."

That's what I'd figured—most men go out with a bang. "How long has it been?"

"Two years next month, though it seems like yesterday." The pain was seeping through her pores.

"I'm really sorry, Sheila. I know how hard that is and how much damage is left in the wake. I presented the flag to a mother at a funeral for her son who worked for me and committed suicide. She couldn't understand why he'd done it and blamed everyone, including me. I guess in some ways we all let him down. Nobody saw it coming." I paused, then added, "My best friend committed suicide too."

"What happened?" she asked as she pulled the ribbon out of her long hair and ran her fingers through it as it fell around her shoulders.

"Shot himself in the head with a rifle. He was having family problems and was on the verge of divorce and losing his kids. The thing is, I'd tried to see him for several weeks before it happened but he kept coming up with excuses to avoid me. I knew the excuses were bogus and that something was wrong, but I let it go. Figured I'd give 'im some space. Then he killed himself. I've never forgiven myself for not doing more."

She scooted closer to me on the couch so that her hip was touching my leg. "Jack, you can't blame yourself. We can't get into other people's heads, no matter how close we are to them. Believe me, I know."

I knew deep down that was true, but the pain and guilt were always swirling around inside of me like a dark cesspool. I took a small sip of my whiskey, knowing if I drank too fast I might end up sleeping on this couch.

She stood up and walked over to the gas fire in her stocking feet, turning her back to the fire. She looked like a dark angel silhouetted against the fire in the dim light. "I didn't see it coming with my husband either. These dark moods would take him over, but he always seemed to pull himself out. Eventually he went into one and never came out. I guess he got tired of fighting it."

Her voice dropped to a whisper. I felt a jolt of anxiety about my own struggles with The Black Dog. "The thing is, I wish I'd known how much pain he was in." Her soft voice was cracking, "I would have done something different. He didn't want help when he went into those moods, but now I think I should have done more." Her eyes flashed with pain in the firelight. "I wanted to retire here in little Port Townsend, but he wanted to be in a big city near his buddies. Maybe if he was around more of his old shipmates in a Navy town, he would've had more of a support network," she said, starting to cry.

I stood up and moved in front of the fire to put my arm around her shoulder. "Hey, you can't blame yourself, just like you told me. And by the way, this is a great town with plenty of retired military veterans. You did everything you could. Didn't you just tell me that no one knows what goes on in someone else's mind? We're all unknowable beings, aren't we?"

She leaned her head into my shoulder. "What about you, Jack? Why is The Black Dog chasing you?"

I let go of her shoulder and turned to stare into the fire.

"An incident in Afghanistan, among other things," I answered in a monotone.

She turned around, standing shoulder to shoulder with me, as we both stared into the red, glowing embers.

"It must've been awful over there," she said quietly.

I nodded, not wanting to think about it. The firelight reflection in the darkened room danced off her face.

"Can I ask you something?" She turned to me.

"Sure," I said, hoping she wasn't going to ask me to spend the night.

"What's it like when The Black Dog is chasing you? Alex never talked about it."

I hadn't expected that question and thought about not answering, but then realized maybe I could offer her a little closure. I turned to face her—the firelight lit up half of her beautiful face, leaving the other half darkened like a native warrior in war paint. *How much do I really tell her?* Nietzsche's words returned to my mind once again. *How much truth is enough?*

"It's like this, Sheila. The Black Dog smells your pain and guilt. It feeds on the carcass of whatever hope you have in this world until there's none left."

She bowed her head and sobbed. *What a jackass! I should have lied to her, given her some BS story, not the truth. Some things are just unspeakable.*

I pulled her in close, wrapped my arms around her and hugged her tight. She was warm and sobbed in my arms. Her hair smelled like roses. I held her for a long time—two souls damaged by war. I closed my eyes and tried to envision her husband Alex. My mind created a scene where I met him here in Port Townsend as Navy vets, we became friends and somehow I saved him from killing himself. Saved Sheila from all this grief and bought myself some recompense for not doing enough to prevent my best friend's suicide. I pulled away and brushed the long hair from her bloodshot eyes.

"I should be going," I whispered. If she didn't want to be alone, I would crash on the couch but she didn't ask.

"Thank you for this evening, Jack," she said. "I really needed someone to talk to."

"Me too."

"Good night then."

"Good night, Sheila."

TWENTY-FIVE

D istant voices carry on the wind during the long daylight hours. No one approaches the cave or comes down the river bed. I study the map in the back of the cave to reduce my exposure until dusk. The canyon we're in runs roughly parallel to the drainage we need to be in to find the village. The valley that leads to the village is to the north of our position. At dusk I would hike out of this canyon, perpendicular to the river bed, then drop into the next valley before daylight set in. It's cold outside, with light snowflakes beginning to fall. I check the girl's pulse and breathing. She's still wearing my Gore-Tex jacket so I pull the hood tight over her head and cinch down the neck strap. The sun has set, darkness is creeping up the canyon walls. Very carefully, I hoist her onto my shoulder and scramble down from the cave to the river bed, loose boulders and sand slowing me down. We reach the river bed and I set her down to rest. After a few minutes I again lift the girl and set off down the river bed for 300 yards until I find what I'm looking for—soft dirt to the right, larger rocks in front of us in the canyon. I lay her on a large flat rock, take obvious steps to the right into the soft dirt, then let my tracks meander into the bushes and loose shale rock heading up the canyon on the opposite side from where we need to go. Then carefully stepping only on rocks, I make my way back down the canyon, hoist the girl and start to climb the opposite side of the canyon. If my path in the river bed is found, that meandering trail to the south will lead them astray for a while.

It's steep going up the ridge leading to the next valley. I zig-zag back and forth to ease the climb on my legs. At 2200, I take a rest under a cedar tree that is growing out of cracks in the rocks. I set the girl against the tree trunk and check on her wound—it's oozing brown puss. The clouds are moving fast but the wind has slowed and a half moon is peeking out of the clouds. After a 20 minute rest, I pick up the girl and resume climbing the canyon face. In half a mile, I come across a steep draw in front of us. It looks like I could get across it and continue up the ridge, but I need to find the best place to cross the draw with the girl. I decide to hide her in the bushes and make my way down the bottom of the draw to scout the best path through it. I pull her in between two large bushes and bend some branches to hide her as well as possible. Making my way down the draw through sharp shale rocks, it takes me 10 minutes to reach the bottom. It's dark in the little valley and I can see small pools of water left over from the last rain run-off. I pull out my two Nalgene bottles and fill them with the murky water. I continue walking down the draw 150 yards until I find an easy place to cross with the girl. Finally, I retrace my steps and work my way back up the side of the canyon. I locate the hide site, pull the weeds away and see that the girl is gone.

TWENTY-SIX

— ◆ —

Joe was polishing the brass diving helmet at the end of the bar. When he saw me, he walked over and poured me a cup of coffee. He was walking slower than normal. "How've ya been, Jack?" he asked without his usual enthusiasm.

"I'm good," I answered, then paused and asked, "How's Jane?"

He closed his eyes and shook his head—it was bad news. I waited, giving him some space.

"She didn't get out of bed again yesterday."

There was nothing more to ask. I nodded solemnly and let the moment pass in silence. The pain hung over him like a stench.

"How was the trip to British Columbia?" he asked, not wanting to talk about his wife any more.

"We found information that narrows down the location of the wreck."

"Did you tell Cap?" he asked as a customer walked in.

"Yeah, he came by the bookstore yesterday."

"And? Was he pleased?"

"Well, he took it as a sign that the treasure is down there. It's beyond a long shot, ya know, but I told him I'd help search for about a week."

"You're a good guy, Jack."

"Nah, it'll be good to go to sea for a week, do some diving, get outta town. I was actually hoping you could lend a hand as the medical expert?" Joe was like a father to me and I trusted him completely, plus I figured he needed to get away from the nursing home for a spell and get some mojo back.

He stopped rinsing a coffee cup and looked down at the bar for a moment. "Lemme think about it, Jack. I'll get back to you." He looked older than he had only days earlier.

"No problem, Joe. A little sea breeze in the face might do us both some good, though." He smiled and nodded sadly.

I stepped outside into a cold rain blowing sideways, thinking of Joe. He lives through the Korean War, hits rock bottom, meets Jane, turns his life around and helps countless people. Now he gets the rug swept out from under him. *Where's the justice in that?* Anger started to boil in me. The fact that his wife was going downhill fast and taking Joe with her was just the tip of the iceberg for me. *If Joe's boundless positive outlook was cracking, what chance did I have?*

I opened the bookstore and slammed the door shut. A rage at the unfairness of life had built up within me like lava: Joe's wife, the girl in Afghanistan, Sheila's husband, the IED that took Micah's leg, his abused niece Sarah, my wife, my life, this fucking Black Dog... I screamed at the top of my lungs until I was out of breath. Emilio jumped a mile high and bolted to the back of the store. I stood there breathing heavily and clenching my fists.

Mrs. Johnson burst through the door. "Jack, I heard a scream! Are you OK?" I was still breathing hard but nodded, then looked away.

She waited a moment, seemingly not sure what to do, then said hesitantly, "Well... if you're alright, I'll leave you alone." I heard the door close but didn't bother looking around.

Sitting down at my desk, I pulled out the bottle of Glenfiddich and poured half a glass. The first gulp was a hot branding iron on my soul. I knew in my gut that the whiskey was not taking me anywhere good, but right now, this instant, it was a better place.

Emilio bravely crept up behind me and rubbed his head on my leg. I reached down to give him a scratch and he leapt up on my desk. He was a sphinx—both paws resting on my deployment journal. "OK, I get the message, little guy." Slowly sliding the journal out from under his paws, I cracked it open randomly, as I always do, and read.

The ancient Egyptians believed that when you die, the Gods ask you two questions before they let you into the next world: Did you find joy in life? Did you help someone else find joy in life?

I'm zero for two here. I wouldn't be getting my invitation to the ancient Egyptian paradise. But Joe was a different story. He'd helped so many people find joy in life. Before Jane's recent spiral, he was more at peace than anyone I knew. I figured people at peace must be happy. I hadn't experienced enough of either to be a good judge. I wrote the quote on a 3x5 card so I could give it to Joe the next time I saw him.

I decided to return to the boxes of old books, do something useful, focus. I searched three boxes, all junk, unfortunately. The fourth was a little larger than a shoe box. I dug through a half dozen moldy paperbacks. At the bottom was a dusty leather-bound volume of Plato's writings. I sat down on the wood floor in the back of the shop, leaned against the philosophy section and cracked open the old book. I read, *"Be kind, for everyone you meet is fighting a hard battle."* It hit me like a truck. *Everyone I know is also fighting a hard battle.* The realization of my own self-absorption was like a branch snapping on a tree that held a nest of pity. *I've been a fucking selfish human. Sure, I've had my share of bad breaks, but kindness is not something I've put much effort towards. Sympathy, maybe, kindness, not really. I've added a lot more suffering to the world than I've taken away from it.* A flashback to Afghanistan flooded in through the door of guilt that I'd left wide open. I tried to force it out of my consciousness. I went back to my desk and poured another glass of golden Glenfiddich.

Emilio and I were in deep discussion about Socrates and the relative merits of Socratic versus Platonic schools of thought when Cindy walked in. "Emilio, I want you to meet Cindy. She's a nice person, full of niceness, the nicest person I know, really nice, super nice."

"Jack, what the...?" She looked at me with surprise and probably a little disappointment.

"I'm introducing you to my cat. Is there a problem with that?" I slurred.

She just stood there looking at me with those penetrating blue eyes. "As long as he doesn't talk back to you, I think you're OK."

I snorted, "He did say he wanted me to read a cat mystery to him."

"I was hoping to have lunch with you, but... why are you drinking at work? Has something happened?"

"I'm normally a procrastinator, so I thought I would get started drinking early today," I quipped.

"OK, Jack, I'm outta here." She turned, shaking her head.

"'Wait! Please. I'm sorry, Cindy... I want to have lunch with you."

"Another time, Jack." She reached for the door handle.

"Wait!" I stood up from my desk, knocked my empty glass over, and sent the cat scurrying. "Joe's wife didn't get out of bed yesterday or today. Joe's always a rock, but I don't know what this will do to him." Deep down I was also worried about losing my Yoda.

Cindy closed the door gently and took a seat in front of my desk. She looked adorable in a baseball cap, blue jeans and a windbreaker. "I'm really sorry to hear about Joe's wife." Most people say things like that, but don't really mean it. With Cindy, you felt it was real.

I looked down at my hands. "Joe is always so positive. His wife is in a nursing home, but suddenly she's on the slide and I can see it affecting him. He's like a father to me." Suddenly I remembered Cindy's dad's bout with dementia three years ago. *Everyone I know is also fighting a hard battle.* I wanted to say something, but I couldn't find the words, especially since my mind was fogged by whiskey. Stuck in my own quicksand of inebriated feelings, Cindy rescued me.

"Bad stuff happens to people, Jack. I'm sure you know that more than most. Somehow we have to make meaning out of it and move on."

I stood up, turned away from her, and faced the wall behind me. I didn't want her to see my face. A picture of me with a beard in Afghanistan hung on the wall caught my eye. The image of a young girl with piercing blue eyes laying in the dirt shot into my heart like a poison arrow. *How do you make meaning out of that?*

I shook my head trying to rattle out the memories and felt a hand on my shoulder. It meant more than shiny words. It was warm, soft, strong, courageous, small, fragile, amazing.

"I've got to go, Jack," she said quietly, as I felt her hand slowly slide off my shoulder. "Are you gonna be OK?"

I nodded, still facing away from her. The door opened and closed softly behind me.

TWENTY-SEVEN

A t 5 p.m. I locked up the bookshop and walked down to the docks, hoping to find Steve Cooley. The rain had given way to a warm fall afternoon. A few other boat owners were out and about on the piers, working on their boats or preparing to get underway on this gray afternoon. I glanced up toward the Harbor Master's office and saw an unmistakable figure standing at the head of the pier: Linda Tomkin. Even from a hundred yards away she was striking. I figured she might be meeting another old crabber for her research. Just then a tall figure strode out of the Harbor Master's office and put his hand around her shoulder.

He was no old crabber. They walked together down the pier parallel to me. I ducked inside the cabin of Sea Wolf. *What the hell?* The man with Linda was Jim Tripper, the guy who Cap said had burned his boat and who Steve had warned me about even before I found out that Micah's brother worked for him. As they walked together down the pier, I had the strange impression that Linda was giving Tripper instructions. She was animated and wagging her finger, and Jim kept nodding his head in deference. They stopped and boarded a sleek Sea Ray yacht.

What was Linda doing with Jim Tripper? It doesn't make any sense. I'd only seen Jim around the docks, but I doubted he had any useful information for Linda's research. Linda said she was not from these parts and certainly hadn't mentioned a boyfriend. I watched the yacht for 20 minutes but never saw them above deck or in the galley. They must have been below deck. I could only imagine what they were doing. I was perplexed by this strange connection.

I found Steve on the docks wrapping up his dive gear and stowing it in the cart. He was wearing his wetsuit bottoms with a heavy wool sweater on top.

"Hey Steve-O!"

"What's up, mate?" he said, bleeding his regulator with a burst of air.

"Can I buy ya dinner?" I asked.

Seawater was dripping off his bushy mustache. "I would never turn down a free dinner. Lemme get home and get this saltwater off of me first."

"Meet you at the Belmont at six?"

"Perfect, see you then."

I walked back to Sea Wolf, grabbed a beer from the fridge and sat on the stern to watch the sunset, which I rarely did. The sight of Jim and Linda together came back to me. Something was very troubling about that. I knew Tripper was unscrupulous, and after Linda had fed me false information about the wreck, I figured she was up to something. But seeing these two together was puzzling, to say the least.

The sun dropped below the horizon but not before leaving a fleeting canvas of burnt orange, purple and blood red. I couldn't sit and enjoy it because I felt the need to work on something, move, head towards a destination, get busy, complete a mission. Why couldn't I sit still, enjoy life? It came to me: *I'm afraid to have time to myself for fear of what I would do or think when there is nothing but the sound of breathing.*

After a quick check of Sea Wolf's vitals, I ambled back to the parking lot. At the top of the pier, Jim Tripper was walking down the dock in my direction. He was tall and lanky. As we approached each other I saw his hair was slicked back and he was wearing gold-rimmed sunglasses. He looked up when we were about ten yards apart and a flash of recognition and even anger seemed to cross his face like a shadow. He stopped as I approached.

"It's Jack, isn't it?" he said without holding out a hand to shake.

"That's right. Jim Tripper?"

"I hear you're gonna help Crazy Cap find lost treasure in the Strait," he smirked.

I didn't respond, which seemed to piss him off.

He shifted his legs into a defiant stance. "Cap is a delusional old man. You're wasting your time."

"He wasn't delusional about his boat burning to the waterline, though, was he?"

He clenched his jaw and spoke in a low tone, "That was deemed an accident by the fire marshal."

Time to see how he reacted. "I saw you with Linda—didn't know she hung out with you, too."

He flashed an oily smile, showing perfectly white teeth. "Yeah, what's it to ya? A woman can spend time with whoever she wants, can't she?" He brushed past me and continued down the dock. I took a few steps, then called back to him. He turned around.

"I hear that guy Jerry works for you."

I could see his jaw tighten again. "Who told you that?" He was moving slowly back to me now.

"I heard it around. Turns out he's not really a book lover. You might wanna keep an eye on the guy around your kids, though."

"I don't have kids and no one named Jerry works for me," he said with a sneer.

"Saw you two together at the Cup O' Joe a few days ago."

"You're starting to piss me off, Jack. You don't want to piss me off," he warned through gritted teeth.

"Is my boat gonna burn down?"

He took a step towards me but stopped, having the good sense to turn and walk away. I unclenched my fist.

I strolled up the bluff to the Belmont Cafe, thinking about the encounter with Jim Tripper. Linda, Jerry, Tripper—they were all tied together somehow. Something was afoot, I just couldn't put the pieces together. A funny thought hit me, though: Linda is by far the smartest and most cunning of the three.

I arrived at the cafe before Steve, picked a booth seat overlooking the Sound and ordered a water. Steve walked in, looked around and nodded when he saw me. He was taller than me, barrel-chested and looked like a heavyweight wrestler.

"Hey, Steve."

"How are ya, mate?" He sat down and flagged the waitress for a beer.

"Not my best day, to be honest," I said. "Joe's wife took a downturn and I did a little extracurricular drinking at the bookshop, made a fool of myself in front of a woman I just met." The waitress brought two cold Rainiers in mugs. "Then I ran into Tripper on the docks after you and I spoke."

"And how'd that go?" he asked, froth on his bushy mustache.

"You told me Tripper is a snake, now I believe you. I've heard he's got this big fella named Jerry working as muscle. Tripper pretended like he didn't know the guy when I asked him."

"I've seen that guy Jerry around the marina. I passed him on the docks with my dive cart. He looked at me with this wild eye and I thought he was going to start a fight. He had this big knife on his belt!"

"Yep, that's the guy," I nodded, sipping my beer. "He and I had a little encounter in my bookshop the other day."

The waitress brought two more beers. Steve took a large gulp and wiped his mouth with the back of his hand, "You think you had a bad day? I just found out my brother is engaged to my ex-wife back in Australia."

Suddenly my troubles seemed small, "Man, Steve, I'm sorry to hear that, bud. That's some real Cain and Abel stuff, huh?"

"Now I've lost two people in my life," he said, staring down into his half empty mug.

"If there's anything I can do, I'm here for you, man."

"My brother probably figures he found a treasure, but all he's getting is a gold digger." He looked out the window into the dark night.

"Speaking of treasure, do you know old Cap, the fisherman?" I asked, figuring he wanted to change the subject.

"Yeah, I've seen him around the docks. Nice old guy," he said, turning back to me.

"He's got this idea that he can salvage a wreck in the Strait and get his fishing boat back with the proceeds from the find."

"Sounds a little crazy," Steve said, but I could see his interest pique with the idea of salvage work.

"I thought it was crazy too, but I did some research for him and found the general location of the wreck. It's an extreme long shot, of course, but I told Cap I'd help him search for one week." I paused for dramatic effect, knowing I had his attention. "So you wanna come along?" I smiled. "I need a diver with your experience." I hoped I sounded persuasive.

"How deep we talkin'?" he asked.

I took a pull of my beer and said, "The ship sank about a mile off the coast. Depending on the tides, currents and drift when it sank, it could be anywhere from 60 to 175 feet of water. I'm not planning on searching beyond 100 feet."

"Does Cap have money to pay for divers and equipment? I've got bills to pay, Jack," he said.

"He told me he could get the money. Tell me what you need and I'll get it for you."

Steve looked out the window again, clearly mulling over my offer. "I can do it for 300 a day." That was a steal for his level of expertise.

"Done. Leave it to me. I was thinking we need four divers to keep up a rotation. I met this woman, Cindy, the one I made a fool of myself in front of? You'd like 'er. She teaches girls in Pakistan, but she's also a certified diver. And a straight shooter like you," I smiled.

"Well, I like her already," he grinned.

"What about that other diver on the docks I see, Chris?"

"No, I wouldn't trust that guy with my life," Steve said, shaking his head.

He was starting to sound very interested. "I've got a friend, Anthony, works down in Tacoma. He's an ex-Marine and solid diver. I'll give 'im a call, see if he can help us out. When are you thinking we'll do this?"

"In about two weeks? I've gotta get some gear together and sort out the logistics." I was pretty sure I'd hooked him, plus I knew he'd probably like a break from cleaning boat hulls.

"What kinda dive rig are you planning on using?" he asked.

"Kirby Morgan helmet and a dive panel. It'll be safer with the back-up bottle and communications cable to the surface."

"Yeah, that'll also be good in case we have to do decompression stops. I've got an old Kirby Morgan helmet and spare hose in my storage locker if you can come up with the bottles and control panel."

"No worries, I'll get all that stuff together," I said, relieved that he was in.

Our food arrived and we ate in silence, enjoying the thick juicy steaks and views of the Sound at night. The bright lights of Seattle created a blue-green glow in the distance to the east. We said goodbye after dinner and I headed home. It gave me confidence to have Steve on board with the salvage job—he was a pro.

I thought about stopping at the VFW, but couldn't go there without having a drink, and knew I'd already had more than my quota today. I jammed my hands in my pockets, hunched my shoulders against the north wind and trudged up the dark road home. I didn't even turn the lights on, just collapsed on the futon bed, with thoughts of Joe's and Steve's raw deals drifting through my fitful sleep. The yellow eyes of a black mangy creature peeked out from the closet and I pulled the covers over my head like a child afraid of the monster under the bed.

TWENTY-EIGHT

—— ◆ ——

I conduct a quick assessment of the location where I left the girl. Two sets of tracks had carried her back down the hill, the way we had come up from the cave. A flood of thoughts enter my head. *Who took her? Where are they taking her? Why didn't they stay and ambush me? Did I make a mistake and allow them to track me?* I know what I have to do. I grab my rifle and start loping down the trail as fast as I can without tripping. The crescent moon shines dimly down the valley, barely illuminating the path in front of me. There's a great danger of running into an ambush, but I don't have a choice. It has to be the Taliban that took her—*who else would be following me at night?*

I stumble to the bottom of the valley where the terrain flattens out but I lose the tracks in the rocky river bed. I scramble back ten yards to higher ground, and scan the other side of the valley across from me in the dim moonlight. I spot movement and dial in my scope—two Taliban fighters with AK-47s slung over their backs are making their way up the valley wall across from me. The one in front has the girl slung over his shoulder. They're about 600 yards away heading up to the ridgeline. If they make it to the other side of the ridge, I'll lose them or they'll have help waiting. I scan around my location, quickly find a large rock and rest my sniper rifle on it, taking careful aim. I have to control my thumping heart and slow my breathing. I quickly decide to take down the one carrying the girl first so he won't have a chance to use her as a shield. I have to hit him low, or I might hit the girl. I aim for the back of his legs and squeeze the trigger slowly. He topples to his left, dropping the girl in the dirt. The other fighter turns across the valley toward me, blindly spraying a volley of automatic weapons' fire. He starts to run for the cover of a stand of tall trees up the valley face. I drop him before he can reach the trees and swing my scope back on the fighter who was carrying the girl. He's dragging her towards a rock outcropping where he would have cover and concealment, and I can't get a clear shot with the girl on his back. For a moment he lets go of her to scramble over a rock and that's when I squeeze the trigger. A clean headshot. He slumps over the rock and doesn't move again. I sling my weapon and sprint up the valley face.

TWENTY-NINE

— ❖ —

I woke up with hope that I could stay on the north side of the line of despair today. On the way to the bookstore, I stopped by to check on Joe. The coffee shop was busy this Saturday morning. A lady with short white spiked hair and horse riding boots was ordering coffee. Several other customers were enjoying conversation by the window on this warm fall morning. Joe nodded when he saw me sit down at the bar. He looked a little better today.

I had the 3x5 card with the quote ready for him, but wanted to wait until he wasn't busy with a customer. After a few minutes he brought me a cup of my usual mud.

"Good business this morning, huh?" I said, nodding at the customers.

"I get a good crowd on Saturdays when the weather is decent," Joe agreed, wiping the bartop with a rag.

"I found something in my deployment journal and wrote it down for you."

He looked curious. I handed him the note. He pulled black reading glasses from his shirt pocket and read aloud, "*The ancient Egyptians believed that when you die, the Gods ask you two questions before they let you into the next world: Did you find joy in life? Did you help someone else find joy in life?"*

He looked at me like he was trying to figure out the meaning, and I explained, "I thought, you know, it might help with your wife and all that."

He gave me that old smile I hadn't seen in a few days. "Thanks, shipmate, this means a lot."

"Of course, an Egyptian heaven might have 40 virgins waiting for you."

He snorted, and it warmed my heart to hear him laugh.

"See ya later, Joe," I said, hoping I'd helped at least a tiny bit.

It was warm and I wanted to be outside. I resisted the urge to ignore the bookstore today because I needed to research logistics for the salvage work. I searched online and found a site where I could order an air control panel that was compatible with the Kirby Morgan helmet. I also ordered two large air bottles from a welding shop here in town. Including the labor for two divers, but not even including food, fuel and moorage, the total cost added up to about ten grand. I wondered if Cap had that kind of money, or if he had any idea what it took to put on even a small salvage operation. He was a commercial fisherman, so he must know the cost of marine equipment and labor. I hoped he wasn't scraping together his life savings.

Next I looked at harbors to moor out of, since we couldn't anchor in the Strait at night because it would be too dangerous and rough. Port Angeles had the most services but was 60 miles from the dive site. My trawler cruises at 10 knots, though, and we couldn't afford to spend six hours transiting back and forth every day to Shipwreck Point. Neah Bay was only 19 miles from our dive site and on the Makah reservation.

It didn't have a lot of services, but there was pierside moorage, fuel and fresh water available. It would be our best place to tie up each evening to resupply and rest. Maybe I could even visit Micah and Sarah.

At 11:00 a.m. Cap hobbled into the bookstore. Emilio, lying in the sun next to the window, stood up and followed him to my desk.

"Good morning, Jack." Cap was in high spirits today.

"Hey Cap, good timing. I just finished pulling some information together for the salvage expedition."

He seemed thrilled, and took the seat in front of my desk. As soon as he sat, Emilio jumped into his lap, padded around in a circle and laid down. That was a first. Cap didn't even seem surprised and began to pet him.

"I talked to my friend, Steve, a commercial diver, and he's willing to help out. We need four divers to keep up a rotation. Steve knows another good diver we can use, and I have another friend who's a diver. Steve has most of the dive gear we need, but we have to get an air control panel and rent some big air bottles. I'll pay for the fuel and moorage costs and we can use my trawler as our dive boat. We still need $10,000 to cover the rest of the expenses. Is that gonna be a problem?"

Cap thought for a second as he stroked Emilio. Finally, he looked up and said, "If that's the cost, I'll get the money."

I knew he had insurance money from his boat, but it seemed like this was more money than he had. I hoped he wasn't gonna rob a bank.

"Are you sure, Cap?" These divers are doing us a big favor and I don't want to leave them hanging."

He stopped petting Emilio and sat up straight, "Yes, I will do whatever it takes to salvage that wreck."

"Cap, we talked about this. I want you to understand that this is for a week of searching. There's no guarantee that we salvage anything. After a week, we're out of money and the divers will have to get back to their regular dive jobs," I said forcefully, immediately regretting it.

He looked up at me with his cloudy eyes like a kid who has just been scolded, and said, "I understand, Jack." I still wasn't convinced he did but there wasn't much more I could do about it, short of calling the whole thing off before we even started, which I knew would crush him.

He left and my thoughts drifted to Steve and what he'd told me last night. What a raw deal, having your ex-wife marry your brother. A deep feeling of loneliness settled in my gut so I cracked open my deployment journal and read, "*The time you spend with friends and family makes you forget how miserable you are by yourself. It masks the reality—you are alone in this world. Everyone else is a bit player on the stage of your lonely life. They come on stage for a time, play a part and move on.*" I wish that wasn't so, but I've never known anything to contradict it.

I was about to close the shop and grab some lunch when Cindy strode in. She was wearing a pink *Life is Good* ball cap, an Evergreen State hoodie and blue jeans. She stood in front of my desk looking serious, like I was in for an ass-chewing. "Jack, I wanna let you know that I need to get back to work."

My heart sank. I really blew it yesterday. "I thought you were gonna help out with the salvage diving for Cap? I was counting on you as the fourth diver and to manage our search patterns and navigation." I sounded too desperate and also like the only reason I wanted her around was to help us.

"I know, Jack, but things have changed and I should get back to work."

What has changed? Probably her estimation of me.

I took a chance, "OK, but first how about dinner tonight at my place? I've got a great view of the Strait."

She looked down for a moment, seeming unsure, then sighed and said, "OK Jack, I'd enjoy that." She smiled lightly.

"Six o'clock?"

"Yes, fine, I'll see you then." She stepped out the door into the autumn afternoon and possibly out of my life.

I sat frozen at my desk, cold regret seeping up my spine. All the negative voices in my head chimed in, "You blew it, Jack. She's leaving because of you. You messed up again."

The walls were pressing in on me so I locked up the bookstore and headed for the gym. I needed a good physical beating. Tommy gave me a 'what's up' nod and tossed me a towel. I punished myself with a hard calisthenics routine that left me sweating and depleted. I threw in a few deadlifts for a change. On the second set something wrenched in my back so I sat down on a bench with a towel over my head to recover.

"Jack, is that you under there?" I looked up to see Linda. She had on tight black yoga pants and a small white tank top that showed a new tattoo on her shoulder.

"Is that a new tattoo?" I asked. It looked like a crescent moon.

No answer, but she quickly pulled a sweater on, as if she was eager to hide it.

"Would you like to have dinner with me tonight?" Her dark eyes were drawing me in. Linda was like plutonium; radiant, but likely to kill you in the end. How could that much beauty hide the dark force that I suspected it hid?

"I'd love to Linda, but I already have dinner plans with a friend."

She put her hands on her hips and I thought I was in for an argument. "OK, suit yourself," she retorted, pouting. "Hey, are you still gonna try and salvage that wreck?"

In spite of you, I thought. "Oh, I dunno, I think it's probably a wild goose chase," I said, trying to be vague.

"But I found that journal entry for you. Doesn't that make a search feasible?" she asked, maybe hoping I would search the wrong site for some reason.

I thought about confronting her about the altered journal entry, but figured I'd hold my cards close for now, and not let her know that we found the real entry. "The tides and currents are tough out there and the water is deep. A salvage dive would be very difficult in that environment."

"But you're a Navy SEAL, aren't you? You thrive on the difficult and dangerous," she said playfully, like I was Superman or something. I noted that I had never told her I was a Navy SEAL, although to be fair, there were more than a few clues.

"I'm a bookshop owner, Linda." I was beginning to regret that I'd ever met her.

She dismissed me with a wave of her long fingers and headed off to begin her workout. I showered and changed. On the walk home, I stopped at the local market to pick up two steaks, salad and a loaf of sourdough bread. A light rain started to fall. My back was killing me but when I got home. I figured I'd better clean up the place a bit. Cindy wouldn't appreciate spider webs in the kitchen and dust balls in the corners. I grabbed a duster to reach for the spider webs when a pain shot through my back. I plopped down on my ratty old couch with disgust; I couldn't even clean up. In the bathroom I found an old expired bottle of prescription pain-killers I'd been given in the Navy. I hated the damn things, but sometimes I needed them when I was hurt but had to keep going to complete the mission. I popped two and went back to cleaning.

I took a shower, put on fresh clothes, made two salads then started the grill on the back deck. It was cold outside but there was almost no wind. The sun had set with an orange, red glow in the west. It was a clear night, and I could see the outline of Whidbey Island in the dusk to the northeast. A large freighter bringing cars from Asia to the Port of Seattle or Tacoma was making its way down the Strait. The lights coming off the cargo ship gave the water an eerie glow as it cruised up toward the Sound. I thought about what Cindy had said, "Things have changed." *How do I un-change things?* I wondered. I didn't want her to leave. I was nervous about having her over for dinner too. What would she think of me when she saw my spartan house: *Empty house, empty man?* There was a knock at the door.

"Hey, Cindy, welcome."

She'd brought a bottle of wine. "I hope you like Merlot, Jack," she said with a warm smile, handing me the bottle. She was wearing a black skirt above the knee, a white long sleeve sweater and low but sexy heels. Her unruly hair fell softly onto her shoulders. My heart raced when I saw her.

I uncorked the wine and poured her a glass but I had no intention of drinking after yesterday's debacle. I grilled the steaks while she enjoyed the rare clear night sky and the lights of ships plowing up and down the Strait.

"Lovely view, isn't it?" I said, turning the steaks.

"It's amazing, I had no idea it was this beautiful up here at night! You really have a spectacular view, Jack."

I served up the steaks, salad and bread on my wobbly card table. She didn't seem to care about my cheap second-hand furniture. I had to place a little piece of cardboard under one of the legs to keep the table from rocking back and forth.

After dinner she helped me clean up the dishes. "How about playing some Acey Deucy?" I said, as I washed the plates and handed them to her to dry.

"What in the world is Acey Deucy?" she asked with a smile as she dried a plate with a towel.

"It's a form of backgammon that's popular in the Navy. It's been around since World War I. I'll teach you how to play, but if you lose, you have to swear like a sailor."

"Is that really a rule?" she laughed.

"House rules."

She laughed again. We moved into the living room and she slipped off her shoes and curled her legs up under her on the couch while I set up the backgammon board, poured her more wine and grabbed a bottle of water from the fridge for myself. "What kind of music do you like?" I asked.

"Oh, just about anything," she said, coming over and taking a seat at the table. I liked Sinatra—his songs brought back memories of happier times. Ol' Blues Eyes was crooning about New York as we started our game.

I won the first game. "Now you have to curse like a sailor." I said teasingly.

"Damn it!" she exclaimed with an embarrassed grin.

"You'll have to do better than that."

She sipped her wine, "OK, OK. Shit!" she yelled.

"Alright, I'll give ya that one, but we have to work on your colorful vocabulary if you're gonna hang out with a sailor."

"Maybe the sailor needs his mouth washed out with soap," she laughed.

"Yeah, my foster mother 'Dialed' me up when I was a kid for saying *bitchin*. Kinda hard to breathe as she was jamming soap down my mouth."

"Oh no, you poor thing!" Cindy giggled, as we set up the next game. She had a lucky roll of snake eyes at the end, and took me out.

"Now *you* have to curse, sailor," she commanded, clearly having fun.

"Shucks, golly darn."

"Now I know you can do better than that, Jack," she mocked, almost spilling her wine as she gestured to me.

"I don't wanna get my mouth washed out again. How do I know you don't have a bar of soap in your handbag for guys like me."

"Geez, Jack, I'm not Mother Teresa, ya know." Her honesty and straightforwardness were appealing traits, especially in such a beautiful woman; I'd never met anyone like her. We played three more games as the moon came up outside my living room window, casting soft shadows on the white walls. We moved to my decrepit old couch and looked out the window into the endless night. I knew I didn't want her to leave Port Townsend. I needed her in ways that I didn't yet understand, but sensed in my gut.

I turned to her, "Cindy, I wanted to ask you, when you said things have changed and you have to go back to work, did I have anything to do with those changes?" She had to know I would bring up the subject tonight, especially if she planned to leave soon.

She took a sip of her wine before answering. "Yes, Jack, to be honest, it was partly because of you. My boss did ask if I could come back early, but after yesterday I had concerns about you. You're so self-defeating, Jack. There's a dark cloud swirling about you that's hard to be around at times."

That was a kick in the gut, but I deserved it. "You're right, Cindy, I haven't been doing so great lately." I hesitated, "I wanna be a better man, I really do, but sometimes I feel like I'm drowning."

She curled her legs back up underneath her and turned towards me on the couch to look directly into my eyes. I hesitated, but knew I couldn't hold anything back tonight, gotta roll the dice. "Something follows me around," I shared. "I call it The Black Dog. It's off in the distance or biting at my heels, but it's always there." I paused to let that sink in to see if she thought I was wacko. She scooted closer and gently put her hand on my arm, just as she'd done on our trip.

"What is this Black Dog, Jack?" She sounded like she was genuinely interested.

Her hand was soft on my arm. Truth can be a jagged, double-edged blade, but it was the only tool I could use and still look at myself in the mirror, so I took the leap. "I wrote a passage in my journal when I was in Ireland after my last deployment to Afghanistan. I've never shared it with anyone. Would you read it? It's the best way I know how to explain The Black Dog."

"Of course I would, Jack," she said tenderly.

I reached over to the 40mm ammunition box that served as my end table and grabbed the worn leather journal, then opened it to the page that I dread and handed it to Cindy. She took it with both hands and stared at me for a long moment before looking down and reading. I've memorized the words, so they ran through my head as Cindy read silently.

The Black Dog: I've been on his trail for years. I was there howling in Afghanistan when he shot the girl and tried to rescue her. I was there in the CASH tent with the wounded and bloody bandages on the dusty wooden floor. I was there when his friend's helicopter was shot down, killing 30 good men. I prowled the streets of Iraq when Terry was shot and 7 good men died. I was there on the bank when the machine gun erupted on the bloody river in Baghdad. I was roaming the dirty streets of Ramadi when the IEDs were taking limbs and lives. I was close by when the helicopter took eight rounds and hit the crew chief. My howl got louder after he came home. I was there chewing on his leg after his best friend killed himself. Got a good bite out of him when two of his friends attempted suicide and a third succeeded. Had him by the throat after he tried to save the girl in Afghanistan, but he shook me off at the last moment. I lunge for him when he looks me in the eye, but he turns away at the last second and I only get a bloody bite out of his soul. I'll take him down when the time is right—he knows it. He didn't used to acknowledge me as I followed him everywhere. Now he looks over his shoulder, sees my yellow eyes all the time in his tracks, bloody spit dripping out of my mouth, a disfigured animal, wolfish gait always on his tail, razor teeth ready to tear out his throat.

The Man: I step out the front door of the bed and breakfast in Kinsale, Ireland and turn right onto a narrow sidewalk heading toward downtown. An aging blue Peugeot sedan rambles on the ancient cobblestone road. It's mid-afternoon. I shouldn't look over my shoulder, but risk a glance—The Black Dog is following 20 paces behind. His terrible yellow eyes are watching me, drooling bloody spit. I look up, try to focus on the evening ahead. It's too early for The Black Dog to be this close—don't usually see him until nightfall. In the day he's just a dark dream shadow. But this afternoon he's already close. This being Memorial Day, he's smelling my grief for lost friends and teammates—have to lose him before he gets too close and howls that terrible death shriek at me. Wish I had a teammate with me today.

But now I am alone—The Black Dog is creeping up on me. His horrible death panting is near. I dare not look over my shoulder so I duck into a pub hoping I can lose him, take a seat at the bar between a tourist looking at her cell phone and a local worker in dirty overalls sipping a beer. I order a pint. The bartender pulls a frothy Guinness and the heavy beer quiets my thoughts for a time. The Black Dog slinks away, but he's only hiding outside.

My wife walks through the door of the pub, spots me at the bar. I nod—she gives me a look of disappointment, resignation and compassion that only a couple married 20 years would understand. She weaves through the crowd of tourists and locals listening to the guitarist sing sad Irish tunes. My wife has never seen The Black Dog, but she can see his reflection in my eyes. She sits next to me, feeling the invisible vibration of hopelessness radiating off me. She knows.

Cindy looked up. Her eyes softened and she shook her head slowly. "Jack, I don't know what to say. There's so much pain here."

"I know, it's a lot. I didn't mean to bring you down. I was afraid you'd think I'm crazy."

"Not at all. It helps me understand some things. The girl in Afghanistan you told me about before. She's in here twice. Can you tell me more about her and what happened?"

I rolled my head, thinking about how I was going to answer. "It was a terrible accident that I haven't been able to get over. Maybe someday I can tell you the whole story, but it's too painful to talk about now. It's a raw wound on my soul, ya know?"

She was quiet and nodded before speaking. "So your wife was with you in Ireland?"

"Yeah, she met me over there on my way home from one of my last deployments. She left me shortly after that. Sometimes I think it was my fault, other times I blame her."

"Do you still love her?"

She surprised me with that one. It was a tough question. I thought for a moment before answering. "I loved her once, loved most of the time we spent together. Part of me thinks I can reach back to the past and fix things, but that ship has sailed. She has a new life now... I wish her well... so no, I don't love her anymore." In a way I was just realizing this myself as I told Cindy.

Cindy finished her wine and stared out the window into the darkness. I knew she had more on her mind about me. "What happened to your best friend?" she suddenly asked. I'd been afraid she would ask about that too.

I cleared my throat and sat back before speaking. "He shot himself in the head." I didn't want to think about how I'd missed the obvious signs—isolation, alcohol, despair. Didn't want to think about the grief of his parents, wife and children. Cindy sensed the edge of the chasm and didn't ask more. She slid closer to me and put her head on my neck. I reached over and put my arm around her shoulder. It was the most serenity I could ever remember feeling. Time stopped. The Black Dog slunk away.

"Jack, look how beautiful the moon looks tonight," she said quietly, gesturing to the sky. She sat up and turned to me. "I really had a great time tonight, but I need to get home, it's getting late."

"Yeah, it's close to the witching hour. I'll walk you home."

"No, no, Jack, that's OK. My mother only lives a few blocks from here." She stood and ran her hands through her hair.

At the door I wanted badly to kiss her, but kept my guard up. She turned around and pulled me down to her, hugging me around the neck and whispering, "You're a good man, Jack."

"But not good enough for you to stay in town for another two weeks?" I blurted out impulsively.

She pulled back, reached down and took both of my hands in hers, then looked up into my eyes. I felt like she was evaluating everything about me. "Good night, Jack," she whispered before turning and walking off into the dim street light.

THIRTY

I sprint to the bottom of the valley, scramble up the other side towards the girl. The terrain is loose. Sharp shale rock and roots trip me along the way in the dark. I reach the site after half an hour of hard climbing. I'm out of breath and head straight to the girl. She's lying next to the dead Taliban fighter. I check her pulse, it's flittering but there. Turning her onto her back, I pull out one of my water bottles, lift her head and pour it into her mouth. She drinks a sip, coughs it up, drinks more. Her eyes open for a moment and she stares at me uncomprehendingly before closing them in obvious pain. I set her head back down and quickly move to check on the second Taliban fighter. I find him near the stand of trees, face down with his AK-47 underneath him, dead. I scramble back to the girl and sit down next to her. I need to rest for five minutes and think about my plan to take her to that village across the next valley.

I don't really want to take her there; too many unknowns I can't control. *Would they attack us? Report us to the Taliban? Take us in? Hold us hostage?* For the girl's sake, I don't have a better option. It could take me too long to hike into a firebase with her. She might die before then. I have to take a chance on the village. I zip up the Gore-Tex jacket she's wearing, cinch the hood down tight against the cold wind, hoist her on my left shoulder, and start my trek slowly down the valley.

THIRTY-ONE

After a terrible restless night, I awoke Sunday morning with an intense desire to shed the fucking Black Dog, be a better man, find a path to hope. I knew I had to find a way forward; this life, if that's even what you could call it, was getting out of hand.

I stepped out back to feel the morning weather—cold and damp. The sun was up, but hidden behind murky clouds. A light mist was falling, snuffing out the color and cloaking the morning in a wet, gray sheet. I stood there shivering, which made me feel alive. Suddenly I heard bells and a thought popped into my head like a red star cluster: *Go to church this morning.* No idea where it came from, but it felt better than the alternatives. I was ready to try anything.

I hadn't been to church in years, the last few times had been funerals for SEAL Team friends, but I felt an impulse that Sunday morning. Seeing the ravages of war along with my crumbled life left me little faith in a god who would allow the world to become this screwed up. Yet, I still yearned for the peace that I had felt as a child. My wrestlings with The Black Dog last night had left me exhausted and strung out. I was willing to try anything to get traction on a new life.

The closest church was a five minute walk up the hill. It was a small white colonial building with a tall New England spire. I meandered through the garden as people filed in, because I had no desire to talk to anyone. I sat in the back row close to the exit. The interior was simple; dark wood pews atop oak flooring. The walls were white, with rows of tall, stained-glass windows on either side. At the front, on the right, was a small pulpit. Two stained glass windows behind the pulpit turned the natural light into an array of colors.

An older man with a ponytail and thick glasses played the pipe organ. There was a point during the sermon when we were asked to turn and greet those around us. I put my hands in my pockets and looked down at my feet, as if studying the grain of wood on the dark floor. A woman in front of me turned around, so I felt obligated to look up. She was old, with gray hair in a bun, and a face lined with age, yet it was a beautiful, wise face. She just looked at me, without saying anything. In that face I saw great loss, but also faith and joy. She focused on my eyes as if seeing into me and reached out a bony hand. I held it gently like a baby bird. It was cold. She didn't speak, but somehow said all she needed to say.

There were a few more rituals, songs and prayers before the pastor spoke. She looked older than me, with long gray and black hair tied in a white ribbon. I was watching glints of sunlight dancing in the stained glass window, not really listening to what she was saying. To me it just sounded like blah, blah blah until suddenly I had a gut feeling and looked up. She was looking directly at me: "I was in a biker gang as a young woman," she was saying, regret in her voice. I knew that feeling well. "I abused every drug you can think of, drank like a fish, and led a wasteful life as a biker's 'ol' lady.' When he was killed in a hail of bullets during a drug deal, I fled the gang. I was homeless, wandered the streets of Seattle, became a prostitute, and eventually hit rock bottom."

She paused, scanned the faces in the pews, and settled back on me. "I was planning to kill myself, to end the pain, and was biding my time to figure out how and when. One evening I was walking down a dark alley near the Seattle Underground when I looked up and saw these words written in graffiti on the brick wall: *Forgive Yourself.* The words hit me like a lightning bolt. I realized then and there that I hated myself...deeply. I'd been unconsciously punishing myself every day for the misguided life I'd lived. I latched onto those words like a drowning woman grabs a lifeline." I leaned forward. She had my attention.

She made it her life purpose to forgive herself for each of the terrible things she'd done. It had taken two years. She went over every screw-up and bad decision in her life. As she recalled each mistake and hurt, she washed them from her consciousness with the thought, *Forgive Yourself,* until each incident was no longer painful and merely became the shell of a memory that belonged to another person, or rather an earlier, more flawed version of herself. From there, she spent another year doing nothing but forgiving everyone in her life who had abused her and led her astray. By the end of three years, she'd become a new person. She now dedicated her life to helping others.

I sat with my head in my hands, riveted to the seat. Burning tears came with a vengeance. I tried to fight them back, but realized I'd never forgiven myself for so many things: for what happened to the girl in Afghanistan, for letting my marriage fall apart, for unbridled ambition, for not reaching out to my friends before their suicides, for letting that fucking Black Dog kick my ass, for being a selfish prick. I quickly stepped outside to avoid talking to anyone. It was drizzling, so I zipped up my coat. Looking up at the gray sky, a thought floated in like the raven soaring above me: *Today... today is what you own, what you have, where you live—all you have to do is live today.*

Monday was a slow day in the bookshop. The cold rainy weather chased away anyone who didn't have to be out and about. I'd organized a few books, but that dark, restless feeling was creeping in. Emilio remained curled up on a chair as I walked to the back of the shop, where I couldn't be seen by passersby, got down on my knees and set down the deck of cards I'd taken from my desk drawer. I turned over the first card: 8 of hearts, did 8 push-ups; turned over the next card: Jack of spades, knocked out 11 push-ups; and continued through most of the pack until I heard the bell on the door jingle.

I walked to the front where I found Cindy standing there in jeans and a rain parka, running her hands over her hair to dry it.

"Hi Jack, why are you breathing hard?" she asked, looking at me askance.

I figured she'd come to say goodbye. "Slow day in the book business, so I was doing a few push-ups in the back." No comment from her—I guess she didn't think that was too strange.

She took off her coat and hung it on the rack. "Can we talk for a minute?" In my experience, nothing good ever came from that phrase, especially when it was uttered by a woman.

"Of course, come have a seat," I gestured while walking behind my desk, which gave me a little distance from her, a space to absorb the blow of bad news.

She sat down across from me, posture erect, legs crossed, hands in her lap. She spoke slowly and softly, as if she was counseling a third grader who'd started a fight on the playground. "I enjoyed dinner with you on Saturday." *Always start with something positive before you drop the hammer—nice technique...*

"Me too," I said in a neutral voice, my insides roiling.

"The thing is, Jack," she paused and took a deep breath. *Here comes the shit hammer.* "I think I understand you better now." *OK, that wasn't terrible.* "To be honest, part of you scares me. You have tendencies towards violence, self-destructive behavior, maybe even paranoia." *Geez, don't sugar coat it.* "But from what you've been through, which I'm beginning to understand a little, I think you're doing your best to move forward and build a new life." A bubble of hope rose in my gut. "Part of me wants to run far away from you," she admitted. "But another part of me wants to stay here and get to know you better."

I couldn't tell if I was supposed to argue on my behalf so I kept my mouth shut. She looked into my eyes, maybe taking one last read before deciding. "I think what you're doing for Cap is really special. I want to stay and dive with you on the wreck. I'll tell my boss that I can't come back early."

A big, uncontrollable smile instantly spread across my face. It was the best Monday I could remember having. I was leaping for joy inside, but played it cool. At the same time, it hit me, *I will be responsible for her safety*. I felt myself shaking.

BOOK TWO

THIRTY-TWO

— ◆ —

T he Ford Lehman diesel engines chugged along at 10 knots as Sea Wolf passed the last marker buoy at the mouth of Port Townsend harbor. The green foamy sea flowed around the hull in lumpy waves, producing a gentle rocking onboard. The large compass floated in its gimbal oil, leaning with the boat's motion. My right hand was resting on the two throttle levers, holding them steady at 1800 RPM's; her best cruising speed. It was a gray, foggy morning. I flipped on the radar bolted to the dash in front of me, noting a couple of large blips on the radar screen—cargo vessels moving down the Strait towards the port of Seattle or Tacoma. The coastline to our port side was shrouded in mist. As we passed Fort Worden State Park, I swung the helm to starboard and steadied on a bearing of 285 degrees towards Neah Bay. After a week of preparation, we were finally underway to try and find the wreck of the HMS Hawthorn. My feelings of excitement about the trip were balanced by the danger I knew we would face running a salvage operation in cold, deep waters.

"How about some coffee, shipmate?" I turned from the helm as Joe handed me a mug. I was so glad he'd decided to come and hoped it would do him good.

"Joe, I'm really glad you came on this trip because I couldn't live without your coffee."

He laughed like old times and re-adjusted his Navy ball cap on his head. "I'm glad you invited me, Jack. I needed to get my sea legs back."

Nothing more needed to be said between us. Sea Wolf gently plunged and rose against the oncoming swells. The warm coffee was a lifesaver on this cool, foggy morning. Standing next to Joe with the helm in my hands, I was back in the game, back doing something vital. There is no past or future at sea, just the now of safely piloting the boat.

"How long until we make Neah Bay, Navigator?" I called out over my shoulder.

Cindy was squinting at a chart spread out on the shiny teak galley table, making little pencil marks on our track with a long plastic parallel ruler. "Well, at this speed we have a full day ahead of us. We should be there by dinnertime."

I'd been flying high ever since Cindy had come to the bookstore a week ago to let me know she was game on for the diving operation. She'd helped me organize the whole trip so all the pieces easily fell into place.

Cap was seated at the galley dinette next to Cindy, wearing his Greek fisherman's cap and a set of grubby green rubber overalls that he probably used for fishing. He'd been teaching Cindy how to navigate using the nautical chart and compass rose to lay out a course and speed. I used the GPS as a backup, but Cap and I both liked paper charts as our primary navigation tools. He reached across the table and picked up a set of metal compass dividers. With a flick of his wrist, he opened them and showed Cindy how to calculate the distance from our position to a marker buoy outside the bay using the latitude scale on the chart. He didn't have his fishing boat back, but his confidence was returning already. He was back in his element, and I was happy for him.

"Cap, you're really good at this," Cindy marveled.

"I've spent most of my life at sea, young lady. I'm more comfortable navigating here than I am on the road to Bremerton," he said, standing up and looking out the window at the hazy horizon.

"What time is Steve planning to meet us in Neah Bay?" Cindy asked, rising from the galley table, and coming to stand beside me at the helm. She pulled the sleeves of her red sweatshirt over her hands and crossed her arms as if she was a little chilly. Her blonde hair was blowing around as usual and one piece of hair stuck in the corner of her mouth. I couldn't help myself and set down my coffee cup so I could reach over and gently move it off her face. She smiled sweetly at me. Steve and Anthony, our fourth diver, were driving Steve's van to Neah Bay with the dive gear, extra food and provisions. That way we would have a vehicle to use at the harbor if we needed to drive to town for supplies or repairs. I hadn't met Anthony yet, but Steve's thumbs-up was good enough for me. He was a Marine, so I knew he would be good to go for anything that got hard.

"They should be there about the same time we arrive," I said.

At noon, Cindy and Joe made ham sandwiches. Then Joe took the helm and I sat down to eat and rest at the galley table as Sea Wolf chugged along against the growing swells. The fog had lifted, but the seas picked up as we made our way closer to the mouth of the channel and the Pacific Ocean. I'd been piloting for four hours, thinking the whole time about contingency plans for the inevitable problems that

I knew would occur. I always rehearsed the "what-if's" in my head for every operation.

"Orcas off the starboard bow!" Joe called out from the helm. Cindy and I stepped outside onto the narrow deck that ran the perimeter of the pilot house.

"Look, look!" Cindy pointed, "A mother and her calf!" Two large black and white shapes surfaced two hundred yards off the starboard bow. "Jack, aren't they magnificent?" she exclaimed, unbridled joy on her face.

"They don't attack humans, but have you seen what they do to sea lions? I look an awful lot like a sea lion with my wetsuit on. I'd rather not get flipped in the air 50 feet and gnawed on," I said, recalling the massive shark that swam under me one night on a hydrographic reconnaissance mission. The bioluminescence in the water had made the shark look like an eerie blue-green torpedo.

The two whales were on the surface now, swimming a large circle around our boat and checking us out. Joe throttled back to idle. The mother orca was leading the youngster around, keeping it close and looking warily at us through huge black eyes. After a full circle around the boat, they dove and disappeared. Joe brought Sea Wolf back to cruising speed, pointing us toward Neah Bay. The event reminded me that the sea is home to beautiful but dangerous creatures.

After two hours, Cap informed us that we were passing over the supposed location of the wreck. He put on a peacoat and stepped up to the bow to get a good look. I walked up there with him. "I feel it in my bones, Jack, the wreck is here," he declared with confidence, scanning the horizon with his dusty blue eyes.

Low-lying clouds were partially obscuring the coast so I couldn't pick out a landmark, but Cap had been tracking our location meticulously on the chart. I'd done several underwater search and salvage operations and knew that finding anything underwater was like trying to find a key you lost on a football field by crawling around in the dark on your hands and knees and feeling for it while wearing boxing gloves. In other words, almost impossible.

"Cap, I promise I'll give it my best shot, OK?" I said, turning to him.

"I know you will, Jack. You've already done more for me than you know. Just being out here on top of this wreck is a dream come true." He turned, put his hand on my shoulder and looked me in the eye. "Whatever happens, I'm grateful, Jack." I felt a burden lift. I was sure he was, as we say in the military, 'front sight focused' on this wreck. Maybe I'd misjudged him.

I took over the helm. Sea Wolf rose and fell on each swell like a big, slow roller coaster. The waves were getting bigger as we approached the mouth of the largest ocean in the world. I pointed Sea Wolf a little north of our track to prevent the growing swells from hitting us broadside and knocking the boat about. She was a deep draft trawler and could plunge through huge waves head on, but a beam sea caused her to swing violently side to side. Once I was abeam of Neah Bay, I turned hard to the south and brought Sea Wolf inside the protection of the harbor. A large rock jetty sticking out into the Strait protected us from the swells. We were heading towards the Makah Tribal Marina. I'd called ahead and made reservations for a forty-five-foot slip with water and electricity—that would be our home for the next week. Sea Wolf glided through the calm green waters of the bay, leaving behind a frothy white wake.

I was able to get cell phone reception and call Steve, who was at the marina office and told me to tie up at slip C-17. I came to idle speed inside the harbor and brought Sea Wolf to the mouth of the marina. I'd studied the chart before our trip and knew where C dock was located. The rest of the crew was on deck throwing the fat blue rubber fenders over the side and getting dock lines ready to tie up. We passed a row of rusty mooring buoys and a flock of gulls floating in the bay, resting before their next fish hunt. Most of the boats in the Makah Tribal Marina appeared to be commercial or recreational fishing craft. The marina was about one third full. I turned toward C dock and spotted Steve and Anthony standing by our slip with dive gear stacked on the pier behind them. There was a slight cross wind which made docking tricky. I brought Sea Wolf upwind and let the wind blow her into the slip. The slip was U-shaped with finger piers on each side, which made getting in and out easier, since I didn't have to worry about bumping another boat next to us. I pulled the throttles back to reverse just before the bow touched the pier. Cindy and Joe tossed the dock lines to Steve and Anthony. We were secure. I shut down the engines and climbed onto the pier while the crew doubled up the mooring lines.

"Hey Steve, you made good time," I greeted.

"Yeah, we got a good start. Jack, this is my friend, Anthony, ex-US Marine and commercial diver in Tacoma."

I shook Anthony's hand. He was taller than me, maybe six-foot-two with curly dark hair and a Mediterranean complexion. He looked Italian or Greek and had a strong handshake and several gold rings on his fingers.

"No such thing as an ex-Marine, isn't that right, Anthony?" I said with a grin.

"Ya got that right, Jack. Semper Fi," he said in a thick New York accent. "I deployed with some SEALs during DESERT Storm," he added, turning to cinch down a dock line. "Were you in that turkey shoot, Jack?"

"Oh yeah, I probably know some of the guys you deployed with. Where're you from?"

"The Bronx. I joined the Marine Corps after high school and moved out west," he said, coiling the dock lines on the pier.

Cindy, Joe and Cap helped Steve and Anthony load the dive gear and bottles onto Sea Wolf while I went to check in at the Harbor Master's Office. The marina office was a small white metal building with a blue roof and a little patch of brown grass out front. Inside there were two racks of fishing tackle for sale, boating supplies and a small interior office. Behind the counter stood a tall Native American in a red flannel shirt and blue jeans. It was Micah, who was balancing on crutches, without his prosthetic leg. I hadn't noticed before that his left eye was cloudy, probably damaged from the IED blast. "Hey Micah! I didn't know you worked here."

"Hey Jack, good to see you," he said with genuine warmth and surprise. "What brings you here?"

"I'm leading a diving salvage operation for a week off Shipwreck Point."

"What're you lookin' for?" he asked, stepping out from behind the counter with his crutches.

"It's a long story. I'll tell you over a beer. But the short version is that I met an old fisherman in Port Townsend who asked me to research a possible sunken ship for him. I really like the old guy, so I agreed to put on an expedition. Not much chance of finding anything, but I could do with a little change of scenery."

"Is his name Cap?" Micah asked, leaning on the counter.

"Yeah, how did you know?" I was intrigued.

"My brother Jerry talks when he's drunk. He mentioned a guy named Cap had been holding out on Jim Tripper and deserved what he got."

"Cap's boat burned a while back after he refused to sell it to Tripper. Did Jerry say he started the fire?"

Micah thought for a moment, "No, but it wouldn't surprise me a bit if he had."

I tucked that in the back of my mind, but had no intention of mentioning it to Cap. I figured Jerry probably had a hand in burning Cap's boat. Apparently, he was even more dangerous than I thought and capable of who knows what.

"We just pulled into C-17. I wanted to square with you," I said, reaching for my wallet.

"For a week?" Micah asked.

"More or less."

He pulled out a map and pointed out the bath house, fuel pier and pump out station. "You let me know if you need anything else," he said, handing me the map.

"How is Sarah? I thought she might come by the bookstore for another book."

Micah ran his hand across his face, looking distraught. "I haven't seen her in a day."

"Whaddaya mean?" I asked with alarm. "Where's Jerry?" I had a bad feeling.

"Jerry's still here. He claims she disappeared in the middle of the night, maybe ran away for a time. She did that twice last year." He shook his head sadly. "I've gotta shut the marina office down," he said.

I didn't know what else to say or how I could help Sarah, so I changed the subject. "Well, lemme know if you hear anything, yeah? We're gonna grill steaks on the boat in about an hour. I'd love it if you could join us. I'd like you to meet the crew." I tried to make it as enticing as I could.

He thought about it and said, "Sure, Jack, I'll come by. Thanks."

"Alright, see you then," I said, hoping it would at least be a welcome distraction while he waited for news. I watched him lock up the back door with the crutches balanced under his arms.

As I was leaving the marina office, a poster on the bulletin board caught my attention. A mountain lion had been recently spotted prowling the reservation. A few cats and dogs were missing, but there were no reported attacks on humans. The poster asked everyone to be on the lookout. I remembered one of the Vietnam vets on my first SEAL Team telling me about a tiger encounter when he was an advisor for the South Vietnamese SEALs. The large cat had tracked their patrol at night and ambushed the last man, a Vietnamese soldier. All they found were small pieces of the guy. I shuddered at the strength and cunning of large cats.

Back onboard Sea Wolf, the crew had the dive gear stowed and the large air bottles secured on the back of the boat. I told everyone about Micah and that he would be joining us for dinner. I fired up the gas grill mounted to the stern rail: gotta feed the crew well if I'm expecting them to work hard. At dusk a sea lion popped up astern of the boat, looking at me with curiosity. His giant whiskers were dripping with green sea water as he barked. I thought more about what Micah had said about Sarah: *Maybe she just ran away for a time?* I sensed deep down it was probably worse.

Micah arrived with a six pack of Rainier beer. "Welcome aboard!" Joe held out a strong hand and helped him aboard. I was grilling on the stern, so Joe introduced everyone. "I'm Joe, owner of Cup O' Joe coffee shop in Port Townsend. This is Cap," he pointed to the galley where Cap sat.

Cap stepped out of the galley and shook Micah's hand. "Pleased to meet you, Micah," Cap said.

Steve, Anthony and Cindy each introduced themselves in turn. Micah was wearing his prosthetic leg again so he was able to walk around the boat by holding onto the rails that ran the length of the pilot house. Cindy was about to reach out and give him a hand but I touched her shoulder as Micah hobbled past her to the stern. "He's lost a lot, but not his pride. Let him do it," I whispered. She nodded.

It was a warm night, and we ate thick, juicy steaks and fresh green salad on the stern of Sea Wolf, as the veterans shared sea stories and war stories, while Cindy talked about teaching and Cap spoke about his fishing days. The lights in the marina sparkled on the water. The stars shone brighter out here away from city lights.

"Are you married?" Cindy asked Micah.

"No wife, no kids," Micah answered bluntly. I watched his face to see if he was going to mention Sarah.

He hesitated, then spoke, "I have a niece... but she disappeared yesterday."

"Oh no, what happened?" Cindy asked with alarm, putting down her fork and leaning closer to Micah.

"My older brother Jerry is an alcoholic. His wife died. He isn't a very good father. He claims Sarah disappeared from their mobile home last night. He thinks she's probably run away for a while. She's done that before."

"What about the police? I didn't hear anything about this on the news," Joe said.

"She disappeared on the rez, so there's not a lot of interest or press about it. These things are viewed as internal tribal matters. The tribal police looked into it, but so far they have no leads," he said, shaking his head. "I talked to them earlier and they told me it hadn't even been 24 hours, and that most of these cases get resolved by themselves."

"Do you have any idea where she could be?" Cindy asked with obvious concern.

"No, I really don't. But Sarah wouldn't leave the rez by herself, not without telling me first. No one spotted any strange vehicles or people around. It's a mystery. She's a sweet little girl—loves to read, and fish and hunt for seashells with me." The pain on Micah's face was tangible to everyone. "Jack met her in Port Townsend. He gave her some books."

My heart was racing as I thought about what could have happened to her. "Yeah, she's a real sweetheart," I said.

"Jack, she left that book you gave her in her room. There was a bookmark in the middle, so she wasn't finished with it yet. I don't think she would've left that book behind voluntarily," said Micah, looking at me pointedly. I didn't have an answer for that.

Hearing about Micah's missing niece put a damper on the rest of the evening. It was not a good time to celebrate the first leg of our journey. After dinner we all said our goodbyes to Micah and he walked home.

I sat on the stern of the boat looking out to the mouth of the harbor while everyone got ready for bed. It would be an early start tomorrow. The mast lines on sailboats were gently clanging, making a soothing, musical sound. Other than that, the harbor was quiet. The wind had died down and a few bright stars were shining through the clouds. Tomorrow was going to be an important day that I needed to plan for, but I couldn't help but think about Sarah.

Cindy came out back and sat next to me after everyone had gone to bed.

"It's beautiful out here, Jack. I'm glad I came," she said, turning to me with a sweet smile.

"I'm glad too, Cindy," I said, looking down.

"What's wrong, Jack?"

"I was thinking about Micah's niece. She's only ten years old." Another young girl's dirty face flashed into my mind. "It just hit me in the gut when Micah told us about her, but I'm OK," I lied.

"Are you?" She moved her head to look directly into my eyes. It was dark and I was glad she couldn't see my face clearly.

"I'm sure," I said quietly. "Time to go to bed, we have an early start tomorrow." I didn't want to talk about it anymore.

Cap and Joe slept in twin beds in the stern stateroom. Steve and Anthony shared the V-berth in the bow. Just aft of the V-berth to the port side was a small single stateroom where Cindy slept. I pulled out a blanket and laid down on the cushioned seats in the galley, the boat gently rocking me. I drifted off, thinking of Micah pulling in a bright silver salmon and his niece reading a book under a shady tree. So much innocence was lost in this world. *How do you get it back?*

THIRTY-THREE

I'm hiding in a tall stand of cedars, half a click away from the village, with a view down into the small green valley. It's six in the morning. I don't want to walk into the village at night, scare the locals and set off a firefight. Plus I want to scout the area and see how many villagers come out at first light, so I can make a plan to bring the girl into the village safely. If the locals are armed and the place looks like a Taliban base camp, I'll keep on moving with her. I check her vitals; she's hanging on. I put a hand under her dirty, matted hair and pour the last of my water into her mouth. She coughs lightly a couple of times, then drinks a few swallows. I check the wound in her shoulder—oozing yellow pus drips out from under the bandage. At least she isn't bleeding heavily. I breathe deeply and wait for first light, shivering under my lightweight camouflage uniform. I'll do my best for this girl. I'm the one who shot her and I'm determined to get her help. Over the course of the trek, a strong feeling has crept into my heart: my life isn't worth that much anyway. I'm ready to face death to protect this girl.

Thirty-Four

— ※ —

S ince I was already in the galley when I woke at 5:00 a.m., I made coffee for everyone. It was dark outside and there was no wind, which made for a quiet, calm morning to think. I poured fresh coffee into a faded SEAL Team mug. The mug had black coffee stains in the bottom from years of use. The complexity of the upcoming diving made me feel alive, like I was preparing for an operational mission. I methodically went through a mental checklist for the day, thinking through each evolution: transit, identify the initial search site, anchor, safety brief, dive brief, first diver in the water, set up marker buoy, set up search grid on the bottom, start search pattern. It was dangerous business diving in deep, cold water with limited visibility and it was my responsibility to make sure everyone was safe.

Anthony was an early riser. He came out of his cabin in jeans and a red Marine Corps pullover.

"Coffee's ready, Anthony," I said, handing him a cup.

"The boat rocked me to sleep," he said. We stood together in the galley looking out the windows at the mast lights of boats, as dawn broke to the east.

"How did you get into diving?" I asked.

"I was in Recon Battalion. When I got outta the Corps, I just kept diving."

"Married?" I asked.

"Divorced," he smirked. "I was married to the heiress of a large food company." He paused, then said with a little laugh, "She turned out to be bat shit crazy. Her father gave her everything. She couldn't handle being the wife of an enlisted Marine and I couldn't handle being a socialite. Her father's army of lawyers made sure I didn't get anything in the divorce."

"That's rough, man."

"Nah, it all worked out. I'm doin' what I love and she's doin' her thing - shopping, or whatever," he said sarcastically.

I pulled eggs out of the small fridge and cracked them in a plastic bowl. "You need help with chow?" Anthony offered.

"I'm good, thanks," I said, pulling out the bacon from the fridge.

He sat drinking his coffee and staring at the chart on the table. "You think we have a chance at finding this wreck?" he asked, skimming his fingers over the chart.

I took a moment to consider my answer. "A small chance, but you never know. One time this guy I was training dropped his machine gun in the river at night. The river was fast flowing and muddy, with alligators prowling the banks. My platoon did 20-foot-deep breath hold dives for two hours and we were about to give up. I gave it one more try and buried my arms in the mud up to my elbows. Believe it or not, I felt the barrel of a gun and ripped it outta that sucking mud. Ya never know when you might get lucky diving, right?"

Anthony laughed, "Man, I'd never get in the water near alligators—that's crazy." He stood. "I'm gonna get a jump on prepping our dive gear before the others get up." He set his cup in the sink and headed out to the stern.

"Roger that."

I made eggs and bacon, the sizzling sound and smell of which woke the rest of the hungry crew as it wafted into their cabins. The day broke partly cloudy with no wind so it was looking like a good start. Everyone got busy after breakfast and prepared Sea Wolf to get underway. I started the engines one at a time, letting them warm up to operating temperatures. The big six-cylinder Lehmans came to life with a satisfying rumble. We idled out of the marina as the sun lit up the day against the low clouds on the horizon. When we cleared the jetty entrance, I swung the helm northeast toward Shipwreck Point. The smell of salty ocean flowed through the pilot house. Seagulls were screeching and diving on a school of anchovies behind the boat. Today was going to be good, I just knew it.

Cindy and Cap had studied the nautical chart and identified a location to start the search. It was about one mile off Shipwreck Point, as Jeremiah Benton had noted in his journal. However, they'd located a spot on the chart that looked to be a little shallower than the rest of the area. We'd start there, see what the bottom looked like. Cindy and Cap were working on the chart, tracking our path. Cap was holding his coffee cup above the table so it wouldn't spill with the rolling of the boat. Joe put on a heavy coat and stepped out on the bow. I wanted to see how he was doing, since this was the first day he hadn't been with Jane in a long time.

"Hey Steve, can you grab the helm for a minute?" I asked.

"No worries, got it, mate."

I walked up to the bow and stood next to Joe without saying anything. We were doing eight knots, with the relative wind in our face. The bow surged up and down, throwing white foam across the blue-green sea. After a few minutes Joe spoke as he continued to stare out to sea. "It's good to be out here, Jack. I haven't done anything like this in a long time. It's like a wet desert. Wide open spaces that force me to think." He turned to look at me, "I hope I can be useful."

"Don't worry about that, we're gonna need everyone to pull this off safely."

I touched his shoulder, he nodded and I headed back to the pilot house; it looked like he could use some time alone. Steve was checking his heading with Cindy and Cap, and handed me the helm when I stepped inside. "What's the dive plan today, Jack?" he asked.

"I was planning to have you go down first, check the anchor, set the marker buoy and start laying out the initial search grid lines," I answered. Steve was our most experienced salvage diver so I wanted him to go first and survey the site. "Anthony can follow you and continue laying out the grid lines, I'll go next and Cindy can dive last." I wanted the most experienced salvage divers to go first, so they'd have time to do a second dive each day, if possible.

"Sounds like a plan, mate, I'll start getting ready." Steve headed aft to get his gear together.

Two hours later we were on top of the search area. The tide was flowing in from the sea at a gentle speed, approaching slack water. I checked the depth sounder: 69 feet, which was well within our safety envelope. I swung the helm and turned Sea Wolf into the current while Steve and Anthony pulled the big spade anchor out of the hatch on the bow and laid out the chain. "Let 'er go!" I yelled out the side door.

They dropped the anchor over the bow with a splash and played out the chain and line as the 50-pound anchor sped to the bottom. I kept Sea Wolf idling over the site against the gentle current. When Steve felt the anchor hit bottom and the line go slack, Anthony let out another 20 feet to account for the tidal change, then gave me a thumbs up. I put the big diesels in reverse and backed her down until I felt the spade dig in and hold fast on the bottom. At last we were on site. I looked over my shoulder at Cap. He was looking out the galley door with a contented smile on his face.

While Steve donned his wetsuit, I set up the diver control panel. It looked like an orange hard plastic suitcase. The vertical back panel handled all of the communications with the diver through wires connected to the dive helmet, and ran down the umbilical air hose to the diver. Communications through the helmet system sounded garbled and tinny, but at least you could talk to the diver. The back panel also contained a 'push to talk' button, speaker, and switches to control volume. The bottom horizontal panel held two big gauges that showed the diver's depth. Below that were gauges that tracked the air pressure from the high-pressure hose coming into the panel from the auxiliary air bottles and the low-pressure air going down to the diver through the umbilical air hose to the dive helmet. There were several regulators and valves to adjust the pressure of the air coming into and leaving the panel to the diver—it was the brains of the diving operation. I tested the lines from the air bottles and umbilical, and noted with relief that everything was working as it should.

Steve was all jocked up, wearing the small bailout bottle on his back as back-up, in the event the air coming to his helmet from the umbilical line failed or the hose was severed. He was holding the Kirby Morgan helmet in his hand so we could talk easily before he started the dive. We were in the stern cockpit, the boat bobbing with the swells. The first dive was critical, and we were all a little nervous.

The crew huddled on the stern. Steve laid out his plan as the rest of us listened: "I'll follow the anchor line down and take the line for the marker buoy with me, then look for a place to tie it off. If I can't find any rock to tie it off on, you guys let the 25 pound mushroom anchor slide down the anchor line with a carabiner. I'll use that to keep the marker buoy in place." He waited for questions.

"Sounds like a plan," I nodded. "After you secure the marker buoy, we'll send down the grid lines, stakes and hammer in a bag and you can start to lay out the initial search grid." Our plan was to lay out four 50-foot by 50-foot squares on the bottom so we'd have a larger 100 by 100-foot square overall, with four smaller 50-foot squares within. We could then methodically search each square. I gave Steve some final directions. "Looks like we're anchored in about 70 feet of water, but the gradient will get deeper to the north as you start to lay out the grid pattern. I'd start laying the grid lines to the south first, in the shallower water, to give you more bottom time."

"Got it, good idea, mate," Steve agreed as he walked over to the stern ladder and prepared to enter the water.

Cap hobbled next to Steve before he descended, then turned back to the rest of us. His voice cracking, he said, "Just being over this site is a dream come true for me. I can't believe it's finally happening." He removed his cap and wiped his eyes, then went on, "I want you all to know how much this means to me." He scanned each of our faces then put his hat back on.

Steve nodded and put one hand on Cap's shoulder in acknowledgment, then put on the helmet. Anthony and Joe helped him into the water and he plopped in with a splash then swam to the bow so he could follow the anchor line down. He gave a thumbs up to Anthony, who had moved with him to the bow, managing the umbilical hose, and Anthony relayed the thumbs up to Cindy, who started the dive clock. She'd keep track of his dive time and depths in a log and, using the dive tables, let us know when we should bring him back up to avoid decompression sickness or decompression stops. Cindy was sitting next to me on the stern, both of us staring at the diver control panel. Anthony and Joe were feeding the umbilical air line down to Steve on the bow. I could feel the excitement in the air for the first dive. No matter how much of a crazy long shot this was, there was always the chance we could find the wreck, and we all knew it.

I toggled the 'push to talk' switch. "Comm check, Steve, how's the water down there?"

"Passing 30 feet," Steve sounded like his head was in a box. "Check." Cindy jotted the time and depth into a log.

"Passing 50 feet."

"Check."

"On the bottom."

"Check. I'm showing 68 feet here on the panel," I said into the mic.

"Same down here, mate. The visibility is only about 10 feet. The current is noticeable, but I can still move around. The bottom is mostly sand and silt. Lemme look around for a place to tie off the marker buoy."

"Check."

After five minutes Steve returned. "Don't see any rocks big enough to tie off the marker buoy; send down the mushroom anchor."

"Check, on its way."

Cap heard the message, gave me a thumbs-up and headed to the bow. He grabbed the mushroom buoy from the storage locker and, with the help of Anthony and Joe, pulled up a section of the anchor line, snapped in the mushroom buoy with a carabiner and let it slide down the anchor line to the bottom, pulling the marker buoy line down with it. When the marker buoy reached Steve, he unclipped it and set it on the sea bed. Joe and Cap tied off a large, plastic orange buoy to the marker line and cast it into the water to mark our spot. That would make it easy to find our location again after we pulled up anchor each day. We'd marked our territory.

Cindy checked the timer and toggled the 'push to talk' switch, "You have 35 more minutes of bottom time, Steve."

"Check, thanks Cindy," responded Steve.

Cap and Joe clipped in the tool bag with the grid lines in it and sent it down the anchor line as they'd done with the marker buoy.

"I've got the tool bag," Steve's voice came over the panel.

"Check."

Steve started laying out the first 50-foot grid square. After 10 minutes I checked on him, "How ya doin' Steve?"

I could hear him breathing hard as he worked on the grid lines, "Freezing my peaches off! It's 49 degrees down here!"

"Don't lose your peaches, man, you might need them later." Cindy laughed and elbowed me playfully in the ribs.

"I'll send some hot coffee down in a bucket."

"Great, can't wait."

It felt peaceful with Cindy sitting next to me, absorbed in the task at hand. She seemed to radiate a positive energy. Cap was sitting on the other side of me, totally focused on the dive. "Do you think Steve might find something?" he asked hopefully. He was moving around the boat like a younger man, helping Joe with the lines and sending equipment down to Steve. His enthusiasm and zest seemed to have returned.

"Cap, unless he sees something obvious while he's laying out the grid lines, he won't be searching too hard. Once we get all the grid lines in, we'll start a methodical search," I explained.

He nodded.

Cindy looked at me, "Steve's bottom time is about to expire, let's bring him up."

"Steve, your dive is up, time for a hot shower," I relayed.

"Sounds good, mate, on my way."

Anthony and Joe gently pulled up the slack in the umbilical, as Steve made his way up the anchor line to the boat and surfaced near the bow. Sea Wolf was rocking up and down with the swells, but held fast by the anchor line. The sun punched through the clouds, making the dark green sea look crystal blue. Anthony and Joe helped Steve aboard as he climbed the stern ladder, sea water dripping off him like he'd just stepped out of a rainstorm. Anthony removed the helmet and helped Steve peel off his gear. I tossed a towel to him as he pulled his wetsuit off.

"How was the dive?" I asked.

"Not much visibility. I kicked up a lot of silt while working the grid lines, but I completed the first grid square."

Anthony was already dressing out and getting ready for his dive. He went down for nearly an hour and was able to lay down grid lines for two more squares on the shallower sections of the search area.

I was up next. Steve took over the dive control panel. After dressing out, I stepped off the stern ladder into the cool green sea. The cold water immediately filled my wetsuit, giving me an instant chill down my spine. I swam on the surface to the bow line, gave Cindy a thumbs-up and headed down the milky white anchor line. The sun pierced the turquoise sea with shafts of light as I made my way down the sinuous anchor line. It became darker the further I descended as the light was filtered out.

"Passing 20 feet."

"Check," Steve's voice came through my helmet loud and clear.

"Passing 40 feet."

"Check."

"On the bottom at 67 feet."

"Check."

At the end of the anchor line, I looked around to orient myself. Visibility was good for 10 to 15 feet, beyond that I could see only fuzzy shapes and outlines and it was dark beyond 50 feet. The bottom gradient was shallower toward the south and started to drop off deeper toward the north. The tide was close to slack water so all I felt was a gentle current. An orange starfish near my feet crawled slowly across the sandy bottom.

I found the tool bag at the base of the anchor line where Anthony had left it and started to lay out the lines for the final search grid. The last quadrant I needed to mark was sloping down towards the deep channel. As I swam deeper, the bottom composition began changing from sand and silt to rocks. At the end of the first line, I pulled the hammer and a 12-inch stake out of the bag, tied off the line to the stake and hammered it into the bottom. There were rock piles all around me. Beyond my position, the sea bed dropped off steeply. My head was down as I was tying a knot when I sensed a shadow pass by me.

"What the hell was that?" I said aloud.

"What's goin' on, Jack?" Steve's concerned voice came through my helmet.

"I dunno, something big just moved past me."

I turned around on instinct to find a sea monster checking me out. I froze. It was a Giant Pacific Octopus with an arm spread of at least 20 feet—Jules Verne type stuff. The huge brown and black beast was 15 feet away from me, fluidly moving closer to check me out, his big eyes watching me intently.

"Guys, there's a Kraken staring me down. I think I've soiled my wetsuit."

"Repeat please, a Kraken?" Steve sounded confused.

I watched as the lithe octopus danced slowly to my right, keeping his eyes on me as his giant legs moved in perfect rhythm over the bottom. His colors changed as he moved from the sandy bottom to a rocky area. My heart was beating like a runaway engine.

"It's a Giant Pacific Octopus! I've never seen one. Hope I never see one again. His arms must be 8 feet long! He's circling me right now."

"Do you want us to pull you up?"

Finally backing away from me, the big octopus squirted an inky black cloud and disappeared over the ledge into deeper water to the north.

"Nah, he's gone. I'm almost done with this square, so I'll finish up," I said, trying to get my breathing under control. *Helluva first dive.*

"Check."

I completed the layout of the final search grid. On the way back to the anchor line, I wanted to explore a rocky area near the deepest corner of the grid square. I was at 80 feet, and only had 10 more minutes of bottom time before I needed to ascend. It was a large rocky outcropping near my last stake. I swam around it and found that the side facing down the channel had a cave-like entrance. I pulled the flashlight out of my belt, stuck my head in the entrance and shined the light. The cave was about five feet tall and fifteen feet deep. My light cast a laser-like beam on urchins, crabs and all sorts of creatures in the dark water. Suddenly a huge moray eel appeared and darted at my hand with monstrous fangs. It must've been six feet long. I dropped the flashlight and bumped my head on the top of the cave, but was able to avoid the attack.

Steve heard me yelling into my helmet, and asked anxiously, "Jack, what's goin' on?"

I was breathing hard. "I found a cave and a huge moray eel was hiding inside and almost got me. I'm heading up now."

"Check."

I carefully retrieved my flashlight near the cave entrance and made my way back to the anchor line, following it up to the boat. The hull of the boat was above me, like a white whale floating on the surface and moving to the rhythm of the sea. I was beginning to shiver. I couldn't wait for that hot shower.

Steve and Anthony helped me into the boat. Cindy already had her wet suit long johns on and was wrestling with the bulky top. Cap handed me a towel.

"Mate, you're a magnet for critters down there. I'm glad I'm not diving with you," Steve joked.

"That octopus was huge!" I exclaimed, my hands shaking, either from the cold or from thoughts of the octopus and eel. "It looked like an alien creature. And that moray tried to ambush me."

I walked in my squishy wetsuit booties over to talk to Cindy before she put on the helmet. "The last grid square I laid is the deepest—you might want to start searching the grid square closest to the coast to give you more bottom time. Also, I don't want you to be lunch for a giant octopus."

She smiled, "Jack, don't worry about me, I'll be fine." She donned her helmet and went over the side like a kid eager to get into a swimming pool. Steve and Anthony were manning the dive control panel. Joe handed me a cup of hot coffee.

"You're a lifesaver, Joe." The coffee slowed down my shivering as it hit my stomach, warming me from the inside.

Cap came out on the back deck and looked at me expectantly, "Did you see anything down there, Jack?"

"Nothing yet. Cindy's gonna start a detailed search on her dive, so maybe we'll get lucky." I wasn't going to tell him that our 100-foot grid was just a tiny fraction of the possible locations of the wreck, assuming Jeremiah Benton was even half accurate in his estimation of where the ship had gone down.

I sat looking over Steve's shoulder as he monitored Cindy's dive, trying not to worry about her. "How you doin' down there, Cindy?"

he asked after she'd reached the bottom and began a search of the first square.

"All good, I'm moving slowly on the bottom back and forth in grid square one. I'm digging down about six inches as I move, stirring up a lot of silt."

I noted she was in 65 feet of water. Anthony pushed the mic, "You've got about 40 minutes left."

She kept up her search for 30 minutes with regular reports. Her excited voice came over the mic, "Hey guys, I've found something. Looks like an old piece of timber. It's rotting but I can bring it up."

"Are you sure you can bring it up safely?" Steve asked.

"Yeah, it's only about two feet long."

"Okay, go ahead and mark that spot with one of the flags."

"Got it, on my way up."

"Check."

I walked up to the bow to greet her. She broke the surface with a black, barnacle-encrusted piece of wood in her hand. She swam towards the railing, handing it up to me. It was severely waterlogged and squishy, but no doubt it was an old piece of timber.

"Nice work, Cindy!" Steve exclaimed as he and Anthony helped her aboard the stern ladder.

Cap was waiting on the stern to get a look at the find. I laid the soggy wood on the deck for everyone to examine. It could've been from anything, but Cap thought it was a good sign. "This is it! I feel it. We're on top of her now!" exclaimed Cap enthusiastically.

Joe was standing behind him and shot me a cautionary look. *Don't be a hope crusher, Jack.* Cap sat next to the sodden timber, poking at it, looking for secrets. The sun was setting off our bow, throwing golden reflections on the wake as we made our way back to Neah Bay. It had been a good first day, better than I had expected. Everyone was safe, the equipment worked, we'd laid down all of the grid lines. The giant octopus and moray gave me chills as I fell asleep on the galley couch that night, totally exhausted.

Thirty-Five

A fast-running creek bisects the middle of the village with mud and timber huts lining the creek up and down the valley. It's first light, time to go. Initial contact is the most dangerous encounter. I'd moved down the valley at night so I could walk into the village along the path that followed the creek. I didn't want the villagers to think I was trying to sneak in. I was familiar with Pashtunwali, the Pashtun rules of these isolated mountain people. It was a kind of moral code that governed justice, hospitality, revenge and tolerance of others. I'm counting on the hospitality part.

I break cover and start walking down the narrow path. At 200 yards from the village, I see a small boy playing with a stick by the creek. He sees me and runs back toward the village. The girl is slung over my left shoulder, the rifle in my right hand, ready. I keep walking slowly toward the village as a tall man with a deep red beard, white cap and dirty white pants and shirt comes out of a mud hut with the boy. He walks toward me and stops about 50 yards away. *Here we go.* I slip my rifle off 'safe.'

I doubt this guy speaks English, but it's worth a try. "I have an injured girl, I need help for her."

He raises his hands, speaks back to me in a tongue that sounds like Pashto. He doesn't seem angry or startled, so I stop and wait. He yells something back towards the village. I wait, fingering the trigger. A young man in his mid-twenties comes running out of the village and stands next to the tall man. In broken English the young man says, "What you want?"

"I have an injured girl, she needs help."

The young man turns to the elder with the beard and speaks to him. The old man nods and the young man speaks again.

"You may bring her to the village," he says to me.

I study the surroundings one more time, picking out avenues of escape and the best route to bust out of here if things go sideways. I nod and walk slowly up the path toward the two men. As I proceed, several villagers step out of huts to see what's happening. A woman covered head to toe in a blue chadar burqa waits behind the men like a fleeting shadow.

I approach the old man, assuming he's the village elder. He speaks over his shoulder in Pashto. The woman in the burqa comes forward quickly and takes the girl off of my shoulder. She smells like cooking smoke and her hands are covered with orange henna. She carries the girl to one of the huts near the river. The old man speaks to me for about two minutes and I wait for him to finish.

The young man translates, "The girl you bring here is daughter of Taliban emir on other side of mountain." He points up the valley, "Taliban look for her. Our village elder welcomes you to village, but you have brought great danger here. I will take you to a place where you can rest."

"Please give your elder my thanks and respect," I say, nodding my head at the old man. The young man translates, walks over, takes my arm, and leads me to a mud-walled hut three doors down from where the girl had been carried.

I duck under the drape covering a low doorway, enter a small room, about 12 x 12 feet. A red patterned rug partially covers the brown dirt floor. I sit down on the floor with my back against the mud wall, facing the doorway and resting my rifle in my lap. I'm dead tired and starving, but resist sleep. I'm dozing off when the young man pulls the drapery door back and steps into the hut with a plate of rice, a piece of flatbread and hot tea in a battered tin cup.

"Thank you very much," I nod appreciatively, suddenly starving. "What's your name?" I ask.

"My name Khan. I work with Americans before. I know good English," he says proudly.

"Yes, you do. How is the girl?" I ask, using the flatbread to pick up a ball of rice.

"We give her soup, put special plants on her wound. How she was shot?" He is kneeling on the rug in front of me.

I think about it for a moment, then figure the truth is the best answer, "I shot her accidentally at night. I thought she was a Taliban fighter with a gun. It was a terrible mistake. That's why I brought her over the mountain to get help."

"You come long way with many Taliban looking for you, I think."

"Yes, I fought many on the way here." I sip the tea; it has a cardamom flavor.

Khan sits on the carpet and motions for me to continue eating. I grab a handful of rice, squeeze it into a ball and stuff it in my mouth.

He watches me eat, then speaks, "In Taliban, young girl not allowed to be with man. They kill her."

I freeze and stare at him. "What? But it wasn't her fault!" I exclaim angrily. "I shot her. It was my responsibility to help her."

"No difference to Taliban," Khan shakes his head as he stands up.

So this comes down to the Taliban's idea of honor. She would have bled out on that cold mountain or an animal would have found her. Well, I think defiantly, *I've got my own honor code.*

"Khan, do you have an extra Kalashnikov rifle I can use? I'm almost out of ammunition if the Taliban come."

"I will ask village elder, he must approve," he explains, and walks to the door, holding the drapery open.

Before he can leave, I ask, "Is that the man who met me when I walked into the village?"

"Yes, he fought Russians and Taliban many times. Brave warrior."

"Thank you, Khan," I say, as he leaves. I try my best to stay awake but sleep settles on me like a lead blanket.

Sometime late in the night I awake to the sound of gunfire.

THIRTY-SIX

—— ❊ ——

Sea Wolf's Lehmann diesels were rumbling in the cool morning, gently shaking the boat to life. The crew was up and preparing to get underway, pulling in fenders, tossing off dock lines. The mist overnight had left a glossy wet coating on everything. The foghorn at the entrance of the harbor sounded a mournful blast. It was 7:00 a.m., we were getting an early start. That soggy timber Cindy had found had given everyone a tangible hope this morning.

We idled carefully out of the marina and harbor. When we cleared the jetty, I turned on the northeasterly heading towards our dive site. The swells were four to five feet this morning, but thankfully rolling straight on to the bow. I was able to rise and fall over them without getting broadsided. Low cotton-white fog crept south out of the Olympic Peninsula, rolling over the Strait and obscuring our path. I switched on the radar and the green reflections on the screen revealed the coast to our starboard side and blips of larger vessels in the mouth of the channel. It was always a little hairy to plow blindly through the fog, trusting the radar.

I mentally ran through the actions of the day. Cap was at the galley table studying the chart and making notations, wearing his Greek fisherman's hat and a wool sweater. Steve and Anthony, both in shorts and hooded sweatshirts, were preparing the dive equipment on the back of the boat. Cindy and Joe were standing next to me at the helm as I followed our GPS track in the dense fog toward our dive site.

The thick and depressing fog made everything disappear. I began to feel The Black Dog creep up on me. I hadn't felt him on this trip, but he was here, somewhere on the boat. I pulled my cap tight over my brow, thinking about Micah and Sarah again. *After what he'd been through in Iraq, and suffering through all those injuries and surgeries, why had it come to this for Micah?*

Cindy was a teacher and practiced at noticing nonverbal cues, so she turned to me and asked, "You're unusually quiet this morning, Jack. What's up?"

The boat rose and sank over a swell as I explained, "I was just thinking about Micah and his niece."

Cindy looked at me and nodded, then said, "I read that in the majority of missing child cases, the child shows up eventually. It's only been two days, Jack. Maybe she really did just run away."

I wasn't buying her optimism this morning; too many things were stacked against young Sarah, but I forced a smile and a nod.

Joe chimed in, "Cindy's right, Jack. Unfortunately, these disappearances happen a lot on the rez. The girl most likely ran away from a bad home situation, maybe went to a relative for help." *She's not just a girl, her name is Sarah,* I thought, remembering her sitting on the floor of my bookshop, quietly reading to Emilio and exploring worlds beyond her terrible home life.

The big diesels chugged along as I approached the dive site, carefully navigating the thick fog. I looked at the radar and saw a new contact.

There was a blip on the screen right where the GPS said our dive site should be.

"Guys, look at this!" I called out. The crew crowded around the radar scope as I pointed out the large object at our dive site. "This has to be some kind of vessel. By the size of the blip on the radar, it's pretty big unless it's a small fishing boat with a radar reflector making itself look big."

"Is it moving?" Cap asked anxiously.

"No, it's stationary. It looks like it's anchored at our dive site," I said, alarms going off in my head.

The fog continued rolling south out of the Olympic rainforest, obscuring our view. When we were within a quarter mile of the site, I slowed Sea Wolf to idle and blew the foghorn. After a few seconds, we heard another foghorn respond. Keeping Sea Wolf at a low idle to avoid a collision in the fog, we crept up on our dive location. About a hundred yards away from the anchor site, I could just make out the outline of a large vessel, maybe 150 feet long, where our marker buoy should have been. We idled closer to the vessel but our marker buoy was gone. The boat was anchored right over our dive site. I maneuvered Sea Wolf around so we could come along the port side of the vessel. There was very little wind. "What the hell is this?" I whispered quietly to myself.

Steve and Anthony jumped into action, threw over the fenders and tied them off as we came alongside the vessel. It was a commercial fishing vessel with a big flat deck on the stern that held a large crane and hoist. As we pulled alongside, I looked up and saw Jim Tripper and Linda Tomkin standing at the rail and looking down at us.

I put Sea Wolf's engines into neutral and stepped up on the bow. "What the hell are you doing here?" I yelled up at them.

"It's a free country. We thought we would do some treasure hunting at this location, try out our new side scan sonar," Jim said pompously. He had on a distinctive gray wetsuit with red stripes on the sleeves. Clearly, he was getting ready for a dive. Linda was at his side and suddenly it all clicked. She'd gone to the museum, found Benton's journal, copied the key information and told Tripper, then changed the wreck location to Kydaka Point and given the journal entry to me, hoping to throw us off the actual location.

"So Linda, I guess you expected us to be five miles from here, huh?" I yelled up to her.

"You're more resourceful than I thought, Jack. I'll remember that," she said with a snide laugh.

Suddenly Cap stormed out on the bow, shaking his fist and screaming, "Damn you to hell, Tripper! This is our treasure, and you're not gonna get it! Get the hell out of here!"

I rushed over to Cap and held my forearm in front of his chest, "Cap, this isn't the time or place," I said, so only he could hear.

"That bastard's stolen from me twice, Jack!" he cried.

I looked into the boat, and caught Cindy's attention. She nodded and hurried up on the bow with Joe. They helped Cap back into the pilot house, where he slumped onto the dinette bench with a look of defeat I'll never forget. He put his head down into his hands on the table. Cindy sat beside him, her arm around his shoulder as she said something into his ear.

"You won't get away with this," I said to Jim and Linda, but there was no point in continuing to engage with them. Sea Wolf drifted off the big fishing boat. I grabbed the helm and told Steve and Anthony to drop the anchor when I gave the signal. We were near our original spot but about 200 feet north from Jim's fishing boat. "Now!" I yelled, as they dropped the big spade anchor to the bottom, where it held.

I gathered the crew in the galley.

"What's goin' on, mate?" Steve asked on behalf of the whole group.

"It looks like Jim Tripper and Linda Tomkin put together a crew to dive on this site. They're trying to take advantage of what we've already found out. Steve, you warned me he was a snake but I never thought he would claim-jump us." Steve shook his head in disgust.

"That woman Linda also asked me a lot of questions about what we were up to. It looks like her interest was more than casual conversation," I revealed. Cindy was looking at me closely, eyebrows raised. I didn't dare look at her. I would try to explain my relationship with Linda later, but now was not the time.

"So whadda we do?" Steve asked, throwing his hands in the air. "With that big fishing vessel, they can stay on site 24 hours a day. We can't compete with that."

It was Joe who spoke with the grit of experience, "We don't give up. It's a big ocean, we keep searching. We're not gonna quit just because we have competition." He looked us all in the eye, nodding with confidence, and something switched on in our collective mentality. We all nodded. We could still do this. Cap raised his head from the table, wiped away the tears of bitterness with the back of his hand, pulled on his hat and stood up, ready to work.

THIRTY-SEVEN

—— ¤ ——

"Alright, let's get the first diver ready. Steve, you're up," I announced. With that, the crew went to work. Cap went out to the stern to help Steve get ready. Tripper's vessel had about six or seven other crew on board that I could see. I figured most of them were divers. One in a black wetsuit was being helped into the water off the stern ladder by two others.

We splashed Steve off the stern and he followed our anchor line to the bottom. I contacted him on the diver's communications set as he descended.

"I'm on the bottom at 71 feet," his voice came through the diver control panel.

"Check."

"Don't see our grid lines. Gonna search around here and see if I can find them. Will head south first."

"Got it. See any other divers down there? Tripper has a diver in the water right now," I said.

"No, but I'll let ya know if I see anyone."

"Check."

Cindy and I sat on the back deck of Sea Wolf monitoring Steve's dive. After Steve started his search for the grid lines, she looked at me, the gears in her head obviously turning, and asked, "So, how do you know that woman, Jack?"

I dreaded this conversation, but knew it had to happen at some point. "I was in the gym one day and she came up to me, asked about Port Townsend and said she was researching crabs for her doctoral thesis. We had coffee at Joe's and talked a bit about the town, then off she went."

"But how did she find out about our dive trip?" asked Cindy, knowing that wasn't the full story.

"She kept showing up at my bookstore, asking if I wanted to get something to eat. I didn't chase after her. I don't even have her cell phone number, but she kept coming on to me." I decided not to tell her about that first date where Linda ended up in my bed. I was regretting that deeply, for a number of reasons. I was just glad it happened before I'd met Cindy.

"I told her in passing that I was going to the Royal British Columbia Museum to hunt for the trapper's journal and apparently she went up there before us and found it."

Cindy looked shocked, "What?"

"She claimed she liked to do research. She gave me a copy of the journal entry, but it was a little different from the original that you and I found. Her copy said the wreck was located off Kydaka Point, five miles from here. I didn't tell her that we found the original entry.

"That's why I asked the archive administrator what the woman looked like, remember? I had a hunch it might have been Linda. It looks like she was trying to throw us off the scent," I said, trying to get a read on how Cindy was taking this news.

Cindy narrowed her eyes. "I still don't understand your relationship to her, Jack."

"I found the grid lines," Steve's voice came up on the communication net, saving me for a few minutes. "It looks like they cut the lines, Jack. They're just waving in the current down here. I'll try and reconnect this first set I found."

"Check. Does it look like they were cut on purpose?"

"Sure looks like it to me, mate."

Cindy jumped on the mic, "Steve, you have 25 minutes of bottom time left."

"OK, thanks, Cind."

I turned to Joe, who was sitting on the other side of me. "If Tripper cut our grid lines, that's taking this rivalry to a new level. It's one thing to squeeze in on our site, it's another to destroy our work."

Joe nodded, "We need to be careful with their divers in the water."

Cindy stood up and walked to the bow, probably disgusted with me.

Joe chose the moment to offer some fatherly wisdom. "Jack, don't worry. Just be straight with Cindy about Linda, yeah? Whatever happened between you and Linda happened before you met Cindy, right? Cindy's pretty special, but I think you already know that."

I nodded. "I know, Joe. She's amazing. I hope my bad decision with Linda doesn't ruin it with her," I said quietly, cursing myself.

"Don't throw in the towel, Jack. Just give 'er some time to work it out."

"Believe me, I wish I'd never met Linda," I said, disgusted with myself.

Steve's voice came over the speaker, "I've reconnected two grid lines, can't tell if the rest of them are cut. There's another diver down here, he's just following me wherever I go."

I checked Steve's bottom time, "Roger that, you have five minutes left."

"OK, on my way up."

Steve broached the surface like a black cork. I looked over at Tripper's boat to see their next diver putting on a wetsuit. Steve made his way aft where Anthony and Joe helped him aboard. Anthony was the next diver up and was already dressed out. Joe and Cindy helped put the helmet on him and he made his way into the blue cold. The fog had lifted slightly, but visibility was no more than a few hundred yards.

Steve was toweling himself off on the stern, a shark tattoo taking up a sizable portion of one of his pecs. "These guys have set us back at least a day by cutting our lines," he growled. "What a pisser. And that diver just followed me around, watching me. He didn't do anything," he spat out.

"Maybe they think we found something and they're too lazy to search for themselves," I suggested.

"Yeah, no doubt. These wankers couldn't find a wreck if it hit 'em over the head." He went inside to dry off and change.

Cindy walked around the back of the boat and sat near me as we monitored Anthony's dive. No small talk, all business. I got the message, and it made me nervous.

"On the bottom at 68 feet, heading west to find the other grid lines," Anthony reported.

"Check."

"Another diver is down here, just following me."

"OK, keep an eye out for trouble."

"Will do."

"Cindy…" I began. I wanted… no, I *needed* to say something to her. She looked at me and shook her head. I felt a chill between us.

Anthony's voice came over the speaker, "They've cut the western grid lines. I'm working on tying them back together. Their diver is still following me. I don't get what he's doing."

"Got it, Anthony, you have 20 minutes left," I said.

"Check."

Good ol' Regret had brought his buddy Guilt along and together they started beating rusty hammers on my tin soul in a hellish rhythm. The Black Dog was dancing nearby.

"I've finished connecting the western grid lines. Heading up."

"Check."

I was next down. Steve took over the dive control panel. I wiped the angst off my face and got ready for the dive. Joe helped me with the helmet as Anthony peeled off his wetsuit.

Joe looked me in the eye before pulling the helmet down. "You OK, buddy? You look a little off."

"I'm fine, Joe," I lied. "Let's get on with it." I looked over to Tripper's boat and saw they were bringing a diver up the ladder. Another diver in a gray wetsuit with red trim, like the one Tripper had been wearing when we arrived, was getting into the water. Joe secured my dive helmet and over the stern I went into the freezing dark water. The fog was obscuring the sunlight underwater and the sea was like a dense stormy sky as I made my way down the anchor line. I planned to head to the deeper grid lines to the north, where I'd seen the larger rock pile cave.

"On the bottom at 73 feet, heading north to check the grid lines," I reported.

"Got it, mate," Steve's unmistakable Aussie accent came over the speaker.

Visibility was only ten to twelve feet, with the lack of sunlight penetrating the depth. I checked my wrist compass, knowing how easy it was to become disoriented when diving. I'd made almost all my dives at night in the SEAL Teams and would even lose track of which way was up in the inky black water. Diving under big ships was the worst—you had to feel your way around the hull in the eerie, pulse-pounding darkness.

I continued to follow my compass north. I could just barely tell the bottom was changing from sand to rocks as I slowly descended. I sensed something behind me, and sure enough there was a diver in a gray wetsuit following me, maintaining a steady distance. He was wearing a scuba bottle instead of the umbilical air hose that we were using, which gave him more maneuverability. I waited a few seconds for him to get closer. Jim Tripper's face was visible in the mask, even in the murky ocean water. He stopped when he saw me looking at him. I hated having the guy on my tail, but figured I should just get on with the dive. Not much I could do.

Something dark loomed ahead of me. I saw the entrance to the rock cave where the moray eel had given me a scare. I passed by the cave, still searching for the grid lines, and turned back to see where Tripper was. I watched as his flippers disappeared into the cave. My first thought was, *Have fun with that eel, Jim,* but I couldn't let the guy get taken out by a moray, even if he was a snake himself. I turned around and swam back to the cave entrance but there was no sign of him. I turned on my light and swam into the cave.

Tripper was in the back of the cave flailing like a madman. He'd kicked up silt and sand, so the visibility was terrible, like looking through a dirty snow globe. He was trying to wrench off the moray eel that had clamped onto his left arm near the bicep. Clouds of blood mixed with silt floated in the water of the cave, like a scene from Dante's Hell. Tripper had the tail of the beast and was trying to pull it off, spinning round and round like a washing machine cycle. The teeth on a moray are like a Chinese finger trap: the more you pull, the harder they are to get out. I reached for my knife from the scabbard on my leg. If I could cut the moray's head off, I could pry the jaws apart. Tripper saw me coming toward him with the knife and went wild. You can actually hear a man yell underwater. He let out a gurgling scream. He must have thought I was coming for him and not the eel. That's when it happened. With the eel still clamped on his arm, he pushed off from the back of the cave wall and threw a sharp elbow to my throat as he blitzed for the cave entrance like a man on fire. He smashed the wall on his way out, causing the entrance to cave in. Rocks tumbled and fell from all sides of the entrance as it collapsed on me. Suddenly I was on my back in blinding pain, pinned to the floor of the cavern under a pile of rocks. I screamed into my helmet. I was trapped 80 feet underwater in total darkness.

THIRTY-EIGHT

I awake from a coma-like sleep to the sound of automatic gunfire popping in the distance. My back has slid off the wall during my death sleep. I'm lying on my side and quickly sit up. There's a rusty AK-47 and a spare magazine on the ground next to my feet. I check my watch: 0630. I sling my rifle, grab the Kalashnikov, stow the spare magazine in my cargo pocket and push through the dirty drape entrance into the alley outside the mud hut. It's dark, but dawn is on the horizon. I run past two mud huts to the place I saw the woman in the blue burqa take the girl. I flick open the fabric door with the AK-47 and carefully step into an empty room. *Where have they taken her?*

Hearing the gunfire getting closer, I step back into the dirt alley and slide between two huts to see where the bullets are coming from. The muzzle flashes of Taliban fighters making their way down one side of the valley toward the village are lighting up the sky. From the sound of bullets cracking over my head, I can tell that the villagers are returning fire from the other side of the valley above the village. They must have evacuated and headed up to a more defensible position above the village. I turn and start to climb up the valley on a well-worn trail, toward the villagers. The gunfire is picking up, rounds are whizzing over my head as the villagers and Taliban fire on each other. An orange burst of dawn peeks over the valley. I stumble on a stack of rough-cut timbers left there for future use. The villagers are still above me, firing across the valley at the Taliban. I need to get through their firing line without being accidentally shot. It looks like I'm close to the left flank of their firing positions, so I run to my left another 50 yards to hook around the end of the firing line. When I think I'm clear of the last villager on the left flank, I run up and turn back to my right to join their firing line.

Immediately I come across a villager using the branch of a tall cedar as a rest for his rifle. He's shooting down the valley at the Taliban. I take a chance and wave my AK-47 at him. He turns, surprised, but then signals me with a hand wave. I'm on the villagers' firing line now. I run behind that first villager toward the sound of others firing down the line. I have to find the girl. I stop at a small rock outcropping to fire at the Taliban as they descend on the village. There are 20 to 25 fighters scrambling down the valley opposite us, shooting as they run. The AK-47 is reliable, but not very accurate at this distance. Pulling the sniper rifle quickly off my back, I take aim at a pair of Taliban running side by side down the valley across from me. I squeeze off a round. The fighter on the left falls forward and continues tumbling head over heels down the canyon. The other fighter stops behind a tree and holds his AK-47 out to the side, firing blindly. The Taliban have figured out where the villagers' firing line is and are now leapfrogging down the valley, returning effective fire. Bullets slap the ground all around. I duck behind a rock pile then sprint further down the line. Coming across several villagers firing through a thick stand of trees, I recognize Khan and grab him by the shoulder. "Where's the girl?" I yell.

Thirty-Nine

The rocks have pinned my legs in place, but I can move my arms. It was deathly black in the cave and a hissing sound like bubbles escaping was coming from somewhere. It was getting harder to take each breath from the helmet regulator. I figured my air line was cut or pinched and the air being pumped down to me was leaking out somewhere. I could open the emergency valve, which would disconnect me from the air coming through the hose and connect my regulator to the bailout bottle on my back. But that bottle was only good for 20 minutes at this depth, and then I was done. I decided to breathe off the umbilical hose until it became too hard to take a breath. Fear was creeping up on me like a snake on meth. This would be a bad way to go, stuck in this dark cave, running out of air. *Focus on the task at hand, don't worry about what you can't control.* Boom boom, boom! I knew I had to slow my heart rate and breathing.

Steve's voice crackled through my helmet mic, "Jack, what's going on?"

"I'm trapped in a cave near the northern grid lines. Tripper was following me but he ducked into the cave and that eel clamped onto his arm. I tried to help him, but he freaked out and hit me in the throat. The cave collapsed as he blasted out the entrance. I think my feet are sticking out, but I'm buried up to my waist." I stopped talking to catch my breath. Time for the bad news, "My air hose is leaking somewhere. I'm having a hard time breathing. I haven't opened the emergency valve yet."

It was quiet for a few moments before Steve came over the microphone, "Hey Jack, Cindy was already dressed out for the next dive. She's coming down to help you. I'll let you know when she's on the way down. I'm gonna increase the air pressure coming to your helmet."

I hated the idea of putting Cindy at risk and wanted to tell Steve that he or Anthony should do the rescue dive, but I didn't. I recognized the obvious problem of nitrogen absorption for Anthony and Steve. Cindy was the best choice and she was ready to go. "Okay, I'll let you know when I hear her."

"Hang in there, mate. We'll get her down fast."

"Roger that."

The hissing sound increased, as the extra air pressure Steve pumped down reached my helmet. I realized I was wearing our only surface supplied dive helmet rig with communications. Cindy would be coming down untethered with a single 80 cubic foot scuba bottle on her back, and no communications to the surface. She wouldn't have a lot of air to work with at this depth.

Laying in the dark and cold, I was starting to shiver. I needed to find my flashlight. I moved my arms up and down the cave floor slowly like I was making a snow angel and my right hand touched something hard in the silt. The flashlight. I flicked it on and it shot a narrow beam of light into the dark cave behind my head. The water was murky with the floating silt that had been stirred up when the cave entrance collapsed.

I was lying on my back and my air hose ran down my left side and disappeared into the pile of rocks on my legs. Bubbles were escaping from the rocks on top of the pile, which meant that my air hose must have been cut somewhere in that pile near the entrance. Rocks were piled so high on my thighs that I couldn't see beyond them. The rocks didn't look too big, but there were a lot of them. The pain in my legs was changing from sharp to throbbing, which meant my legs were probably going numb. Breathing out of the helmet regulator was hard; I was starting to get moisture in my mouth with each breath. The severed air hose was leaking a small amount of water into my regulator with each breath and it would only get worse.

I heard clicking to my left. Shining the light under a rocky ledge, a red spiny lobster was poking his head out and looking at me. His two big antennae sticking out two feet from me.

I pushed my hands into the cave floor behind me and sat up to see if I could move some of the rocks, but bumped my head on the cave ceiling. Bending my head to the side, I hinged my upper body closer to my legs without hitting my head. I could now reach the rocks piled on my legs, but couldn't sit up straight.

Steve's voice boomed into my helmet. He must've turned the volume up, "Cindy's on the way down, Jack, should only be a couple of minutes."

"Roger that," I gurgled.

I set my flashlight on the cave floor next to my leg and tried to grab a rock on the top of the pile, but couldn't budge it—I didn't have enough leverage. I was hesitant to pull rocks from the bottom of the pile and cause it to collapse even more, but that seemed the lesser of two evils; either break my legs or die in this cave. I grabbed a rock halfway up the pile and set it next to me. Suddenly I felt something pulling on my foot, realizing it must be Cindy outside the entrance signaling that she was here. I tried to wiggle my foot in response. She pulled on my foot again to communicate that she felt the movement. I looked at my watch: 2:15 p.m. Cindy would only have about 30 minutes of air at this depth. *God, it was great to have her down here with me.* My hope surged.

When I'd heard that Cindy was coming to rescue me, I tried to suppress the terrible fear that she would be killed or injured trying to save me. I knew I would never be able to deal with that. Now that she was here, the fear of losing her came back like a runaway train. I dealt with it the only way I knew how: focus on the task at hand, get moving. I reached for another rock and pulled it off the pile, then another. Every few minutes I felt Cindy give my ankle a squeeze, as if to say, "I'm still here."

Up until that point, I'd been in a kind of panic mode, but now I was angry. *I'm not gonna die in this damn cave.* I started tearing at the rock pile with everything I had. After I moved two or three big boulders, there was a shift in the stack of rocks and my air stopped completely. I took a deep inhale, but nothing came out of the regulator. *This is it.* I reached up to my helmet to turn on the emergency valve. *If this doesn't work, I'm done.* Some primordial fear of death tried to paralyze me, but my training took over. I reached up, turned the valve, felt a rush of fresh air, and took a deep breath. I now had about 20 minutes of air in the bailout bottle on my back. I was completely disconnected from the air hose. I grabbed my flashlight and held it up to my watch. It was 2:30.

Cindy squeezed my ankle again. I could hear her working on the rock pile outside now. I tore three more rocks down and tried with all my strength to move my legs. I felt a little movement, but was still stuck. Focusing on the rocks right on my legs, I dislodged several of the large ones. Suddenly there was a shaft of light in front of me. Cindy had broken through near the top of the pile. She stuck her arm through the hole as far as she could and I reached up and squeezed her hand. It took everything in me to let go of her. If I was going to die, I wanted to die holding her hand. I realized then that I could take on anything with her hand in mine.

My rational mind took over. I let her hand go and tore into the rock pile. The opening where she had reached her hand through was now widening and letting in more light as she attacked it from the outside. I could now reach the hole, and began tearing off rocks around the opening on my side. Another slide bounced a few rocks into my lap, but I quickly swept them to the side. The opening was bigger now. Cindy pushed her head through and saw me for the first time. I saw her blue eyes through her dive mask and realized I'd never seen anything more beautiful. She pulled her head out to keep working. I reported to Steve, "Cindy has broken through the pile." No response. After a second try, I realized that the communications cable running down the air hose must have been cut or pinched along with the air. I had no communications.

The pile was smaller now; Cindy and I had attacked it with everything we had. I tried to pull my legs out one more time. Using my arms to push against the rocks remaining in front of me, I felt a little give. I pulled one more time with all my remaining strength and my legs came loose. With my legs free, I spun around to my knees as the rock pile settled. The opening in front of me that Cindy had made was about a foot in diameter. I rotated my legs underneath my body so I could use them as power and leverage. Putting my head right in that hole, I pushed off my legs, doing a giant squat. The sides of the hole gave in and my shoulders pushed more rocks out of the way. Cindy grabbed my arms, put her feet on the rocks in front of me and pulled as I pushed. It was as if I was emerging from the devil's birth canal. With one final pull by Cindy, the bailout bottle on my back cleared the opening and I was out of the cave, laying on the sea bed. Cindy put her dive mask right up to my face as if to kiss me. She was breathing heavily.

I checked my watch: 2:40 p.m. We had to get to the surface now before one of us ran out of air. I spun around to the rock pile, grabbed my air hose, yanked it hard and cleared it from the rocks. Grasping Cindy's hand, I pulled on my air hose three distinct times, and felt three pulls in response. We began to ascend as the crew on board pulled us to the surface using my air hose. We had to ascend slowly or risk trapping expanding air in our lungs and causing a deadly embolism. The rule of thumb was to ascend no faster than the bubbles around you. I felt another tug on the umbilical. They were checking on us. I let go of Cindy's hand and gave a tug in response. Turning back to grab Cindy's hand, I saw to my horror that her eyes were closed and she was drifting towards the bottom. I reached out for her, but the top side crew kept pulling me toward the surface.

FORTY

K han is firing his AK-47 down into the village as the remaining Taliban fighters descend the valley and assault the empty village. I grab him by the shoulder from behind. He stops firing and looks at me.

"Where's the girl?" I yell over the gunfire.

"Village elder, he take her with him."

"Where is he?" I yell between the staccato of machine gun fire.

Khan raises his AK-47, fires another burst at the village below us. He stops firing and turns back to me, and it looks like he's debating whether or not to tell me. "That way," he points down the firing line opposite from where I'd come.

I turn and sprint down the line, passing villagers shooting from behind any cover they'd been able to find. A group of two men in a small ditch are firing in the prone position. I leap over them, continuing down the line. A lone villager in the crook of a large tree, using one of the branches to rest his AK-47, fires down into the village. A bullet cracks overhead and the man in the tree falls headfirst at my feet like a bag of melons. The bullet has taken off half his head. I move past him and keep working down the line to find the village elder.

The Taliban have entered the huts and are starting to move up the valley wall towards the villagers, who continue to pour fire into the village. The gunfire from the Taliban is increasing, and sporadic bullets are slapping the ground all around us. I have to find the girl. I keep running down the line until I come to a group of four villagers along with the elder firing from a man-made trench supported by timbers on the downhill side to provide good cover. They're kneeling in the trench and firing down the mountain. I move behind them so they don't see me. Behind their firing line the ground flattens out for a few meters before rising again up the valley. This would be a good place to stash ammunition, or maybe the girl. I search behind rocks and trees in the flat area and then I spot her. She's wrapped in several blankets, with her head sticking out of a woolen cocoon. I touch her cheek and one eye opens—she recognizes me. I know what I have to do. The Taliban are here because of me and the girl. I have to get her off the mountain, out of this valley and down to safety and good medical treatment. The villagers are engrossed in fighting the Taliban as I lift the girl to my shoulder. The closest American firebase is due west, so I set off traversing parallel to the bottom of the valley towards the firebase. I have to put distance between me and this village or I might have two hostile groups chasing me.

FORTY-ONE

— • —

Cindy dropped into the depths of the ocean like a sinking rock. I yanked on the air hose with all my strength. The crew obviously didn't know what was going on and kept pulling me to the surface. I reached to my right ankle, pulled my serrated dive knife from its sheath and ripped the knife across the air hose and communication line, severing them both and immediately stopping my ascent. As far as I was concerned, that serrated knife was my most valuable piece of equipment, having also one night saved a buddy of mine who'd gotten entangled on the deck of a submarine. I swam down after Cindy as fast as I could kick my legs. I'd lost sight of her but knew where she would have fallen. I would run out of air any minute. She was laying on her back on the seafloor, and I swam to her as fast as I could. Her eyes were closed and she wasn't breathing. She'd run out of air. Her scuba bottle had a reserve valve on it, so I flipped the valve open, which gave her a little more emergency air. I put my face to her mask but still didn't see her breathing. *Please God, no! Take me instead.*

Grabbing her by her vest, I started to swim to the surface. Her buoyancy compensator vest had an emergency toggle that would fill the vest with CO_2 and shoot us to the surface. I pulled the toggle but nothing happened. It must have malfunctioned. I reached around her waist and unlatched her weight belt, which fell to the sea floor. She was now positively buoyant, so I could bring her up quickly. Her regulator was still in her mouth; I could see a small trail of bubbles coming out of her mouth. As I was kicking her to the surface, I reached over and hit the purge valve on her regulator, which shot a last blast of air into her mouth and lungs. She didn't seem to be breathing off the regulator, so I pushed the purge valve again.

I checked our depth on my gauge: 35 feet. Suddenly, my air ran out. I tried to take one more breath, but it was like sucking on a plugged garden hose. Kicking as hard as I could towards the surface, I blew out air as it expanded in my lungs. In the SEAL Teams we practiced the traditional Underwater Demolition Team breath holding and freediving techniques. I'd passed out holding my breath during training, but my swim buddy had saved me. As we approached the surface, the symptoms of blackout came on, led by tunnel vision. Ten more feet to go. I blasted to the surface with a final kick of adrenaline, anger and fear. We broached the surface 15 yards from Sea Wolf. I turned Cindy onto her back and yelled towards the crew, "Over here, HELP!"

Cindy was floating on her back with her face just above the surface of the water. The cold blue-green swells gently washed over us. I ripped my helmet off and attempted to give her CPR, holding her nose and breathing three breaths into her lungs. Nothing. I looked up and saw Sea Wolf motoring next to us. The engines were running so the crew couldn't hear me scream, "NO, NO, NO!"

FORTY-TWO

Traversing a small animal trail parallel to the bottom of the valley, I move as quickly as possible, but the slope is steep, forcing me to slide down to my right. The sound of gunfire is close behind. I'll never make enough speed to evade the Taliban at this pace. I need a new plan. I have to take another risk. Directly below me is the flat valley floor. I could move much faster there; nobody would expect that I could run out of the valley. But I'd finally gotten sleep and a hot meal, was in good shape and had been training at this altitude for months. It was a change in pace they might not expect. I follow another animal trail that traverses across an open area of sharp scree and eventually leads to a small ravine thick with cover. I creep into the tall bushes, set the girl down, pull out my water bottle and pour her a few sips. She slowly opens her eyes as the water spills from the sides of her mouth and runs down her cheeks into her matted hair. I check her pulse: weak but readable. I pull out my escape and evasion map, note the distance to the closest US firebase—18 miles due west, and make a decision. This will be the last leg of the journey. I need to get her medical help today. I can't afford to stop and hide in the daylight again. I'll hike straight to the bottom of this valley, start running west as the valley descends to flatter ground, then run another 10 miles across open country to the firebase.

Taking off all my gear, I stash my load-carrying vest and backpack in the weeds. My radio was already damaged so I crush it to bits with a rock. I leave the AK-47 and all my other gear behind. I keep one water bottle, the pistol on my belt and sling the sniper rifle over my shoulder. Everything else I leave behind. I pick up the girl on my shoulder and start moving rapidly down towards the valley floor. I descend through scrubby pines, patches of loose rock and dead wood, zig-zagging to the bottom of the valley floor. There's distant gunfire to the east. The valley floor gently slopes to the southwest. A meandering creek flows across small boulders in the middle of the valley floor.

This is it. I've endured more physical and mental hardship in my SEAL career than most people could imagine. *I can do this. I have to do this.* I breathe in deeply, set the girl down, take a knee, do something I haven't done since I could remember: bow my head, "Please help me get this girl down to safety." I stand up, like I've done so many times in my life when I was beaten down. This path ahead is a familiar mental place for me—a seemingly insurmountable physical obstacle, that in its essence is really a mental challenge. I check my watch: 1:30 p.m., and set off running. The girl is bouncing too much on my shoulder at a trot. I reposition her to sit piggy back style on my back with the rifle in my hands. She can't hold on to my shoulders or neck and flops around. I keep her in place by leaning forward, tying my poncho around her back and cinching it into a knot on my chest. I run down the valley, focusing on blotting out the growing pain in my body. I'd seen, too many times, how pain and fear could stop a man in his tracks. Crunch, crunch, crunch—just keep moving forward.

FORTY-THREE

The Coast Guard helicopter was hovering above Sea Wolf. The down blast from the rotors was deafening as it whipped the sea into a white froth all around us. The aircrew was lowering a basket out the side door of the helicopter with a hoist. We were all standing on the bow of Sea Wolf with Cindy, who was lying unconscious, wrapped in blankets. The pilot expertly maneuvered the helicopter to lower the human-shaped basket onto the bow of Sea Wolf. As it approached the boat, Anthony and Steve reached up and grabbed the big cage and eased it to the deck. Joe and I gently lifted Cindy into the basket and secured the straps across her body. I looked into her face one more time, swept her hair from her closed eyes. Steve gave a thumbs-up to the pilot and Cindy was slowly hoisted up into the helicopter. When the aircrew had her safely inside the helicopter, they closed the side door and sped off towards the hospital at Port Angeles.

Sea Wolf's top speed was only 12 knots, but I had the two diesels whining as I surged the throttles forward and pointed Sea Wolf towards Makah harbor. Tripper and his boat had disappeared. Cap moved to stand beside me as I flicked on the GPS. He put a hand on my shoulder and I turned from the helm to look at him. Tears were running down his face. "This is all my fault, Jack. You told me it would be a dangerous business and I didn't listen. All I thought about was the treasure."

I tried to make him feel better. "It wasn't your fault, Cap." I should've said more, but couldn't think about anything except Cindy. I kept seeing her hand reach through the gap in the rocks where I was trapped, giving me the hope and strength to bust out of that pile of death. She had laid it all on the line to save me. She must have known she was running out of air as she worked feverishly to free me, but kept going until I was clear. Cap sat down at the dinette, tears still streaming down his face.

Seeing Cap cry and thinking about Cindy unconscious in that Coast Guard rescue basket made me cry. Stinging tears of regret and guilt flowed. *Why had I talked her into coming on this expedition? Why did I let myself get trapped in that cave by Tripper? Why didn't I check her air supply before we ascended?* It was all too much, and I asked Joe to take the helm. I went out to the back and stood at the stern, watching the meandering green wake. For a moment I thought about jumping into that wake, sinking into oblivion, and washing away all my mistakes. I might have done it, but Steve and Anthony came aft and stood by my side. They didn't say anything, just stood on either side of me. After a minute they each put an arm around my shoulders. I couldn't let my friends down, especially Cindy. I wiped my eyes and got on with it.

"Sorry about cutting your air hose, Steve."

"Ya kiddin', mate? I'm just glad you had a sharp blade."

"How long until we reach the Makah reservation at this speed?" I asked.

"About 90 minutes," Steve said.

"Well, that's enough time to clean up and get all this gear stowed," I said.

"Roger that, Skipper," Steve replied, and he and Anthony went to work.

Joe pulled us into the Makah harbor, and we tied up Sea Wolf at the marina. During the transit, we'd come up with a plan. Steve, Joe and I would jump in Steve's van and head to Port Angeles to be with Cindy at the hospital. Cap and Anthony would spend the night at the Makah marina and bring Sea Wolf and all our gear back to Port Townsend in the morning.

After we tied off Sea Wolf to the slip, Steve and Joe jumped on the dock and we hurried down the pier to Steve's van. On the way I stopped in the marina office to let Micah know what had happened and that we'd be pulling Sea Wolf out early. I also wanted to know if he'd heard anything about Sarah. He looked tired and haggard, like he'd been sleeping in the same clothes since we'd last seen him.

"Aw, Jack, I'm so sorry to hear about your friend Cindy. Sometimes bad things seem to happen all at once, don't they? I know you've gotta go, but Jack, I received a ransom note," he told me, the words tumbling out of his mouth. "They want $100,000 or they'll kill her!" He looked down at his missing leg, then back at me, "The note says if I go to the police, I'll never see her again. They gave me three days to come up with the money."

It was worse than I could have imagined. "Why did they send you a ransom note instead of Jerry?"

"I don't know," he said with a look of utter despair.

"Did you talk to him?"

"I tried, but he disappeared too. He won't answer his phone and he's not at home. What am I gonna do, Jack?"

"Micah, you have to go to the police. They have the resources and experience to deal with a kidnapping. They'll probably bring in the FBI."

"I won't do it and put her life at risk," he said adamantly.

I stood there thinking. "OK, lemme ask you something, Micah, how much disability payment did you get from the government for your injuries in Iraq?"

He thought about it for a second and I could see I was on to something. "About $100,000."

"Micah, obviously that's not a coincidence. Someone knew you received that payment, so they grabbed your niece, figuring it was the best way to get it outta you. I don't know if your brother is in on it, or a victim, but you need to think hard about what you're gonna do if you don't go to the police. Sarah's life is in your hands," I said as forcefully as I could. I paused, "I'm sorry, man, Cindy is being airlifted to the hospital. She saved my life and now she's in critical condition. I gotta roll, but call me later and let me know what you're gonna do. If I can help in any way, just let me know."

"Thanks, Jack," said Micah. "I know you're right. It is too much of a coincidence. I didn't want to believe that someone I know took her, or that Jerry could be involved, but I've twisted it around in my mind a thousand ways and can't see any alternatives that make sense."

"Jerry disappeared just as that note showed up, right? I mean, maybe he's a victim too, but you need to think about who else would do this."

"I've gone over and over it in my head, Jack. I can't think of anyone who would do this." He ran his hands through his long hair and rolled his head as if the thought that his own brother could be a part of this was physically painful.

"OK, man, let's just say that your brother is part of kidnapping his own daughter for ransom. Where would he take her? You must know these lands like the back of your hand. Can you think of anywhere they might hide out with her for that long?" I asked.

A lightbulb seemed to go on in his head. "There's an old abandoned hunting cabin at the western edge of the reservation that Jerry and I found when we were kids roaming the land and hunting. I haven't been there since then."

I put a hand on Micah's shoulder and looked him in the eye, "Listen soldier, I'll be in touch, so whatever you do, don't go out to that cabin by yourself. If anyone contacts you, tell them you're trying to line up the money... just stall them for a little while. Remember, it's the money they want, and they know they won't get it if they hurt Sarah. I'll help you get her back, Micah, I promise." It was a promise that would have consequences I couldn't have imagined.

I ran outside. Steve had the van running at the curb. I jumped in and he stomped the gas and headed for Port Angeles. It was a typical overcast day on the Olympic Peninsula with a light rain coming down. I sat in the back seat as Steve drove, with Joe in the passenger seat. Dark cedars and spruce lined the road, and beyond them, low clouds obscured everything. I could hardly keep my eyes open, as I was deathly tired and going in and out of consciousness. In my semi-dream state, I saw a small white hand reach up to me for help. Was it Cindy, Sarah or the girl in Afghanistan? Or was it the fickle hand of fate, beckoning me forward to the unknown?

FORTY-FOUR

The valley is slowly descending towards the west. I can see out into the high desert plane where the closest US firebase is located. After eight miles of running down the valley, I need a water break; the temperature is warming as I descend. Finding a shady spot in a stand of tall pine trees near a creek, I set the girl down on her back in a patch of soft, river-bed sand. I grab my near empty Nalgene bottle and squat on the bank of the creek to fill it up. The water's running fast and clear, and smells sweet. I'm about to sit up when someone jumps on my back, throws a choke hold around my neck and knocks me off my feet face first into the water.

The attacker holds my head underwater as I struggle to get leverage. I'm on my stomach at the bottom of the creek. The man is strong and heavy on my back. I feel myself running out of air. With a burst of strength, I do a push-up off the bottom of the creek for a split second, enough to grab a gulp of air before he stuffs my head back into the water. His stranglehold on my neck is tightening, and my vision narrows; blackout is seconds away. There's one more move in me before I pass out and die. I crunch my body into a ball, get my legs under me, feel my feet hit bottom, and thrust my whole body backwards with all of my remaining strength. The attacker and I are both propelled out of the shallow water onto the bank of the muddy creek. He's still on my back, the chokehold in place, and I reach for his arms around my neck, trying to loosen his grip. I grab his wrist and suddenly hear a sickly thump, like a cantaloupe being smashed with a hammer. Immediately the attacker lets go of my neck and falls backwards. I whip around. The girl is on her knees with a large rock in both her hands. The rock and her face are covered in blood, brains and bits of skull from the Taliban attacker. She looks at me with vacant blue eyes, then falls face first into the mud. The bloody rock rolls out of her hands into the creek.

I pull her out of the mud and wipe the blood and brain matter off her face with my wet hands. "I'm sorry, I'm sorry... " I mutter as I try in vain to wipe the blood from her hair. My tears fall, mixing with blood and mud and all the other earthly elements of hell.

BOOK THREE

FORTY-FIVE

— ∗ —

I wrap the girl in my poncho, hoist her on my back again, pick up my rifle and head off running down the valley. The dead Taliban fighter was likely a fast scout sent ahead to find me. I can't lose any more time. I need to get the girl to that firebase—ten miles to go. I can see the bottom of the valley now, brown and dry. A surge of strength and resolve flows through my veins; my training has prepared me for this. My legs are like jello, my back is killing me, the rifle feels like lead in my arms, but I keep up a steady pace. I'll get this girl help today.

It's late afternoon, the tall trees are giving way to open grassy country. The deep green creek has now become a wide muddy river. I reach the bottom of the valley and kneel under a shady tree to drink the rest of my water. I don't want to lose time by setting the girl down, so I take a one minute rest on my knees. In the distance I hear gunfire. Time to get moving. At the bottom of the valley, I have to cross the river to get to the firebase. I start looking for a shallow spot to cross safely. The river takes a bend to the right and there's a small sandbar in the middle, indicating shallow water. I step carefully down the river bank and wade across. It's about knee deep, but freezing cold. I trip on a hidden hole in the river bottom and land on my knees without dropping the girl. I'm now soaked up to the waist. As I clear the opposite river bank, a shot rings out up the valley and a round lands six feet from me, splashing in the river. *This is it, Jack, run now for all you're worth.* I tuck my head and sprint.

The trees give way to waist-high bullrushes, reeds and water plants that thrive around the meandering river. They're not tall enough to conceal us completely, but we'd be hard to see in them. I spot an animal trail through the bushes and follow it down the valley. Another shot rings out but nothing lands nearby—probably reconnaissance by fire. After an hour of running, I stop to take a short rest. I find a clearing among some tall reeds where I can set the girl down for a minute. I pour drips of water into her mouth, but it spills out. I listen for her breath and discover that she's making a wheezing sound. I check my GPS: five miles to the firebase. This will be our last stop. I'll make it to the firebase tonight.

I drink the last of my water, secure the girl in the poncho and set off following the river. In a mile I exit the green valley and move out onto high desert plains with undulating terrain devoid of vegetation. The wind is blowing from the south, kicking up fine dust that reminds me of powdered sugar. I run through an empty wadi that meanders to the west so we can't be spotted up on the plains. According to the map, the firebase is located on a small hill, which would give the soldiers a defensible position against attackers. Eventually the wadi flattens out into a dry sandwash, so I run in that for two miles. The soft sand is easier on my knees and back, but absorbs more of my energy. The sun is setting as I creep up the bank of the sandwash to have a peek. I see the firebase lit up on top of a hill about a quarter mile from me. The sandwash starts to flow in a southerly direction, but I need to get up onto the exposed high plain in order to make it to the firebase. I decide to wait a few minutes until dusk. That will give me a chance to enter the firebase out of sight of any Taliban on my tail. A few stars appear to the east above the jagged peak I've left behind. The firebase has an exterior perimeter guarded by Afghan National Army troops. I don't want to surprise them and get into a firefight; they're in the middle of bad guy country.

I find a rough dirt road that looks like one of the access points in and out of the firebase. I walk down that road in the open so it doesn't look like I'm trying to sneak up on the guards. In the faint light of the stars I see a perimeter fence of concertina wire and HESCO barriers filled with sand. At two hundred yards from the perimeter, I stop in the middle of the dirt road and start yelling, "I'm an American and need help!" A large spotlight lights up the sky from a guard tower on the perimeter wall and the operator shines it in my general direction. When the beam hits me, I set the girl down on the sandy road, lay down my rifle, get down on my knees and put my hands behind my head. The light continues to shine, blinding me. Voices and shouting come from beyond the perimeter. A gate opens and a Humvee crawls down the road, and I can see an Afghan soldier manning a .50 caliber machine gun in the turret. The Humvee stops 25 yards from me and a US soldier exits the passenger door with his rifle aimed directly at me.

"Who are you?" he shouts in English.

"I'm with the Special Operations Task Force," I respond. "I've been evading the Taliban down this valley. I have an injured girl who needs immediate medical attention. My name is Jack Thibideaux."

I awaken with a terrible headache from dehydration. I'm lying on a green nylon cot inside a small makeshift room with sandbag walls and a sagging plywood floor. Sergeant First Class Eric Swanson from the Army Special Forces Detachment at the firebase is standing over me. He's short and stocky with curly black hair and a scar on his left cheek.

"How ya doin', sailor?"

"My head is killing me, but I slept like a stone."

"We contacted the Special Operations Task Force. They're sending a helicopter to get you later tonight. Boy, were they surprised to hear that we had you here."

"Like happy surprised or pissed off surprised?" I ask with a dry mouth.

"I would say both."

I sit up. My back feels like someone hit me with a sledge hammer.

Swanson hands me a bottle of cold water. "How did you get down the mountain with the girl?" he asks.

"Long story, but I was lucky." I sip the water and think about telling him the full story. I know I'll have to give a detailed debrief at some point.

"Yeah, we've been picking up intel on the Taliban chasing someone down this valley."

"How's the girl?" I ask.

"Our medic jumped into action right after you brought her in, but there was nothing he could do. She'd already bled out. She was dead before he could start an IV."

I just stare at him. My hand falls and the water from the bottle pours onto the plywood floor. My mouth opens to scream, but nothing comes out.

FORTY-SIX

C indy's hospital room at the Olympic Medical Center in Port Angeles looked out over the Strait of Juan de Fuca to the north. It was a small room with green linoleum tile, bent blue metal shades and stark white walls. A framed picture of an Orca hung on the wall. The sparseness of the room reminded me of a military hospital. I sat next to the window in the only chair. It was a red fake leather recliner so a visitor could sleep uncomfortably if needed. I'd been here for two days. Cindy was in a coma. She was propped up in bed with pillows behind her head. There were two IVs in her arms and a tube down her throat. I'd moved the recliner next to the bed so I could hold her hand and talk to her. The doctor said it could stimulate brain activity and help her wake up. Cindy's mother had been here all day yesterday and today but had gone back to Port Townsend late this evening to get a few hours of rest and would be back early in the morning.

I squeezed Cindy's hand and said, "Hey, did you see that Orca on the wall? It looks like the one we saw crossing the Strait." I squeezed again. "Your mom's been here all along but had to leave for a bit. She'll be back soon. She's not taking this well, but I told her you were gonna wake up any minute and that she shouldn't worry." Silence. I just kept squeezing.

There were things I never spoke about, experiences I'd bottled up inside, events that haunted me. I told her everything, and hoped I was doing it for her sake—to wake her up, but the truth was that I needed to tell her about Afghanistan. Maybe I was a coward for telling her these terrible things when she couldn't respond, but I had to talk about them once and for all.

"Remember I told you I shot a girl in Afghanistan? What I didn't tell you is that she'd saved my life... but I couldn't save hers." I paused, dropped my head, then continued. "It's something I can't think about without an avalanche of pain and guilt crushing down on me. Since then, this Black Dog has been haunting me day and night. He's always there in my mind, taking bloody bites out of my hope and any chance I have for happiness. He tempts me, Cindy: jump off a building, put a gun to your head, step in front of a train."

I raised my head to look at her soft face, but there was no eye movement. I continued. "I couldn't even tell my wife what happened in Afghanistan. She eventually left me and I don't blame her." I squeezed her hand. "You're the only person I've ever talked to about what happened to that girl. I wake up in the middle of the night and she's staring at me with one eye open. She never says anything but that blue eye bores into my soul. She's trying to communicate with me, but I can't understand her. Her eye closes and The Black Dog comes charging in, gnashing his teeth."

"I've tried everything to stop the pain, Cindy," I say as I squeeze her hand. "Alcohol, pain pills, sex. They mask the pain, but nothing ever changes. You probably figured out that I'd slept with Linda before I met you: just another huge regret that I was ashamed to tell you." I looked at Cindy's face to see if there was any reaction. Nothing. "I'm not religious, but I was at my wits end, so I prayed for all I'm worth for God to kill this Black Dog or else take me. I didn't think God answered my prayers, but then you showed up in my life, and now... just this minute... I've realized that you were my answered prayer. When I'm with you, The Black Dog stays away."

I lifted her hand to my face, tears dripping onto her slim white fingers. "Please, please, wake up... I need you... I'm in love with you, Cindy. And I don't think I can do this anymore without you."

FORTY-SEVEN

— ✳ —

Mrs. Johnson returned first thing in the morning and I gave her my seat. She smiled kindly at me and I could see the mixture of hope and terror in her expression.

"Thank you for staying with my girl, Jack," she said gratefully. "I know she's pleased you're here."

I asked the nurse for another chair and stayed until late in the day, but I really had to get back to Port Townsend, to check on my shop and Emilio. I was also worried sick about Micah and Sarah. I hadn't heard from him in 24 hours. I'd been calling him from the hospital but he didn't answer. It was only an hour's drive home, so I would return early in the morning. My old Toyota pickup chugged down the dark, tree-lined ribbon of road. A cold rain fell, making the road shiny and slick. My mind was in a haze. The Black Dog wouldn't stop terrorizing me. *Cindy's coma is your fault. What if she never wakes up? What will Mrs. Johnson do without her daughter? How could you be so stupid and selfish to let this happen? What if Sarah is never found?* My masochistic reverie was interrupted by my cell phone.

"Hello?" I said, after fumbling for the button.

"Jack, it's Micah."

"Micah, I've been trying to get in touch with you! What's going on?"

He ignored my question. "I've gotta talk to you." He sounded almost out of breath.

"I'll be back in Port Townsend in 45 minutes, I can meet you at the bookstore."

"Alright, see you there at 7, and Jack..." he hesitated, "please don't tell anyone." He hung up.

Micah sounded different from the man I'd come to know. Either he had new information or he was planning to take action. Hopefully he was ready to go to the police, but I had a feeling that wasn't gonna happen. I decided I'd do whatever I could to help Micah get Sarah back. I owed a lot to humanity, the bill was coming due.

I parked the truck near the bookstore. The sun had set, and the rain left dirty puddles on the streets and sidewalks. As I moved to open the door of the bookshop, I noticed it had been forced open with something, probably a screwdriver. I opened the door slowly. It was dark inside, and the streetlights cast an eerie glow on the front of the store. I tiptoed quietly to my desk and took out the 9mm pistol from the bottom drawer. I heard a crunching noise to my left and spun with the pistol at the ready. Emilio was playing with a mouse under the coffee table.

Mrs. Johnson had taken care of the cat while I was on the salvage trip. He looked fat and happy; maybe she'd fed him muffins. I turned on the lights but no one was there. As I was putting the pistol away, my eye fell on a folded piece of paper on my desk, and I sat down and opened it. Written in fine cursive, it read, "You are going to pay for what you've done." No name or signature. My sins are many, but

I couldn't think of anything I'd done in Port Townsend that would cause someone to threaten me. I put the note in my desk drawer just as Micah walked in, limping on his prosthetic leg and wearing a jean jacket, cargo pants, boots and his Army ball cap, as if he was ready for a mission. He walked over to my desk and sat down in front of me without saying a word.

"Micah, what's going on?"

"Jack, I think I know where Sarah's being held," he said without preamble.

I slid to the edge of my seat. "Tell me."

He took off his cap, placed it on my desk, ran his hands through his long black hair, and began. "I told you about that cabin on the far edge of the reservation, right?" I nodded and he continued, "Well, it's a perfect hiding spot, Jack: remote, only one way in, hard to find. I drove out there and stashed my truck down an old logging road and hiked up to a small hill above the cabin. I sat and waited." He paused. "That's when I saw it."

"Saw what?" I asked, now on the edge of my seat.

"A black SUV drove down the dirt road to the cabin and parked. Two people got out and went into the cabin," he said.

"Did you get a look at them, could you identify them?" I asked.

"No, I was pretty far away. I just waited, and a half hour later they got back into the SUV and drove away. I was tempted to hike down and check in the cabin, but it was just a scouting mission and I wasn't armed." He put his hat back on his head and looked straight at me. "That's why I'm here, Jack. I need your help."

"Anything, my friend. How can I help?" I leaned forward.

"I have to get inside that cabin, and if Sarah's there, take her back."

I thought a minute before speaking. I wasn't sure if Micah understood the difficulty of what he was suggesting. It was a high-risk hostage rescue mission with no support or back-up, probably even illegal. I knew in my gut that I'd help him, but I needed him to understand that we'd have to do it on my terms, not his.

"Micah, I'm all in on this, but we're gonna do it my way, OK?" He nodded. "OK, we need to strike fast, before they get a chance to move her, assuming she's there." He nodded again, this time more enthusiastically. "Tomorrow, after dark," I said.

I pulled some sheets of blank paper from the printer tray and spread them out on my desk. Micah looked up at me with a quizzical look. "We're gonna plan this out in detail, by phases. Each of these papers represents one phase of the operation. For each phase, we'll work out everything we need: logistics, weapons, communications, movement, actions, etc. Then we'll work out the possible contingencies if things go wrong." *As they usually do,* I thought.

After three hours of considering every detail, we had a plan. He headed back to the reservation and I called Mrs. Johnson to check on Cindy. She picked up on the third ring.

"Mrs. Johnson, Jack here. How is Cindy?"

She sounded exhausted. "Oh, Jack, there's no change. She's still asleep."

"Listen, Mrs. J, I won't be able to be there tomorrow. There's something I've gotta take care of."

There was a long pause, "OK, Jack, I understand," but the tone of her voice told me she was disappointed and probably judging me. She might even be blaming me for Cindy being there in the first place. I know I was blaming myself.

"It's something Cindy would want me to do, Mrs. J., I promise you." The line went dead—she'd hung up. I couldn't fault her for being upset with me. Get in line.

The rescue planning with Micah had given me a focus, but the news about Cindy had brought on damn The Black Dog again. I drove home alone in silence with despair glaring at me from the passenger seat. As if guided by another hand, I turned and parked at the VFW. I needed to think this out and didn't want to be alone.

I was relieved to see Sheila alone at the bar, and I walked up behind her. She had two empty shot glasses in front of her and a half full one in her hand. I sat next to her without saying a word. I figured she'd try her voodoo mind reading on me. I was right.

"Jack, you look like hell," she said, turning to me. She waved over the bartender, a young woman I hadn't seen before with dark hair and a gold nose ring. "What're ya drinking, Jack?" Sheila asked.

"Whatever you're having," I mumbled.

"Two shots of vodka please," Sheila instructed. The bartender nodded, grabbed a tall bottle behind the bar and poured two overflowing shot glasses.

"You're having another?" I asked, looking at her two empty glasses and the third in her hand.

"They're both for you, Jack. You look like you need it. What's going on with you? I sense some real bad news forthcoming."

Where do I begin? I told her about the diving accident, how Cindy had saved my life, her coma and then about Micah and the ransom on his niece. In retrospect, it was a lot to dump on her. But I'd had a terrible few days and needed to tell someone. Sheila was a good listener.

She turned and looked straight at me. "I think I know you, Jack. You're blaming yourself for Cindy's accident. I can see you've put another heavy rock in your rucksack, and you're carrying that guilt along with everything else. It's weighing you down somethin' fierce, honey, I can see that." I stared at the drinks lined up in front of me as she spoke. "And there's something else, Jack. I sense it clearly in you: like I said before, you're in love," she said simply. This time I didn't argue with her.

"Jack, look at me." I turned and her wise eyes were locked on mine. "Listen," she began, with a hardened look I hadn't seen in her before. "You have to be stoic here. You can't do anything for Cindy right now. You have to drop that weight and take charge of what you can control. It's in your power to help Micah, and that poor little girl." Her eyes were aflame with passion and her voice was steely as she continued, "You go out to that reservation, you find that girl and you kill those bastards who took her. Chop them up in little pieces and bury them out there where they'll never be found." *Definitely a side of Sheila I hadn't seen before.* "Then you come back with your head held high, knowing you saved an innocent life." She stopped, and returned back to the woman I knew. I felt like the Spartan who was told by his wife to come back with his shield, or on it.

She turned to the bar and tossed back her last shot. "You haven't touched your drinks," she said calmly, as if she hadn't just sounded like a general preparing her troops for battle.

I twirled the shot glasses on the bar, but didn't drink them. "I'm not feelin' it tonight, Sheila," I admitted.

She nodded understandingly. In truth, I was dying for a drink, but right now I needed the pain, not the numbness. I needed the pain to sharpen my aggression and hone my resolve. A quote by H.L. Mencken came to mind, "*Every normal man must be tempted, at times, to spit on his hands, hoist the black flag and begin slitting throats.*" Sheila was spot on. There was blood to be spilled.

FORTY-EIGHT

—— ◆ ——

"Sergeant Swanson, I want to have the girl buried according to Muslim tradition. Her body has to be washed, wrapped in linen and buried within 24 hours," I explain, standing in the doorway of his makeshift office.

"I don't have the time or men for that, Thibideaux. We have imminent operations. Looks like you stirred up a hornet's nest out there with the Taliban and local tribes. The girl's body will be taken to the local authorities for disposal," he says, shuffling papers on his plywood desk.

"Bullshit, Swanson, I'll dig the grave myself right now."

"Suit yourself, shovels are in the shed out back," he says, pointing behind his room.

"Do you have any females here in the compound?"

"Just one, our intel specialist."

"Can I speak to her?"

He thinks for a moment then says, "She's down the hall in the SCIF. Just hit the buzzer on the door." He picks up the phone on his desk as I walk out.

I make my way down the dim, dusty hallway. Exposed lightbulbs throw shadows on the walls. The old mud walled building must have been some sort of community center before the locals allowed the firebase to operate there.

The SCIF, or sensitive compartmentalized information facility, was the intelligence hub for the firebase. There's a black SCIF sign above the door. I hit the red buzzer button, and in a few seconds a short female dressed in gray Army PT gear steps out from behind a makeshift metal door. She's African American and her hair is tied in a bun.

"My name is Jack and I'm with the Special Operations Task Force."

"Yeah, I heard all about it," she cuts me off.

"Listen, I've got a favor to ask you. A girl died... I mean... I killed a girl and I want to bury her according to her religious customs."

"You need me to wash the body?"

"Yeah, it would mean a lot to me."

She looks me in the eye then down at the ground before answering, "Let me check with my superiors. I'll get back to you in a few minutes. Wait here." She disappears behind the heavy black metal door. I wait about ten minutes, then the door opens and she steps out. "OK, I'll do it. The girl is in the medical bay right now, I'll have the medic help move the body to the female latrine."

"I'm gonna dig a grave out back. I can come get her when you're done."

"I'll let you know," she says, nodding and turning to walk away.

"I can't thank you enough. I didn't even get your name."

"Specialist Amy Jackson," she says, turning back towards me.

"Amy, it's nice to meet you. I really appreciate this." She smiles lightly, then I reach out my hand and she shakes it.

The ground behind the firebase is rocky soil mixed with light brown powdery dirt. I jam the shovel in the ground and it reverberates with the ping of steel hitting rocks. I dig the grave, bit by bit, clouds of fine dust swirling around me. After an hour and a half, it's four feet deep. I climb out of the hole and stand on the edge, looking down. The grave is surrounded by HESCO barriers, sandbags, piles of spent cartridges, empty ammunition boxes and mortar holes. *What a shitty resting place,* I think despondently.

Specialist Jackson walks out, wearing her Army duty fatigues. "I've washed her body. You can come get her now."

She leads me into the building, down a narrow corridor to the lone female bathroom. She opens the door and I see the girl's body lying on a bench, wrapped head to toe in a white sheet for burial. She looks like a mummy. I gently pick her up and Amy leads the way to the gravesite. On the way she speaks to one of the Afghan security guards. He leaves his post and walks with us to the grave.

At the gravesite I step down into the hole and lower the girl into the rocky dirt. It's the last time I will carry her to a resting place. Tears fall on the white sheet as I set her down gently for her final rest. It feels like it should be me lying here, not this child who was simply in the wrong place at the wrong time. *What future has been snuffed out? She'll never smile again, be a mother, get an education, watch a sunrise, grow old.* I don't know what to say.

I climb up out of the hole, wipe my face with the back of my hand. Amy reaches over and touches my shoulder. The Afghan soldier starts to recite verses from memory in Pashto; it sounds like a poem. I don't know what he's saying, but he has a beautiful voice. He stops and nods to me to signify he's finished. I pick up the shovel, but I'm suddenly frozen. I can't bury her. I just stare at the grave. Amy reaches over and slowly takes the shovel from my hand, and starts to bury the girl. I stand there like ice, watching. As the soft brown dirt covers the clean, white sheet I realize that everything good in my life is being buried alongside this young girl.

FORTY-NINE

— • —

I was lying in a patch of tall wet ferns, cold droplets dripping onto the back of my hands. We were in a primordial old growth forest deep in the Makah reservation that had clearly never been harvested for timber. The huge spruce, pine and cedar trees blocked out the ashen sky. The incessant rain covered everything in a damp coating. It had been easy to creep into this position, as these prehistoric ferns were four to five feet tall and provided excellent concealment. I could move quietly without being seen, crouched on my feet and knees in this deep green sea of fern. My M-14 rifle was aimed at a small cabin 30 yards away. Trees had grown up all around the structure, as if it was now a part of the forest itself. A large cedar with a deep reddish-brown trunk grew in front of the cabin, its branches covering the front porch. A crooked door with leather hinges and one small window were the only entrance to the cabin. I could see no other windows. Despite its obvious age, the cabin stood strong, without a sagging roof or walls. It was clear that someone had been taking care of it. I'd been watching for an hour. Three hours ago, Micah and I drove slowly down a dark logging road, hid my truck along a narrow side trail and started to patrol silently to this cabin. It was an eerie and wild place.

I pushed the talk button on my UHF radio, "Micah, seen any movement?" There was a click and then I heard him say, "Negative." It took him longer to crawl into position with his prosthetic leg, but he was now set up on a small knoll about 60 degrees from me. He had a view of the other side of the cabin and the entrance. I couldn't see him through the trees and dense cover, but knew exactly where he was. We'd picked out these locations on a 1:24,000 topographic map during our planning session. He was carrying my Remington 1187 semi-automatic shotgun loaded with six rounds of double 00 buckshot. I figured one lethal scatter-gun might come in handy if things got messy.

We had discussed how we would play this out, depending on the variables. The biggest question was Micah's brother Jerry. We didn't know if he was part of the scheme or a victim himself. If he was a victim, we'd put priority on getting the girl out, but would do what we could to rescue him as well. But if Jerry was mixed up in kidnapping his own daughter, then he'd just be collateral damage, like anyone else in our way of recovering Sarah.

The other big variable was how many people might be on the target besides the girl, if she was even in the cabin. I figured there wouldn't be more than two people to watch a 12-year-old girl. The more people in on it, the greater chance they would be found out and the smaller their cut of the ransom money, so I knew it would be a small group. Bottom line, this wasn't gonna be easy. We had to be patient and smart.

Micah's voice came over the radio, "We've got a black SUV coming up the dirt road near your location."

"Roger that," I whispered back.

In a few minutes I heard the crunch of rocks and twigs as the SUV crawled up the forgotten and overgrown dirt road and parked in front of the cabin. I peered through the passenger side of the vehicle, but couldn't get a good look at the driver as he stepped out. He was tall, and wore a ball cap and a windbreaker, his arm was in a cast. He scanned the area before moving up to the porch. That's when I realized it was Jim Tripper. He entered the cabin by the front door. "*Son of a bitch*," I muttered to myself with fury, a wave of rage sweeping over me.

"Micah, did you get a good look at that guy?" I asked quietly over the radio.

"Yeah, I've seen him on the rez talkin' to my brother. Figured he was an insurance agent or somethin'."

"No, that's Tripper. He runs the marina in Port Townsend. He tried to take over our dive site and almost got me killed. He's why Cindy's in a coma," I explained quietly into the mic.

Voices were coming from the cabin. The door swung open and Tripper stepped out, followed by a heavy-set Native American man in jeans and a flannel shirt. He had long black hair like Micah, and a red bandana around his head. I couldn't get a good look at his face from my vantage point, but it sure looked like Jerry to me. He had a pistol in a leather holster on his right side.

"Is that your brother?" I whispered over the radio.

Micah replied coolly, "Yeah, I'm gonna give him a chance to come clean right now."

"Wait, Micah, that's not the plan!"

He clicked off. *Damn it!* While Tripper and Jerry talked on the porch, Micah slowly stood up from the ferns where he was hiding. He was holding the shotgun in front of him, but not raised or ready to shoot. *What the hell was he doing?*

"Jerry!" Micah called out to his brother. Tripper and Jerry nearly jumped out of their skins. They turned toward Micah. Jerry pulled his pistol out and aimed it at his brother. Micah was still holding the shotgun in his hands, but low, not ready to shoot. "Brother, let her go. You and I can work this out," Micah said in a strained voice. *Aim that gun, Micah! Brother or not, these guys are not gonna reason with you.*

Tripper jumped behind the SUV opposite Micah and yelled, "Shoot him!" Tripper was on my side of the vehicle now. I had a clear view of his back. Jerry was still on the porch aiming at Micah, who was standing in waist deep ferns with his hands down, holding the shotgun at his waist. Either Micah couldn't bring himself to shoot his brother or he was tired of this life and was going to force his brother to pull the trigger. I couldn't let either of those things happen. I'm trained to shoot to kill, but for Micah and Sarah's sake, I put a round through Jerry's right knee. His leg buckled like a straw and he fell sideways onto the porch with a terrible scream and thud. The pistol fell off the porch onto the ground. Tripper realized the shot had come from right behind him so he stood up, raised his hands over his head and yelled, "Don't shoot, don't shoot!"

I stepped out of the ferns in my dark green camouflage uniform and pointed the M-14 at Tripper. His eyes widened as the big 7.62mm barrel stared him in the face. "Get down on your stomach," I commanded. "Now!"

Keeping Jerry in the corner of my eye, I walked through the ferns over to Tripper. That pistol was just off the porch from Jerry's reach. I held the rifle aimed at Tripper but kept a close eye on the pistol. When

I got to Tripper, I patted him down, pulled his arms behind his back and zip-tied his wrists and ankles. I walked around to the driver's side of the SUV, pulled out the keys and tossed them into the dense ferns. No one was gonna drive outta here except me, Micah and the girl.

"You've got it all wrong, Jack, I've got nothing to do with this," Tripper pleaded. "I was just trying to help negotiate a bad situation." *Bullshit.*

"Shut your mouth," I spat, shoving his face into the wet earth, holding it there until my vengeance was temporarily satisfied. Cindy was in a coma because of this lowlife. I let go of his head and he raised it, gasping for air and spitting out moss and twigs. The message was clear: I wasn't in the mood for conversation. My blood was boiling.

Micah had hobbled to the front of the cabin, and was standing over Jerry, who was laying on his side making a low guttural moan like a wounded buffalo. I left Tripper tied up and walked over to the front porch with my rifle trained on the door. We still didn't know if there was anyone else in the cabin who might want to step out and catch some lead in the chest. I glanced at Jerry; he wasn't bleeding out—the bullet had missed his artery. Lots of blood, bone and tissue damage, but no gusher. While Micah glared at his brother, shaking his head in disgust, I took Jerry's bandana off his head and wrapped it around the wounded knee, then zip-tied his wrists.

Micah opened the door of the cabin and walked in while I was still tending Jerry. I jumped up and followed behind him with my rifle at the ready to clear the room.

"Sarah!" Micah exclaimed with a sudden low sob, running to her. There were beer cans and whiskey bottles strewn across the cabin floor. Sarah was sitting up in a filthy wooden bed against the far wall. She had a rope lashed tightly around her right wrist, and the other end was tied to the headboard so she couldn't get out of the bed. The stench hit me first, then I saw the filthy sheets; they'd forced her to use the bed as a toilet. My head started to spin, so I turned and quickly headed back outside. I didn't make it to the edge of the porch before I began retching with disgust and white hot anger. Bent over at the waist, horror dripping from my mouth, I stood up in a rage and kicked Jerry hard in the ribs. It produced a satisfying cracking sound as he screamed. I'm not proud of that, but it felt good at the time.

FIFTY

— ‖ —

M icah called out to me in a strange voice, "Jack, come in here!" I wiped my mouth with the back of my hand, and returned inside. That's when I realized the mistake I'd made, on multiple levels. Linda was standing next to Sarah with a .45 pistol aimed at her head. She was dressed all in black, and had on gloves and hiking boots. Her hair was tucked away in a big, black scarf, like a Hijab. She must have hidden in the cabin when she heard the commotion outside. I hadn't finished clearing the room before going outside to puke and now we were all in a bad spot.

"Put your gun down, Jack. If you raise that weapon, I'll put a bullet through this girl's head. Believe me, I'll do it." Her voice was as cold as steel, and her accent was more pronounced. Her eyes were two dead chucks of black ice. I had no choice. I slowly set the M-14 down on the floor.

She pointed the big pistol at Micah and ordered, "Tie him up." She kicked a small roll of rope over to Micah. He picked it up and limped over to me, tying my hands behind my back. "Tie his ankles together too," she said, smiling.

"Linda, what is this? What're you doing?" I tried to make a connection with her, but she seemed like a completely different person.

"Just shut up, Jack. All will be revealed to you, don't worry."

Micah finished tying my ankles. I stood there helpless, unable to move unless I hopped across the floor. I looked over at Sarah, with her right arm still tied to the headboard. She was holding her left arm across her face as if to block out the horrible scene unfolding in front of her. I couldn't see her eyes.

Linda stood with the pistol aimed at Micah, then walked over to the door and picked up my M-14 and slid the pistol behind her back. She aimed the big rifle at Micah, then spoke in a low, menacing tone. "You fought in Iraq, you came as a conqueror, you killed my people, you fought against the establishment of a pure Caliphate and the true believers. Your reckoning has come." The shot from the M-14 was deafening in the cabin. Sarah screamed as a huge hole opened in Micah's chest. He slumped against the wall, slid to the floor and fell to his side, dark blood pooling across the dirty wooden floor. My jaw dropped, I couldn't speak. *What kind of a monster is this woman?*

I couldn't take my eyes off Micah. After all he had been through, he didn't deserve to die like this. Several realizations hit me at once, like machine gun fire: I had lost another friend in the war—same enemy, different battlefield; the war had followed me to this place I thought was a refuge but there really was no escape from my actions, no place to rest and heal; Micah was a hero who died saving his niece. He'd paid a heavy price in Iraq and now had sacrificed himself for a child. It was up to me to save Sarah now. The responsibility that came with that was like a rock in my gut. There are fates worse than death, and I knew that if this girl died, I wouldn't be able to live. Somehow Linda knew this too.

I heard a metallic click and snap and turned to see Linda removing the magazine from the rifle and checking the ammunition. She stared at me with those dead eyes, then stepped outside with my M-14. Tripper yelled out, "Linda, I'm over here!" I heard Linda step off the porch. A few seconds later, Tripper screamed out, "Linda, NO!" and then I heard the distinctive boom of that 7.62 round. I heard her step back onto the porch as Jerry cried out, "No, don't shoot!" followed by the M-14 firing again. *My God.*

The door opened and Linda stood there, her face aflame. I didn't know what hatred really looked like until I saw it in her face at that moment. "Sit down Jack, you're going to need your strength," she said, practically dripping with sarcasm. I hopped over and sat on the edge of the bed. Sarah was sobbing. I tried to sit next to her, figuring it might comfort her.

Linda sat down in a rickety chair by the door, with the M-14 resting on her lap, her head slumped down like she was in a trance. After a couple of long minutes, she sat up straight and said, "I'm going to tell you why all of this is your fault, Jack. You're going to pay for what you've done." Just then I remembered the note that had been left on my desk.

She looked beyond me, as if telling a tale around an ancient camp-fire. "I grew up in the shadow of the Hindu Kush, no-man's land between Afghanistan and Pakistan. The Soviets came and my father and his brother joined the Taliban and made the Soviets pay in blood until they left our lands. My uncle grew strong in the Taliban, while my father joined the Al Qaeda brothers who helped us fight the Soviets. When the American soldiers came, we fought again. Our village was bombed." She paused and the look on her face changed from hatred to anguish. "My mother and brother were killed, along with all of my uncle's family, except his daughter. My father sent me away. You see, he couldn't stand losing his last remaining child. I fled to Pakistan, secured a visa to England then applied for a student visa to the United States." A powerful shiver went up my spine—I had a hunch where this was heading.

She stood, looked out the only window, and continued, "My father told me that my uncle's daughter, my only cousin, Azeera, was killed by an American soldier. He described how the American had shot Azeera, captured her, took her away from her people and family, and how she had died in the hands of foreigners and invaders. Infidels!" My heart was banging, realization setting in. The girl's name was Azeera.

"My father had connections with Al Qaeda, so he used them to find out where the American who had killed my cousin lived. I was already living in this area, so they asked me to take our family's revenge, and I gladly accepted." She turned from the window and glared at me. She wanted to see the shock in my face. I think it gave her some kind of twisted pleasure.

"Your little mind is wondering about the diving, Tripper and all that," she continued. I needed help to get you out here to this cabin, to make you pay, to take the vengeance that belongs to my family. I paid Tripper and Jerry to help me. They're both idiots and had no idea who I was or what I'd planned. Tripper's payment was that ridiculous sunken treasure. I gave him the information in exchange for his help. Jerry was just a piece of shit drunken father. They were both useless and weak." I glanced at Sarah; her sobbing had stopped. She was looking at me with fear and a silent cry for help.

"Now Jack, it's time to finish this, for you to pay for what you've done to my family and my people." She set down the M-14, pulled the pistol from her back, strode to the bed and reached for a sharp knife on the floor to cut Sarah loose. Sarah remained on the bed, sobbing and still looking at me. Linda reached under the bed and pulled out a noose connected to a length of rope. While holding the pistol on me with one hand, she threw the noose over an exposed rafter ten feet above us and tied off the end to one of the old wooden vertical posts that was holding up the rafter. She set a chair on top of a small table and pushed the table under the noose. Grabbing Sarah by the wrist, she yanked her onto the table. "Climb up on that chair," she barked. I couldn't believe what I was seeing and felt completely powerless. Sarah looked at me, then stepped carefully from the floor to the table onto the wobbly chair. "Now put that noose around your neck," Linda spat venomously. Sarah was trembling uncontrollably, but slowly reached up, grabbed the noose, and put it around her neck. I watched as if in a nightmare. *She can't really be doing this! Killing an innocent young girl who had nothing to do with any of this?*

Linda stepped up onto the table, flashed that same knife so I could see it and plunged it into Sarah's collarbone. Sarah howled. I yelled, "No!" but it was too late. Linda jumped back down off the table and trained the pistol on me. *This monster has even more horror in mind.*

"Get up, Jack," she sneered.

I stood up, though it was difficult with my hands and ankles tied. "Hop over here," she pointed to a spot next to the table. I hopped like a human pogo stick. She looked up at Sarah who was still screaming and bleeding and said, "Put your feet on his shoulders. Do it or you die right now." Sarah obeyed, stepping off the chair onto my shoulders with both her feet. I realized Linda's plan. What a sick puppy this woman was. She kicked away the table and chair and Sarah almost fell off my shoulders, but I held strong, giving her a solid platform on which to stand. Her blood dripped onto my head and down into my eyes.

Linda came over and got right in my face. I could smell her breath. Her eyes were burning with evil, her nostrils flaring like a demon. "You took my cousin's life, now you're going to pay with another girl's life. You see, Jack? There's no escape from your actions." I had to agree with that. "I could kill you now, but that would be too easy. I want you to suffer like my cousin and the rest of my family suffered." She flashed the blade in my face with a twisted smile, then plunged it into my chest—not enough to kill me, just hurt me bad. Muscles and flesh tore, pain seared like a lightning bolt through my body. I almost toppled but held strong to keep Sarah on my shoulders.

Linda stepped back and looked at us: her masterpiece of revenge. For a second, I wondered how long the crazy bitch had taken to think this one up. "Either you or the girl will give out soon. Enjoy that moment, Jack," she sneered with unbridled hatred. "You'll never see me again. I have a flight to Karachi tonight. I'll rejoin my family and the fight against the infidels. Oh, and if you do survive somehow, you'll have to explain how everyone was shot with your weapon." With that, she turned and walked out the cabin. Almost immediately I heard her step back onto the porch and the door swung open. "Where are the keys to the SUV?"

Well, finally I had an advantage. "I threw them in the bushes. You'll never find them, you psycho."

For the first time, I saw something like fear replace hatred in her dead eyes. Her meticulous planning had gone slightly off the rails. "Give me your keys!" she shouted.

"You'll never find our vehicle. We hid it in the forest and covered it with bushes," I lied. She was considering three bad options: hunting for the SUV keys in the deep underbrush, trying to find my truck in the dark forest at night, or hiking to a main road to flag down a vehicle for a ride or hijack. Her face twisted in anger as she spat a curse at me in Pashto. I couldn't understand the words, but I sure knew the sentiment. She kicked open the door with a bang and was gone.

FIFTY-ONE

— ⬩ —

I looked up at Sarah, "Stay with me, Sarah, I'm gonna get us out of this, OK? You have to stay on my shoulders. Don't fall! Do you hear me?" I heard a low moan, like an animal caught in a trap. I didn't have much time before one of us passed out. My chest was killing me, great circles of throbbing pain arcing across my body. Linda's wacko revenge plot was working. There had to be a way out of this.

Sarah was wavering on my shoulders, her legs becoming weak, the blood loss taking a toll. If I stayed put, she would slip and die, or I would pass out and we'd both die. I wasn't going to let that happen. Her sticky blood was dripping off my face and forming a dark pool at my feet, mixing with my own blood dripping down my chest. I looked around the room and saw only one viable plan. I was out of time.

"Sarah!" I yelled up at her. "Listen to me!" I looked up. She bent her head and looked straight down at me. This was it. "I'm gonna stand on my toes. That will raise you a few inches. When I do that, I need you to grab the rope above the noose with your good arm and wrap your hand around the slack in the rope. Do you understand, Sarah?" She nodded at me tearfully. "When you get the rope around your hand, you need to yell," I explained. She nodded again. "When you yell, I'm gonna jump away. Your hand will get squished and hurt like crazy, but you won't choke. Do you understand, Sarah? I'm gonna get you down, I promise. OK?" One final nod.

"Are you ready, sweetheart? I know you can do this, Sarah." I bent my knees slightly for lift, then arched on my toes as high as I could. I looked up, saw her wrestling the rope with her good arm. "Grab it, Sarah!" She yelled, "Got it!" I hopped out from underneath her and she screamed as the rope went taut, but her left hand caught the brunt of the tension. I took two large hops, then rammed my shoulder with all of my strength against the vertical post holding up the rafter she was dangling from.

The post held fast and knocked me on my ass, but moved a few inches off its base. Sarah was dangling above me. She stopped screaming, her face turning blue. I scooted on my butt towards the post, laid on my back, put my head against the wall for purchase and pushed the base of the post with all the strength in my legs. The bottom of the post slid out, then gave way, followed by crashing and splitting wood. The end of the rafter holding the noose crashed to the ground. Sarah landed in a heap next to me. She didn't make a sound.

I struggled to my knees and inched towards her. My hands and feet were still tied. Her eyes were closed. "Sarah, wake up. You're gonna make it, I promise." She didn't move. I put my ear to her mouth and heard shallow breathing. "We're not gonna die here, Sarah! Wake up!" I screamed from the bottom of my soul. One of her blue eyes opened, then the other. It was like two bright stars rising over the horizon.

She was awake, at least for a minute. "Sarah, get up. You have to cut me loose." The blood loss had taken a toll on both of us. She was groggy and weak. I was feeling light-headed. She made it to her knees, then fell back to her stomach. "Sarah, remember in the Swiss Family Robinson? The boys didn't give up when they were attacked but fought back as hard as they could. You can do this, Sarah!" She rose to her knees again. "That's it! Get the knife, sweetheart. It's on the floor near the table—see it?" She looked to her left and nodded. "Go get it, Sarah!"

She crawled towards the knife, then grabbed it with her good hand and crawled back to me. I was sitting up now with my legs in front of me, blood pooling down my leg. "Cut the rope around my hands, Sarah. You're doing great." I felt her grab the rope and push the knife but nothing happened. "Saw it, Sarah, you know, like you'd saw a log?" I felt the knife move back and forth, and finally my hands were free.

I grabbed the knife from her hands as she fell over on her side. I cut the rope around my ankles and turned back to Sarah. Blood was seeping from her collarbone area. I grabbed the pillow from the bed, stripped off the pillow case and cut the cotton into small patches. I knelt over her, "This is gonna hurt, sweetheart, I'm sorry," I said, stuffing a wad of cotton into her wound, but she didn't make a sound. I quickly cut a long strip of the pillow case and fashioned a large bandage and sling for her arm. She couldn't sit up, so I propped her against me and secured the bandage and sling. I took another piece of that sheet and jammed it into my chest wound, which felt like a hot poker. I wrapped a section of sheet around my chest to hold the bandage in place. I had to get her help before she bled out. No way was I gonna let that happen again.

I grabbed the dirty blanket from the bed, hoisted Sarah onto my back with her arms around my neck, and tied the blanket around my waist to keep her from falling off my back. I picked up the knife with my good arm and walked out the door of the cabin. The gray clouds had given way to a rare starry night. Somewhere in the distance a sound like the scream of a wild animal wafted through the dense forest. It suddenly hit me that I'd been in this situation before. I stepped around Jerry's body and off the porch and ran down the dark winding dirt road towards my hidden truck. Nothing would stop me.

FIFTY-TWO

— ❋ —

Tall pines and cedars lined the side of the road leading away from the cabin, creating a corridor of darkness with beady eyes peering at me from nighttime nests. I was still getting used to the black night; it would take at least 20 minutes for my night vision to kick in. Only the dim stars were visible above me. My feet crunched across twigs and weeds on the overgrown dirt road. "Sarah, you with me?" I needed to keep her awake and conscious. "Mm-hmm," a faint voice responded. The left side of my body was throbbing with excruciating pain from the stab wound. I reached up with my right hand and felt blood oozing out of the bandage, then looked down and saw it dripping down my pants onto my boot. I didn't have time to stop and sort out the bandages; I needed to get help before Sarah passed out.

I jogged about half a mile from the cabin to the main dirt road that ran east to west. Micah and I had ditched my truck down an overgrown path to the west, off the main road. I needed to take a left on the main road, go another mile and look for a break in the foliage to the north, where we'd hidden the truck.

"Sarah, what's your favorite book?" I asked, trying to keep her mind active.

She whispered, "Swiss Family." I knew it hurt her just to talk. I tried to run cat-like without bouncing her.

Suddenly a tingle up my spine made me pause, like something or someone was following us. A decorated Vietnam era SEAL had taught me to patrol through the jungle, forest and desert. He would set up ambushes in places we would least expect, always training us to stop, listen and check our tail periodically, since that was the most likely avenue of attack.

I quietly stepped off the right side of the road, made a small circle in the dense underbrush and crawled back to the edge of the road, where I could see if anything was coming up behind us. I kept Sarah on my back in case we had to move fast. Kneeling behind a large rotten log, I waited. There was a shape, low to the ground, in the distance. It appeared to stop, go flat and lie down. It was at the far edge of my range of sight; a black, blurry figure, but definitely something. It was hard to judge distance at night, but I estimated it was 50 yards behind us. I waited ten minutes, watching, but it didn't move. *Maybe I was seeing things in the pitch-black forest. Maybe it was The Black Dog gaining on me?* Then again, we were dripping blood. That would attract any number of animals in this area. I had to take a chance, get moving and get Sarah to a hospital.

I stood up and moved as quietly as I could back onto the road. The ferns and underbrush were so thick that there was no chance of walking through the forest to remain undetected. If I didn't use the road, we would never make it to my truck. I could only see 10 to 20 yards ahead in the dark with the curves in the roads. Finally, I recognized a large bend in the road and knew my truck was hidden down a path to the right of that bend.

I passed the bend, slowed down and carefully scanned the forest to the north. I was looking for a rarely used logging road to the right after the big curve. It was carpeted with tall grass and weeds, and barely visible. The break in the treeline gave it away. I recognized the trail as it wound downhill to the north. Micah and I had found a good place to turn the truck around and cache it in a small opening of trees.

I took a right on the path that led to the truck, picking up my pace. I felt Sarah's head lolling around on my shoulders. "Hey Sarah, we're almost there, wake up!" I barely spoke above a whisper, not wanting to arouse any of the predators in the inky black forest. She didn't respond so I started to run faster. The road widened and opened into a small clearing. In the ambient starlight, I could see my truck parked off to the left near the edge of the forest. I ran to it, kneeled down and untied the blanket holding Sarah in place. She spilled off my back, falling gently onto her side. Her eyes were closed, but I could feel her breath on the back of my hand. A crunching sound came from my left. Spinning my head around, I saw a figure step out from behind the other side of the truck. "Hello Jack, what took you so long?" said Linda, training the pistol on me and grinning.

"What are you doing here?" I gasped, getting to my feet and keeping Sarah behind me for protection. Linda stood ten feet away, the pistol held in both her hands and aimed straight at me, ready to fire. She was close enough to take a sure shot, but just far enough that I couldn't lunge at her.

"I tried to hitch a ride, but there's no one on this road at night. I found your truck and was about to hot-wire it when I heard you coming down the trail. I don't know how you escaped that cabin," she hissed, "but I can assure you that this is the end of the line. Your death is all I've dreamed about for years and now I'm going to enjoy watching it." The starlight shone through the trees, casting a dim light on her contorted face. *How had I missed the evil behind those eyes?* "I'll give you a choice, Jack. Who do you want me to shoot first, you or the girl?"

I knew I had to charge—maybe take two rounds before I reached her. As long as they were not headshots, I would have about two minutes to kill her before I bled out. It was my only play. She sensed the tightening in my muscles and backed away two steps towards the treeline, keeping a steady aim on me. Out of the dense primordial forest, a blazing fast shape leapt from behind a tree and knocked Linda to her back. In a split second, I saw the mountain lion rake its razor claws across her body, tearing huge gashes while she screamed, before it clamped its jaw on her neck. The cougar must have been a hundred and fifty pounds. It started to drag Linda into the forest. I was momentarily stunned by the speed and ferocity of the attack, but the sight of Linda's pistol on the ground woke me up. I ran for the pistol, grabbed it, aimed at the cougar and fired. It was so dark, I doubt I hit the lion, but the sound of the shot chased it off.

Keeping the pistol at the ready, I walked carefully into the woods until I found Linda. She was on her back, her black sweatshirt shredded, huge gashes on her chest slowly spewing blood. The bite near her throat was a ragged puncture wound with two large holes pulsing her life fluid into the damp, earthy forest floor.

After the unimaginable cruelty she'd inflicted at the cabin, I burned with hatred for her and had thought of many ways to make her pay. But now I knelt beside her. I didn't feel compassion, but it came to me that she too had been a victim of the horrors of war. She deserved to die, but maybe not to be dragged off into the forest and chewed on by animals. I took hold of her hand and her deep brown eyes winced and opened to look at me. Her lips mouthed something, but no sound came out. I put my ear to her lips. "Kill me," she begged.

A hundred thoughts raced through my head at once. On one level I would have loved nothing more than to take that pistol, stick it deep into her mouth and blow the top of that vengeful head off, but that wasn't me. A warrior and a killer are two different species, though they look alike to the untrained eye. I wouldn't kill her, but I couldn't leave her here to be dragged off by the cougar. I reached under her back and scooped her up. Her head and legs dangled off my arms as I carried her to the truck. It was only a two-seat truck, so I set Linda down in the bed like a dead deer. I picked up Sarah and set her in the passenger seat next to me. Both of her blue eyes opened for a second before her head fell back onto the seat. I jumped into the driver's seat and tore down the gloomy path towards any light I could find.

FIFTY-THREE

———— ❦ ————

T hat night I'd driven out of the forest with Sarah and Linda, I called 911 as soon as I picked up cellular coverage and an ambulance from the rez clinic met us. The EMTs started an immediate IV on all three of us, then raced to the Forks Community Hospital near the western side of the reservation. Linda and Sarah lay strapped to thin metal beds in the back of the bumpy van. Blood from both of them pooled on the floor, mixing gently as the van swerved through the turns on that dreadful night.

I sat on the floor as an EMT in blue coveralls worked on Sarah. I tried to sit up and look at Sarah, but the pain in my chest knocked me back down. "How's she doing?" I asked. The EMT looked at me for a second but didn't answer. He was busy hooking up an IV to Sarah.

When he was done with the IV he looked down at me, "She's lost a lot of blood, we need to get her to the hospital asap. What happened out there? Did a mountain lion cause all this?" *How could I really answer that first question?*

"No, the lion attacked her," I said, nodding towards Linda. Just the thought of the suffering and bitter revenge Linda had inflicted on all those around her made me feel like a hot poker had been stuck in my gut. To realize that the world contained people who hated that much was like eating a rotten apple. It made me sick to think we were both human. I never really hated the enemies I met on the battlefield. I just had a job to do and they were on the wrong end of American foreign policy. It was just business. It's not that I never hated anyone, like say Jim Tripper, but I just couldn't make hating someone the major motivation in my life. But with Linda, I realized, it was beyond personal, it was like her blood, her DNA, her life. She was damn good at it. Best hater I ever met, world class.

We reached the hospital in Port Angeles in the early morning hours. A swarm of nurses with two gurneys met the ambulance as we pulled into the emergency lane. I hopped down out of the van and waved the nurse off who tried to put me into a wheelchair. I grabbed Sarah's gurney with one arm and tried to help the nurses rush her into the building, but they shooed me off. I felt helpless.

I spent that night in the hospital. It was the best place to keep an eye on Sarah plus the ER doctor kind of insisted after stitching up my chest wound. In the morning I escaped my hospital room and snuck into intensive care, dragging my IV bag on a pole, padding down the shiny linoleum floor in my hospital socks, and wearing an open-backed gown that had more ventilation than I was used to. From around the corner, I saw the duty ICU nurse start to make her rounds. I waited until she went into a room and quickly dragged my accessories into Sarah's room. She opened her eyes when I walked in and granted me a beautiful, heartbreaking smile. I knew right then that she would be OK, and a huge weight lifted off me.

The duty nurse came round and chucked me out of Sarah's room. She was a matronly, plump woman with short red hair, a petite nose and freckles on her pink cheeks. She was peeved that I used stealth techniques to sneak into Sarah's room. As she escorted me down the hallway and out of ICU, I turned to her and asked, "What happened to the other woman I brought in?" She stopped walking. It had clearly been a tough night for her, and a frown crossed her kind face.

"She died last night, honey. Blood loss led to heart failure. I'm so sorry." I nodded neutrally. I thought I would feel triumph, but all I felt was sadness.

FIFTY-FOUR

The pastor was speaking at the funeral, but my mind drifted to a convoy in Iraq. Micah was driving us through dirty streets on the outskirts of the Green Zone in a desert-colored Humvee. He took a sharp turn down a narrow alley. A huge lorry crossed in front of us and stopped. Micah stomped on the brakes, turned to look at me in the back seat, and tried to tell me something. The bomb must have been radio detonated. After the explosion, everything went silent.

The pastor's long salt and pepper hair was tied in a black ribbon. A red rose tattoo from her days in the motorcycle gang poked above her clerical collar. The small church was filled. Joe sat next to me, along with Steve, Mrs. Johnson, Anthony, Sheila and Cap. It was cloudy and raining outside and the normally vibrant stained glass windows appeared monochromatic and dead.

"Forgiveness," said the pastor in a strong voice full of empathy, "is what we all need today. We have to forgive others for all the violence they have inflicted on us mentally and physically, but most importantly, we need to forgive ourselves. By failing to forgive ourselves, we bury the good in our lives in a pit of despair, hatred, regret and guilt." An image of a shallow grave in Afghanistan and a flashback of Micah looking at the bloody, gaping hole in his chest blasted into my mind.

I gripped the side of the pew until my hands went numb. I bowed my head in grief and guilt and Joe put his arm around my shoulders. I couldn't remember how many funerals I'd been to, but it came to me, very clearly, how many I'd been responsible for.

There were only a few of us at the graveside service. The simple green casket was lying at the bottom of a six-foot hole. A cold rain fell from the leaden sky. The pastor spoke one more time, as we all bowed our heads in prayer. Everyone turned to head back to their cars as the icy drizzle continued to fall. I stayed behind, walked over to the tool shed, and took out a shovel. The pile of dirt next to the grave hole was muddy, heavy and smelled of pine and seashells. I dug in the shovel and tossed a heavy glob of water-soaked dirt onto the casket. It made a hollow thud. I paused and thought of something I needed to forgive myself for. The list was long. I tried to scoop up each bitter regret into the shovel with the putrid earth, and then throw it into the hole. I let the next searing regret come to my mind, like a muddy river depositing rotten debris on the bank. I mentally picked that one up, put it into the shovel full of muddy earth, and tossed it into the grave. The fountain of regret and pain in me was seemingly endless, flowing like a broken sewer pipe. The more I thought about a painful incident, the more the regret flowed and tried to drown me. There was no end to my river of anguish.

I threw countless piles of earth and bile into that hole until I was empty... spent. I scooped up one last pile of dark earth with my hands, got to my knees, and placed the muddy glob carefully on top of the casket, smoothing it out. Sarah's face came to my mind. I saw her on the floor of the dirty cabin, blood pooling down her shirt, her filthy matted hair mixed with blood, one eye staring at me. I realized then that there was too much to forgive. I couldn't do it.

I stood by the graveside. Micah would always be my friend. He'd been a good man—a soldier, a patriot, a loving mentor to his niece. He'd served his country, recovered from unimaginable trauma, and made a positive impact on a young girl's life. He'd died trying to protect her. I stood up and rendered a sharp hand salute, "At ease, soldier, rest in peace."

FIFTY-FIVE

A t the funeral I'd asked Cap to meet me on board Sea Wolf that evening. I walked down the pier in the dark. Pools of yellow light from rusty lamps spilled across the weathered dock planks. Boats tugged gently against their lines, making a squealing sound that reminded me of nights in the jungle. I reached Sea Wolf. Cap hadn't arrived yet. I put the canvas bag on the table in the galley, turned on a light, sat down and waited for him.

I heard slow steps coming down the pier towards Sea Wolf. Cap appeared at my dock step: I stood up and waved him in. He slid open the small door and stepped gingerly into the cabin.

"Hello, Cap, thanks for meeting me here."

He took off his Greek fisherman's cap and held it in his lap, "I'm so sorry about Micah."

"I know, Cap, me too. It's terrible."

He nodded with an expression that knew the cruelty of man.

I asked you to come down tonight because I have two things for you and one request. He looked puzzled, but said "OK," hesitantly, not sure what to expect.

"First thing," I said, opening the bag in front of us. I reached in and pulled out the timber that Cindy had recovered from the sea bed of our dive site. He looked surprised and smiled.

"I sent this to my buddy at the University of Washington and he was able to get the lab guys to test it. Guess what? It's over 200 years old... and on top of that, they determined that it came from an oak tree native to England."

"We might have been right on top of the site!" he gasped in awe.

"It's possible, Cap, so I wanted you to have this," I said.

He reached across the dinette table and lightly touched the piece of timber like it was a holy relic.

"Second thing," I said. I placed the keys to Sea Wolf on the table between us. He grimaced like he'd bitten into something rotten, trying to understand.

"I want you to have the boat, Cap. You can live aboard and take her out whenever you feel like going fishing."

His jaw dropped. Speechless, tears started to form at the corners of his salty old eyes and drip onto the table. He bowed his head, then shook it in disbelief.

"The last thing is a request," I said. "When you're done with the boat, I want you to sell it and give the proceeds to Micah's niece, Sarah, or else just put it in your will that she will inherit the boat."

Once he had gathered himself together, he spoke in a choked-up voice, "Of course, I'll do that, Jack. I don't know what to say. Are you sure about this, son?" he asked.

I smiled and we embraced, then I left him to his new home. From the pier, I looked into the window of Sea Wolf as I walked past and saw Cap grasping the helm, a thousand good memories flooding into his head. My memories were taking me in a different direction.

FIFTY-SIX

I drove alone to a deserted beach just west of Port Townsend. The ocean had always been my solace, my place to rest and reset. I also knew, deep down, that it would be my final resting place. I parked at the end of a twisty gravel road and climbed down a small rocky bluff to the secluded cove. It was a typical dull, cloudy day, with offshore gusts meeting the incoming tide, creating choppy swells. Small foamy waves were lapping onto the shore to the rhythm of the sea. I sat down in the sand and looked out at the vast expanse of the Strait. The sea and sky blended into a horizon of gray. I hadn't planned to drive to this beach, The Black Dog drove me here. Deep down I knew what that meant, I just didn't want to think about it... yet.

My terrible mistake in Afghanistan had finally caught up with me. I thought it would subside, go away, become less menacing, like Joe had said. But it had followed me here, snowballing into a bloody mass of hatred, violence, revenge and death. It led to the deaths of four more people and to a young girl losing her father, her uncle and her innocence. It led to Cindy's coma. All of this because of my need to succeed at all costs, my untethered ambition, my unchecked desire to win, my pride and hubris. For a time, it seemed like there was a path forward, but now I felt there was no light at the end of the tunnel, no way to stop the speeding train of pain and guilt, no process to come to terms with the destruction in my wake, no way to be sure that more people wouldn't suffer because of me. I had made a promise to myself but I couldn't fathom how to keep it.

I stood up, took off all my clothes except my shorts and stepped into the icy water. I stood there for a moment, the cold like red ants biting my feet and ankles. I looked for the sun, but it was nowhere to be seen. The ashen and spiritless day matched my soul. I stepped further into the 52-degree water, now up to my knees. I saw pebbles on the bottom, but my feet were too numb to feel them. I waded up to my waist, and turned around to look at the shore one last time. A dark green forest amphitheater surrounded me. The wind in the trees clapped, as if it was the end of my performance on earth. I turned back to the water, waded up to my neck and started swimming out to sea. the offshore wind picked up, slapping the back of my head with frothy waves, pushing me further out into the Strait. The chill wracked my body with uncontrollable shivering. Swimming until I was too cold to continue, seeping hypothermia slowly shutting down the shivering, I knew what happened next: numbness, a slow descent, the end of pain and suffering. I floated on my back now, ready to return to the slime below me, atone for my mistakes, drown The Black Dog. Cold had reached my brain, thoughts started to freeze up.

I floated in the icy life-giving fluid of the earth, suddenly seeing images mixed with feelings of my life in fast forward mode: the sheer joy of playing on a warm beach as a child, the exhilaration of riding a motorcycle for the first time, the pride I'd felt earning my Trident as a US Navy SEAL, the unselfish love I'd felt at my wedding, the despair at the suicide of my best friend, the guilt that came with the death of the girl, Azeera, in Afghanistan.

What came next was a total shock. I saw Sarah walking through a dense forest, heedless of the animals all around her that were hidden in the shadowy corners of the woods. She came to a Y in the overgrown trail, stopped, turned her head and looked straight at me, as if to ask what path she should take. Somehow, I was above her, like a drone view. I could see that the path to the right wound through tall trees and opened into a bright meadow with a gentle stream running through it. I looked the other way and saw that the path to the left started out green and lush but slowly the trees died off, sharp rocks took their place, and eventually it led to a desolate, barren black desert. Sarah stood there waiting for me to give her directions, a look of complete trust on her face.

That's it! It had been right in front of me my whole life. You don't live for yourself, you live for others. That makes it all worthwhile; all the effort, the pain, the suffering. What a fucking selfish thing I'm doing, easing my pain, giving in to The Black Dog instead of trying to make the world a better place. I thought of Sarah again. How was she going to make a life for herself after all that had happened: the death of her mother, an abusive father, the killing of her uncle in front of her eyes, the murderous and vengeful acts of a demented woman who'd tried to murder her. Sarah was going to have to sort all this out and I wouldn't be there to help because I felt sorry for myself? Because I couldn't see roses and rainbows ahead of me? Something flipped in me. *To hell with that!* A surge of warmth and strength flowed into me like a burning hot drug. A thought vibrating from the depths of my soul bubbled to the surface of my groggy consciousness. "Drop it all, Jack, you have more work to do."

I flipped over to my stomach, turned around and scanned the shore in the distance. Bobbing up and down as the rollers carried me slowly out to sea, numb in my body, but warm now in my mind, I knew what I had to do. I had a purpose. I turned toward the shore and swam for all I was worth, my arms and legs like waterlogged deadwood. I paused after a minute, raised my head, and saw that the shore wasn't getting any closer. I put my head down and stroked against the unforgiving density of the ocean until my arms felt like they were plowing through wet cement. I looked up—still no progress against the onslaught of the wind and sea. A wave hit me in the mouth, cold seawater spilling down my throat and causing me to cough and spit. I took a quick bearing; the beach cove was about 400 yards ahead of me, but the offshore waves and wind were right in my face, pushing me out to sea. I'd never make it. A hundred yards to my right was a rocky outcropping. Waves were beating violently against it, but it was my only shot. I turned to the right and swam like I was being chased by a shark. My hands and arms were numb, my feet like anchors behind me. I stopped and took another peek. I was getting closer to the rocky point, white foam splashing into the air off the large rocks like small geysers. The cold was overtaking me but I had to give it one more try.

I took a final bearing on the rocky point and dug in. Without the wind and waves in my face, I made progress. I reached the shore and tried to stand up, waves pounding me against the rocks, tossing me around like flotsam. I was stuck, pinned to a large rock by the force of the sea, frozen, unable to climb or walk to shore. My arms and legs were failing to respond.

I looked around and saw a decent size wave coming my way. I had one chance. As the wave approached, I timed a huge push off the bottom and the swell carried me to the top of the rock. The frothy water receded, leaving me on my stomach, clinging to the rock like a giant white barnacle. I lay there shivering. *That's a good sign. I'm not going to die here.* I struggled to my knees and started to climb slowly off the sharp and slimy rocks towards the safety of shore. I tumbled over the last rock and fell to the sand, landing on my back. The wind was still gusting, taking with it my chances at warming up. I rolled to my stomach, raised my head and looked around. I saw a bit of blue material wedged in the rocks, spit out by the lowering tide. I crawled towards the debris. It was a tattered old tarp. I grabbed a corner of it and rolled myself in it like a human taquito. That's how Joe found me.

FIFTY-SEVEN

—— ✦ ——

"I'm not going to ask how you ended up on that rocky beach," Joe said as he handed me a mug of hot tea with honey. I was sitting in Joe's faded brown leather recliner covered in musty wool blankets as a crackling fire threw dancing shadows against the white walls of his small living room. I was relieved he'd come right out with that: I figured he already suspected why I was nearly incoherent on that beach, yet he was wise enough to let it go.

"How did you find me?" I asked, shuddering as I thought of the icy cold that had pierced me to the bone. I was barely conscious when he'd picked me up, carried me to his car, still rolled in the tattered tarp, and drove to his home. The tea and honey along with the blazing fire were having the right effect. I was finally warming up to the point that my mind was clear.

Joe sat down on the small couch adjacent to my recliner. He stared into the fire and said, "You left me a voicemail saying you were going for a swim on that beach. It didn't make any sense on a cold day like today and I had a gut feeling something was wrong. Plus, I figured if you left me a voicemail, I had permission to check on you." I nodded, realizing that the voicemail to Joe had been a kind of subconscious cry for help: hoping he would answer the phone, sense something was not right, knowing that there was a strong, invisible thread connecting us to each other. Sometimes life hinges on a single phone call.

"You good now... I mean... everything sorted?" he asked without looking me in the eye.

"Yeah, I'm good, Joe." I paused, thinking about how much I should share. *If I couldn't talk to Joe, I couldn't talk to anyone.* "Ya know what, Joe? I had a kind of epiphany out there in the water." He looked at me attentively, then turned back to the fire. "I never told you, but there is a Black Dog chasing me and taking bites out of my life," I revealed, pausing to see if he would react to that. Nothing. "I've tried everything, but I can't seem to shake it. Out in the cold water, staring death in the face, it came to me: I'm lousy at it, but I need to help other people, try to make life a little better for others. That's the only thing that will keep the Black Dog at bay. D'you know what I mean, Joe?"

Joe sipped his tea thoughtfully and looked at me with that wise face before saying, "Yeah, I know exactly what you mean, buddy. Did you have anyone specific in mind?"

"As a matter of fact, I do. I wanted to get your advice on an idea I have, something that's a completely foreign step for me. I need to know if you think I can handle it and I know you'll tell me the truth."

The roaring fire had died down to glowing embers. Joe stood up, threw on another log, turned to me and said, "I'm all ears, shipmate, what's on your mind?"

FIFTY-EIGHT

—※—

Cindy was reclining in a chair with her feet on my desk. Down the first aisle of books, Sarah sat on the floor with Emilio purring in her lap. Sarah had a sling on one arm and was brushing the spoiled cat with the other hand. An open book lay haphazardly on the floor next to her.

The fact that Cindy had awoken from the coma and asked for me and a cheeseburger, not in that order, had been called a miracle. I was sitting at my captain's desk staring at her, enjoying the magic of the moment, of just being in her presence. She looked sexy in her red turtleneck, jeans and Doc Martens.

"Why are you looking at me like that?" she asked, turning to check on Sarah.

"Sorry, I'm just so glad to see you out of bed."

"So you don't want to see me in bed?" she teased.

"Wait a sec, don't twist my words," I shook a finger at her. She giggled, and the sound warmed my heart like nothing else could.

"What's the latest on Sarah? Does she have other relatives on the rez?" she asked quietly.

I paused before answering, "Cind, there's something I wanna tell you." I lowered my voice so Sarah wouldn't hear. "I applied to adopt her." Cindy sat up straight, eyes wide, and mouth dropped open, but in a good way. "It was a long shot. The Tribal Council had to approve it. They usually want a tribal member to be raised by another person of the Makah nation, but her circumstance is unique, so they've approved me." I was grinning. "It won't be effective until they finish the background check, though."

A smile spread across Cindy's face like a sunrise in the mountains, "Jack, how are you gonna raise a girl by yourself?"

"Well...uh..." I reached across the desk and took her soft hands in mine. I wasn't sure how to say it so I just spat it out. "I don't know how you'll feel about this but I was kinda hoping you'd help me?"

She stared at me for a moment. "What are you asking, Jack?" she squinted at me playfully.

I cleared my throat, "I'm asking you to help me raise Sarah." She looked shocked. "Maybe it seems kinda quick to you, but I'm in love with you, Cindy, and I'm hoping you'll consider marrying me." Her eyes filled with tears as I pulled a small ring out of my drawer and set it on the desk in front of her. She looked at the ring then at me with what seemed to be utter amazement.

"What is that, Jack?" she asked breathlessly, mesmerized by the stone.

"When you rescued me from the cave, I grabbed this pebble from the pile and stuffed it in my wetsuit bootie. It will always remind me of that moment when your hand broke through that death trap and gave me hope." She picked up the ring, slowly turning it in her hand, remembering that frightening afternoon when she had almost died saving me. "I had a jeweler set the pebble inside the piece of turquoise glass you found on the beach. Remember the one you gave me when we went crabbing together?"

She recognized the glass shard, and tears ran down her cheeks like waterfalls of joy. "I put that piece of glass in there to remind you to keep looking for the good in me, even when I can't see it." She stood up, reached across the desk, put both her warm hands on my cheeks, and kissed me. It was a kiss I'll never forget.

"Does that mean yes?" I asked nervously.

She nodded, then said the words I wanted so badly to hear, "Yes, Jack, I will marry you."

Sarah's court-appointed guardian from the rez came by at 4:30 to pick her up. Sarah hugged me on the way out the door. I handed her a package I had behind my back. "Go ahead and open it, sweetheart," I said. She smiled and tore the wrapping off. She held the book in her hands and looked up at me with awe. It was a First Edition of *The Swiss Family Robinson*, very rare and in good shape. She held it to her heart with both hands. I gave her a kiss on the forehead and the guardian ushered her out the door.

I closed the bookshop at five o'clock and walked Cindy home to her mother's house. As we walked, I reached over and took her hand. She held tight: it was my first solid grip on a new life—one with real hope.

We reached the door to her mother's home. I turned to face her, holding both her hands, "I want you to know that I support what you're doing for those girls in Pakistan. It's important work, I'll take whatever..." But before I could finish, she leaned in, put her hands around my neck and pulled me to her for a passionate kiss. My arms naturally slid to her waist. I buried my head in her sweet neck, smelled her wild, unruly hair and my heart raced. We held each other until the world and all of its pain disappeared for just a moment. A thought came to me slowly, like the opening of a beautiful rose, possibly from an angel, I have come to believe. I was responsible for the death of one girl, but I'd also saved two girls, so even though my debt wasn't fully paid, I'd made a down payment. The warmth of that realization crept into my blood, lit up my heart, and I could feel a glow emanating from within. A lightness flowed into my body, and a mangy black dog skulked away, a dirty tail between his legs.

EPILOGUE

As I was fulfilling online orders one day at the bookstore, my cell phone rang. It was an unknown number.

"Hello?" "Um... is this Jack Thibideaux, former Navy SEAL?" The hesitant voice sounded familiar but I never gave out that information.

"Who is this?" I asked a little sternly.

A moment of silence before, "This is Sergeant First Class Eric Swanson, First Special Forces Group."

My mind was spinning hard. *Swanson? Where had we met? I knew that name.*

"You walked into our firebase in Afghanistan with an Afghan girl."

Warning bells went off. *Why was Swanson contacting me? That was almost two years ago.*

"I remember you, Swanson. What can I do for you?" I asked suspiciously.

He hesitated, then said, "I need to talk to you. I have something to tell you."

The warning bells became red star clusters. "What's that?" I asked, trying not to sound angry.

"I'd rather talk in person. Can I come see you this afternoon? I'm not far from Port Townsend. I'm stationed at Fort Lewis so I can be there by six."

"OK. I have a bookstore, Sea Wolf Books—you can't miss it. I'll meet you there at six."

The rest of the day my mind looped in circles. *What did Swanson have to tell me? And why couldn't he tell me on the phone?* It didn't make sense.

Swanson walked into the bookstore at ten till six. I recognized him instantly: short, muscular, dark hair, small eyes, scar on his cheek. My heart rate went up. Whenever I met someone I knew from Iraq or Afghanistan, bad memories usually gushed in.

"May I sit down?" he asked.

"Of course," I nodded. He sat in front of the desk. I waited.

He took a deep breath. "There's something I need to tell you, Jack. It's been weighing on me. When I found out you were living here, I knew I needed to talk to you."

"Spit it out, Swanson, you have my attention."

"OK, bottom line, you didn't kill that girl, Jack."

What was he saying?

He saw my confusion, then my shock, but before I could respond he said, "Let me finish. The night you walked into our firebase, the whole valley was up in arms. We'd just worked a truce between the villagers up and down the valley and the Taliban. You inadvertently broke that truce. All the tribes were mobilizing against an onslaught from the Taliban in revenge for the help the villagers had provided to you and that girl. When you walked in with her, you gave us an opportunity to stop the fighting, prevent more bloodshed, and resurrect the truce.

We patched her up, Jack. She survived. The girl you buried was a local girl who'd been killed by a roadside bomb. You had too much of an emotional connection with the girl you brought in. You would've gone berserk if you knew the plan."

I was breathing hard and beginning to shake with anger. He could see it on my face.

"We brokered a deal with the local tribes and the Taliban leaders: we'd deliver the girl to the villagers and they would give her to the Taliban. For that exchange, the Taliban would retreat and respect the truce. Five days after you left the firebase, we gave the girl to the villagers. That action prevented a lot of bloodshed, Jack. I know you understand that."

I stood up and turned away from Swanson. I simply couldn't believe my ears.

He continued, "I thought about how bad you must have felt, thinking you'd killed her. You saved her, Jack. I needed to tell you that."

I paced around in a daze, my head down, muttering to myself. So many questions. *Was she still alive? If she was alive, why did Linda say that she was dead? Where was the girl now? What was she doing? Had she fully recovered?*

Swanson stood up and walked to the door. "I hope you understand, it was a military imperative." He turned and looked at me, but I said nothing. My expression told him it was time for him to be out of my sight. He opened the door gently and stepped out onto the wet sidewalk.

I sat down against a bookcase, head in my hands. A gentle white light crept across the floor until it shone on my face. The moon was rising. A twelve-year-old girl with a dirty face opened both her deep blue eyes and smiled at me.

Acknowledgments

I'd like to thank two amazing editors, who have both become good friends. Lisa Messinger brought my writing into the light. She is such a pleasure to work with. Randall Surles, a former Special Forces officer turned editor and writer helped me see the big picture.

I'd also like to thank my wife for her endless patience with me along with my son and daughter for their tireless encouragement. My good friend Commander (retired) Pam Kramer was a great help.

Finally, I want to thank all the providers and counselors out there helping veterans overcome the physical and psychological wounds of war. You are true heroes.

I hope you enjoyed reading Black Dog Escape. My intent in writing this novel was to shine a light on the struggles that veterans experience after traumatic events in their military careers.

If you would like to follow my author web site below, you can sign up for a newsletter and get notified about upcoming books and events. Thank you!

https://www.wlbachauthor.com/

 Please leave a review on Amazon. Thank you very much!